A *Weave* of **Old** and **New**

A Historical Novel

Susan Posey

Great Rock Press
Asheville, NC

ISBN 978-1-7366300-2-0 (Paperback)
ISBN 978-1-7366300-3-7 (Digital)

Printed in the United States by
IngramSpark Lightning Source

Dedication

To my husband Bill for his deep love and commitment.
Here's to the next 50 Years!

Acknowledgements

I want to thank all of the intrepid critiquers from our
ongoing Grove Writers Group for your crucial input!

**Characters from *A Home on Wilder Shores* who appear
in *A Weave of Old and New*:**

Ardath Rhys, elder of two Welsh sisters, age 19 in 1753

Gwyn Rhys, younger of two Welsh sisters, age 16 in 1753

Carys Rhys, mother of the sisters, a midwife and healer

Dougie, Carys's adopted son, age 2 in 1753

Ibrahim, Muslim ship's doctor on the Atlantic, works from his apothecary shop in Philadelphia

Mrs. Perry, or Mrs. P, housekeeper for the sisters and a seamstress.

Samuel Booth James, a British army major, 3rd son of an Earl, married to Ardath, called "James" by his American family and "Sam" or "Sammy" by his English family

Elizabeth, James's younger sister

Stephen and Richard, James's older brothers

Gregory Smythe, a friend of James and the sisters, a solicitor in Philadelphia, in love with Gwyn

Alex Whitsun, First Mate, then Captain, on the Atlantic voyage

Omar, father and master carpenter, Isa, mother and good with herbs, and grown son Ahmed, a blacksmith: Africans freed by the sisters

Thomas Reese, an Episcopal minister, the sisters' uncle (wife Priscilla)

David Reese, the sisters' first cousin, lives in North Carolina, son of Thomas, loves Gwyn

Other characters:

Caroline, Countess of Redfern, James's mother

Aunt Charlotte, widow of Caroline's brother

John Stewart, courts Elizabeth

Charles, James's houseman

Margaret, a nanny

Colonel Ellis and wife, James's commanding officer

Chapter 1

Gwyn
Summer 1753

As we sailed into the wide mouth of the Delaware River, the waters a dull blue under a molten cobalt sky, I just wanted to be home. I lifted my eyes to the huge old trees that came into view along the banks. Soon we would be able to make out their patterned bark and dark summer leaves. The breeze at least was fresh and pushing us up towards Philadelphia. Though we had only landed from Wales two years ago, the city was so firmly our home that I could imagine no other place for me, anyway, than Philadelphia and the cabin we had built in the woods.

We had gathered our family together in Wilmington and found room aboard a small ship, which carried only us, leather bags of mail, boxes of indigo, and sacks of rice. I could sense a faint muddy and earthy smell from the indigo, sometimes known as "Blue Gold," and valued as a precious dye.

Having found our mother, Carys, and Ardath's husband, James, in North Carolina, my older sister Ardath and I counted our journey down the Wagon Road a great success. James was solicitous of my sister as she was expecting their first child. He didn't seem to notice her impatient toe tapping as we made our way slowly up the coast. Mother spent most of her time watching over her adopted son, Dougie, who wanted to toddle about the deck of the ship with unsteady legs.

The river took a bend to the east. Soon eagerness arose in my heart; we were in sight of the docks and warehouses of the city. The warehouses wore many colors, green, maroon, straw, and dirty white, all faded by the sun. Strangely, the docks, usually bustling with men loading and unloading ships, lay mostly empty and quiet, with no large ships to be seen. More, the harbormaster's boat failed to greet us for inspection.

Very strange, indeed. And I noticed a yellow quarantine flag sagging over the central flagpole. Could this mean an epidemic of some kind cursed the city?

After all her impatience on our way north from Wilmington, Ardath should have been the first off the ship when we finally docked, but, no, it was I who leapt onto the boards and commenced to pound past the few brawny workers gathered to unload the vessel. It was a gasping hot and wet day. My boots splashed up mud from the street onto my clothes, though I had gathered my skirts as I ran. It was perfect weather for disease to spread.

And where do you think I went first? Why, it was to Ibrahim, our Moorish doctor friend, who would surely know all that had happened while we travelled the Wagon Road, and what disease might be in the city.

The streets were oddly deserted, while the sun glared down. I struggled to breathe in the humid air, almost as thick as we had experienced in Wilmington. When I passed the hospital, I saw more signs of life, and of death too. Two rough men with handkerchiefs tied over their noses grunted as they pushed a cart heaped with dead bodies through the clogged mud. This and a yellow quarantine flag above the hospital building again indicated an outbreak of contagion. I rushed on, with an ominous feeling in my throat, to a nearby street.

My heart lifted as I saw the apothecary door ajar. Ibrahim came out just then stretching his arms and back. His brown face lit with delight to see me.

"Gwyn, my sweet friend. How wonderful to find you back on these shores after so many months!"

Soon I was enveloped in his warm arms. "Ibrahim, how are you? How are you all? Is Omar back? What has happened while we were gone? Did you not get our letter that we were coming?"

"We did not get a letter. The mail has been somewhat slow because of the yellow fever epidemic," he said briefly. His sad brown eyes showed what that sickness had meant for him, surely hard work that never ended, and death all around.

"Oh, yellow fever! Is, is, Isa well? Ahmed? Smythe? Mrs. Perry?"

"None have the fever. There is much to catch up on. But, where is Ardath?" he asked.

"Oh, there is much to tell on our side too. We are all well. We should wait for their arrival to tell it all, I suppose. But what have you heard of Omar? He has been on our minds since we had to leave him at the Fairfax house in Virginia." I'm sure I conveyed the guilt and worry that had troubled me since Omar's accident on the Wagon Road.

"Omar is here with us and gets about quite well. Ahmed went to fetch him when he was able to ride in a wagon. Omar blesses you for the good job you made of his broken leg."

"Oh, good then. Is anyone else here today?" I asked, peering around him because we had not yet stepped inside.

"Just myself and a patient with the fever," he said. "I'd rather you didn't come in just yet."

"We found our mother! And James is with us. And—but the rest can wait."

"Your mother! I had little hope of it," said Ibrahim. "What a blessing. I must return to my patient now, but, Gwyn, please get everyone to your house as soon as you can. It lies higher than the rest of the city, which may help prevent your contracting the disease. It seems to be claiming more victims in the lower-lying places near the river. We've had many deaths already. I've sent Omar and Isa to your property to live in the tent there."

"I understand. Can I help you with the sick?"

"My dear one, I appreciate your offer, and you are a fine healer, but I want you all to be safe. Don't come down here until I send word."

With that, he turned and closed the door in my face. I knew he wouldn't be abrupt with me unless he was really worried. I went back to Mulberry Street, thinking of Omar, our African friend whom we had met on the Atlantic journey. He and his wife Isa and grown son Ahmed had been slaves brought on board by a slave trader. After the man died in the small pox epidemic on board, we took them with us to Philadelphia and freed them legally as soon as possible.

On Mulberry, our party was moving along well. A small handcart followed the group, pulled by a dockhand. Dougie rode on top of the piled-up goods, grasping the rope that tied him on, with a happy grin. He looked like a triumphant Roman general being paraded down the street.

"Gwyn, where did you go?" asked Mother as they drew close.

"I've been to see Ibrahim. He asked us not to venture close

to the apothecary, but to go home and stay there. There's yellow fever in the city."

"Oh, I heard a dock worker speak of it when they unloaded us. I know how deadly it can be. I hope it isn't a bad outbreak," she said.

I didn't tell her about the bodies I'd seen. "He thinks we are safer if we stay up higher," I said.

Ardath sighed. Even her straw hat seemed to droop. James put a supporting arm around her. He made no comment, but picked up his pace. We all proceeded as fast as the muggy heat allowed.

Mrs. Perry was hanging out white sheets to dry in the sun when I ran into the yard. She turned, startled, as I rushed to her side. Spitting out the clothespins she held in her mouth, she draped the rest of the clothes over the line and clasped her hands together before hugging me to her ample breast.

"Oh, Gwyn. How I have missed you! What news, my darling?"

"We found our mother, Mrs. P! And we have a new brother, Dougie, and James is with us, and I am so happy to be home."

"No more happy than I am to see you, believe me," she said. "But where in the world shall we put all these people?"

"Time to build additions to the house, I'd say."

"We already have the tent up here, for Ibrahim has banished Isa and Omar," she said.

"I know; I saw him. He said you had not received our letter. He almost pushed me away from the apothecary."

"Aye. There's no cure for this fever, he says." Her lips tightened.

"Well, we have plenty of money and it is summer. We'll make do with another tent, though it must have a floor of boards to please me. I've had enough of camping in the grass."

Mrs. Perry's expression had darkened as soon as I said we had plenty of money.

Before I had time to ask her why, she said we must go and fetch cool water for the rest of the family, and that luckily she had made a cake that very morning. So we set about making a little welcome snack for the others on the hearth table, putting out mugs and cutting the orange cake, which smelled of oranges, honey, and vanilla. By the time we had that in readiness, the rest had reached the front door, where we heard the thuds of boots hitting the floor, and cries of "Mrs. Perry? Gwyn?"

"Welcome home," I said to them all. "Mother, this is our precious Mrs. Perry, who came across the Atlantic with us and has lived with us since, to our great good fortune! Mrs. Perry, our mother, Carys Rhys."

"How do you do?" each said, with smiles all around.

Mrs. Perry went from person to person, greeting and hugging until she reached Dougie. She stooped down to his level.

"What a fine young man. Wherever could such a boy be found?"

Mother answered. "Why, he is from Wales, whence he and I sailed to the West Indies. On the island of Jamaica we found your old friend Captain Whitsun."

"Miracle after miracle!" Her plump ruddy face turned a shade lighter from the shock of it. "He somehow survived the shipwreck, then."

"He did, and he took Dougie and me in. Eventually, we got to Wilmington, where we found Ardath and Gwyn and James ready to come back home. Well, that's the short of it. There's much more to be told around the fire this winter!"

"Of that I'm quite sure," said Mrs. Perry. Her mouth seemed set in a permanent O of surprise.

I saw Ardath sink into the biggest chair, her feet turned to the side. "James, we have refreshments," I said nodding toward the hearth table. He patted Ardath's shoulder and went to fetch her a plate and cup.

Dougie saw the table and asked Mother, "Me?" to which she nodded yes. I helped him with the cake, which made his little face shine with anticipation.

Mother turned to Mrs. Perry. "I have heard such wonderful things about you from my girls."

"Well, don't be believing each and every thing you hear!" she said, and to my surprise, she blushed. "In particular, Mrs. Rhys, I have no idea where to put all these folks."

"Please believe me, we have been in all sorts of accommodations and lack thereof on our travels. We are not expecting you to solve the dilemma of our sudden arrival," said Mother.

At this point, James appeared at my side. "Ladies, I believe my first piece of business would be to obtain another tent. Certainly, the menfolk, that is Dougie and I, can camp there most comfortably." Dougie, hands and mouth sticky from cake, came to hold onto James's britches. "Shall we, Dougie?"

"Yes, camp!" Dougie said with great enthusiasm.

"Oh, James, thank you but—"

"In fact, I must go immediately to the Colonel to report in. I'll ask for a tent, or to have one made. Gwyn, please keep an eye on Ardath for me?"

"Of course," I said.

"Well, we do have material for pallets," said Mrs. Perry. "We could stuff them with some clean straw. I don't have batting and Ibrahim has forbidden us from going to town. Major James, do not linger down there."

"That I will not," he said, turning on his heel to go.

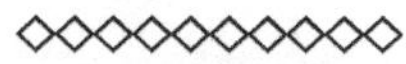

We all washed our hands. Mother and Mrs. Perry set about sewing the cloth covers for the pallets. For now, Ardath and I would sleep in the full bed upstairs and Mrs. Perry and Mother in the small beds across the hall. We would set James and Dougie in the main room on the pallets, or they could use a tent if need be.

"I'm going to look outside," I said. "Dougie, would you like to come?" He nodded eagerly. I checked on Ardath, who seemed comfortably asleep in the big chair, then took Dougie by the hand to the back.

The first thing that met our eyes was the large canvas tent set up far across the field. In the foreground was a neatly tended vegetable garden and to our right, a pen of chickens.

"Dickies," said Dougie, jerking from my hand to run to them. Of course they weren't used to him and squawked as if they were caught by a fox. I noticed that they were securely penned in all around and across the top of the enclosure as well to keep out wild animals. Our folks here had done a good job with the upkeep of our land.

While Dougie hung on the chicken yard fence, I went on to the tent, calling, "Isa, Omar." Their dark faces peered out at me in surprise and (I hoped) with joy.

"Gwyn." said Omar. "We didn't know you were here."

"Omar, I am so glad to see you, and Ibrahim says you have

healed well." I couldn't help throwing myself into his arms, where he hugged me tightly.

"Oh, yes, good doctors, I say." his grin beamed at me.

Isa appeared behind her husband. She looked into my eyes and suddenly began to weep and to cover her face. "Oh, Isa, I'm sorry our letter didn't make it here to let you know we were coming."

"No, no, is good, but oh so sorry…."

I hugged her, unsure what she was trying to say. When I pulled away, she bent from her middle and wailed. I looked around, remembering that no one had mentioned Ahmed since we had come back.

"Where is Ahmed?" I asked. "Omar?"

Now both of Ahmed's parents looked at me with tragic expressions, seemingly unable to speak.

Chapter 2

Ardath
1753

I had dozed off for but a moment in our padded chair when I heard a primitive wail from the back of the house. Gathering my skirts around me, I lumbered to the garden, where the following scene greeted me.

Omar and Isa stood near Gwyn and Dougie, Isa keening like an ancient Welsh woman in sorrow. Omar held her by her shaking shoulders.

"What is this?" I asked, perhaps too loudly.

"I don't know, Ardath," Gwyn answered, as she turned to me. Dougie looked confused and a little frightened. His thumb went to his mouth.

"Omar, please, explain what happened."

"Oh, my ladies. Oh, oh!" he said. I had never seen him with such a sad face, not even before we rescued them from slavery in the hold of the ship crossing the Atlantic. "We have caused a great trouble to you, a great trouble!"

"Omar, nothing can be this tragic. Speak, please, but first let's get out of this sun," I said.

We all moved to the shade of our massive oaks.

Gwyn turned to Dougie. "Dougie, can you find your mother, please? Ask her to come here, then you go see the dickies."

He nodded and toddled towards the house, yelling "Mama."

Omar dried his cheeks on his shirtsleeves. "I am so sorry, so sorry!"

I took a steadying breath. "Omar?"

"It is Ahmed. He has brought us into disgrace. I know not how to say to you. He took your coins, gold and silver, all. Isa and I now will be your slaves. You can sell us to have what you need. We are in disgrace, my ladies!"

A groan escaped me before I could stop it. Here we had returned home thinking all was secure, ready to use our father's coin and the slaver's gold to continue our lives. I glanced toward the animal room, beside the stairs and under the bedrooms, where I had buried those coins so many months before. Only Mrs. Perry had known where they were, but somehow the thief had sniffed them out. This was my fault for not listening to our solicitor friend Smythe and putting all our resources into a bank. James didn't make much as an army officer, and he had no income from his father, the Earl, so it looked like we were back to a state of abject poverty.

Gwyn hastened to encourage Omar and Isa. "Of course you aren't slaves. We will make this right together, as we always have. Where is Ahmed now?"

Isa, who had been sobbing quietly, again wailed into her hands.

"Gone, dis mont' past, we know not where," said Omar. He pulled Isa into his arms and murmured in their Mandinka tongue to comfort her.

I cursed under my breath. This! After all I had promised Mother that we could do to improve our lot in life. She had never known anything but penury since she married our father twenty years ago in Wales. It was unfitting. She deserved to live like a noble woman, the life she had been born into. And James and I would not have the means to start a trading business with the Cherokee who had befriended him on his expedition south. The funds for upkeep of the apothecary would only be what we could make in that enterprise. We couldn't afford to set up a separate dressmaker's shop for Mrs. Perry. One dream after another disappeared like a puff of dust.

Mother came to us just then. Though I hoped I hid my distress, she always knew what I felt. She put her arm around me and gathered my hot body to her.

Gwyn explained in a low voice what had happened. Mother said to the whole group, "Don't be distressed. We'll work this out. Come in and get refreshments. It is cooler in the house."

With her example before us, what else could we do but follow?

When I entered the kitchen door, I saw that Mrs. P looked quite guilty. She had known, then, about the theft, but I supposed it wasn't her duty to tell us about Ahmed.

After we were seated around our scrubbed wooden table, I said, "It seems so unlike Ahmed to do this. What happened?"

Mrs. P answered, as Omar and Isa still were silent. "Well, there's no excuse for it, is there?" she said, wiping her hands on her apron and tightening her mouth. "But Ahmed was severely burned at the forge. The pain could only be eased with laudanum. When that was gone, he thieved opium from Ibrahim. When that was gone, he turned to strong drink. He soon became a layabout, to the horror of his good mother and father. He consorted with bad fellows. One was that gimpy little fellow with the crooked nose; the other was tall with a scar down the left side of his face. They were as much villains as they looked too. Somehow they picked the lock, because I always had the key on a thong around my neck. I heard them and went down with my lamp, and I could see them as they ran away."

My glance fell on his parents while she told this tale. I thought they might feel even more guilt from hearing it, but they merely nodded, acknowledging the truth of it.

Omar continued. "My ladies, we tried to bring Ahmed to his senses! But it came to not'ing. Soon he had no more money to buy da drink. We asked Mr. Smythe not give him da money we had saved."

"We didn't t'ink Ahmed knew where you put your coin. Den one night, as we were in de tent, we heard men hurry away from here. He and de other layabouts had taken everyt'ing."

Once again, I felt stunned by the hopelessness of it. "You told Smythe, I hope."

"Oh yes, we all told Smythe, of course," said Mrs. P. "He reported to the constable, but the yellow fever made it hard for him to do more than send out messages to other towns hereabout. Even then, we didn't know which way those fellows went."

I wished yet again, as I had so many times in the last months, for my usual strength. I'd have taken a horse and gone after them myself, were I not so heavily weighted down by the growing babe I carried. I knew this was another time when I must rely upon the vigor of others. Thank God for James and his strength. I had learned to value it without feeling I must be even stronger. I yearned for him to return from town with all speed.

Chapter 3

James

I hurried down the ominously empty streets, to Colonel Ellis's house. The maid peered around the barely open door.

"I am Major James, reporting to Colonel Ellis."

"Oh, yes, sir, if you would please wait here, I will let him know." She gently shut the door. Obviously, the colonel was being careful with whom he saw.

She returned soon. "Please come in," she said, leading me toward his office. He stood to greet me. I was not surprised to see him in full regalia, even in the hot weather.

"Sir," I said, saluting him.

"Ho, ho, don't stand on ceremony. It is good to see you again, Major. Please forgive your reception. We are being very cautious, to avoid contagion. Mrs. Ellis has fled to New York for the duration."

"I'm sorry to find such a situation here," I said. "My wife is suffering from the heat as well, being heavy with child."

"Well, you rascal," he said. "Gave her a good sendoff, did you?"

I smiled, though I thought he was being rather condescending. "I hope you have received my dispatches from North Carolina," I said.

"Yes, I thought them well-done, full of information. We need to cultivate the Cherokee as allies."

"Yes, I was hoping I might eventually serve as a liaison with the tribe."

"We are not at that point yet, but we may be in the future." He took up his pipe, tamping the tobacco down. "Oh, speaking of missives, I have received one from your family's estate in England. It seems it might be important." He rummaged in his desk, producing a thick paper sealed with the Ensleigh emblem.

"Thank you, sir," I said and tucked it into my pocket.

"Welcome back. There's not much we can do until this illness slows down. Be careful."

"Yes, sir, and you as well." I saluted him and turned away.

Leaving the colonel's house, I went directly to the tent maker. No one answered the door there, but I could hear hammering from the back.

"Mr. Campbell," I said, startling him so that he dropped his hammer.

"Oh, sorry, Major," he said, eyeing my uniform.

"I am sorry to surprise you, but I'm in need of a tent."

"How soon?"

"Immediately, I'm afraid."

"Aye? I have lost my assistant to this horrible plague, so I'm working slowly. I do have one made for the army, which I can't imagine they will need soon. You can take that and I will start on another for them."

"That would be a great help," I said. "Please deliver it to us and I shall have the coin for you then." I gave him directions to the cabin; he promised to deliver it that day.

It was well that I hurried home, for when I arrived, I found the whole household gathered around the hearth table in strained silence. Even Dougie looked solemn, holding onto Carys's skirts.

"Oh, James, thank goodness you are here," said Ardath, looking at me as if I would surely offer the remedy for whatever ailed them. That called up everything protective in me. I put my arm around her shoulders.

"What is the matter?" I asked.

"Our funds are completely gone!" she said.

"But…how?"

"Ahmed and two others have dug up our coins and fled with them, weeks ago." She looked up at me in distress.

I felt stunned at this information. I thought no one knew of the spot where they had been buried. Also, all the Africans had seemed devoted to the Rhys sisters. I shook my head to clear it. "But, some of your funds are held for you by Smythe, at least."

"Yes, some, but not the fortune we had here," she said.

I looked around the table. Grim expressions greeted me, especially those of Isa and Omar.

"There will be a way for us going forward, I feel sure," I said. "For one thing, it is doubtful Ahmed could have spent it all. Has the constable been notified?"

"Oh, yes," said Mrs. Perry. "But no man of the law has found them anywhere. We advertised a reward of course, but still nothing." Her lips were drawn in a thin line. She was fiercely loyal to Ardath and Gwyn.

"I will meet with Smythe in the morning. Or perhaps he can come here to give us more news about where we stand. Omar, can you go to his office to ask when we may see him?" I said.

Omar looked relieved. "Of course, sir, I will go now."

"Good. Ask him to bring my funds with him," I said. "If he can come now, please wait and accompany him here."

"Yes, sir." He hurried away.

To the others, I tried to give hope of some recovery. "I'm here now and I believe we will be able to resolve this predicament." I also gave the information about a new tent available to us. They seemed to draw comfort from my assertions and sat straighter in their chairs.

"I'll get the pallets ready for you and Dougie," said Mrs. Perry, as she rustled up from her seat. At that, the group broke up and each went to attend to her separate concerns. The two sisters went upstairs to change into lighter-weight gowns. Carys ushered Dougie along behind them for a nap. Mrs. Perry bustled around in the hearth area, muttering under her breath about Ahmed. Isa went to care for the garden.

As for me, I found the house quite full of women for whom I felt responsible. I could only hope that Smythe wanted to help me untangle some of this. Thank God that the fall and cooler weather were on the far horizon. The epidemic was likely to lessen and then we'd have Ibrahim's brain to pick as well.

I retreated to the front porch. A welcome breeze sighed in the trees around me. The missive still weighed down my pocket. With a jerk, I pulled it out, split the heavy wax seal with my thumb, and read.

TO: SAMUEL BOOTH JAMES, Philadelphia, Colony of Pennsylvania:

Your presence is required in England at the Manor of Ensleigh forthwith, upon receipt of this letter.

Caroline, Countess of Redfern

I flushed with anger. Typical of Mother to send a demand that would play havoc with my life, and without explanation or affection! I calmed myself with breathing deeply and resolved to think this out before taking action. As I moved in my seat, a small note written in a cramped hand fell out of the folded letter. It read:

Sam, please come with all haste. Father is very ill. Both our brothers are on an expedition to further family business on the continent. They have been gone too long, with no contact. We fear for them. Mother is mismanaging the estate and won't let Mr. Appleton overrule her. She has never been so cruel to me as she is now. I am desperate and have no way to escape. Please come, Your Elizabeth.

Ah, my dear sister, trust her to give me the true picture. My heart ached for her. But what was I to do? My own wife and family needed me here, rather desperately, with financial concerns, and especially with the babe due within the coming months. I couldn't make a trip to England and back before that time came, even if I stayed only for a brief term. My loyalties wrestled and strained with one another. It might be that my brothers would come back just as I got there, or even before, while it was certain that I was needed here.

What I could do about the estate, I had no idea, having

never been taught anything about it as my older brothers were. I might be able to escape, rescuing my sister, though Mother might send the sheriff after us. Most of all, I hated to hear that Father was ill. He never gave up on his duties to the estate or the crown, ever, so he must be very ill.

I turned as the door to the house opened. Ardath stood there, holding her bulging middle. She nestled down beside me, taking my hand. Her hands were cool and she seemed calm.

"What's the matter?" she asked.

I smiled. "Oh, other than thievery and penury, you mean?"

"I know you, how you are when worried," she said, curling her fingers through my hair.

"What is this?" She had picked up Mother's letter and gazed at it, looking incredulous.

"This is my mother, demanding that I return to England." She looked at me, chestnut eyebrows peaked. "But you will understand more when you read this." I gave her my sister's note, which she read quickly.

"Much goes on at your home," she said. "What will you do?"

"First, my home is with you. Then, I know not yet what to do. This letter has been at least some weeks in making its way here. There is no way to know what is happening now."

"Your sister, it seems, needs help rather desperately."

"Yes, it tears at me to know she is so miserable. I've left her alone in that situation for entirely too long. If Father is ill and my brothers missing, there is no one but Mother in charge and she can be both ignorant and cruel. I don't understand where my brothers could be, but it is ominous that they are gone so long, on such a short journey."

"Oh, no. We have finally come together. I was depending

on you to be here." She paused, sighing, and intertwined our fingers. "At the same time, I believe you must go, James."

"That is generous of you, but I want to be here for you and the babe."

"If I weren't with child, I'd go with you, but as it is, I should stay. You know that I have plenty of help and love here." She brushed a stray curl from my forehead. "James, I married a soldier and knew that you might be called away at any time by duty. You still have a duty to your family in England as well. And it's not like I am a shy and helpless maiden. But," she grabbed me by my waistcoat, "you must promise me to return as soon as may be."

She kissed me, distracting me for only a moment.

"But what about your financial situation and the need to apprehend Ahmed and the other thieves? I can't do anything for us if I am traveling abroad, except leave some of my back pay to help out."

"We will work all that out somehow. We aren't destitute. Thank you for the extra money. We can use the coin we have to buy livestock to see us through the winter. Smythe will surely help us manage; in fact, I see Smythe coming now."

The tall, slim figure of my friend appeared on the path walking towards us. Omar came behind him and vanished towards the backyard.

"James, Ardath, well met!" said Smythe. He and I shook hands and clapped each other on the back.

"Congratulations to you both!" he said, glancing at Ardath's expanded waist.

She hugged him and asked, "How do you fare, Smythe? How good to see you."

He gave a crooked grin. "I'm better since I heard you are all safely home, and have found your mother to boot."

"Yes, we are truly fortunate to be here, alive and well," I said. "And happy that you seem to be the same."

"I am blessed with health so far," he said. "Before we go to greet the others, I will tell you that your coin has increased during your absence, partly from the work of the others, though Ibrahim doesn't charge enough for his wonderful care. No one has felt any want. Your pay," he said to me, "has continued, of course, and has mounted up nicely, though none of you are rich." He took Ardath's hand. "I am dreadfully sorry for the loss of your capital through Ahmed's actions."

"We have been discussing it just now, and this missive from my mother ordering me home." I handed him the letter and Elizabeth's note.

"Good grief!" Smythe said, rubbing his forehead.

"I think he has to go," said Ardath. "No one else knows about it yet."

"A shame, James," Smythe said, shaking his head. "However, if you must go, I shall help as vigorously as I can here."

My heart warmed at his words. He was a good and faithful friend. I knew that I would leave my women in capable hands.

Chapter 4

Gwyn

As usual, I had worried how it would be to see Gregory Smythe again, after my brief but fierce alliance with my cousin David Reese in North Carolina. As usual, I needn't have worried at all. As soon as I saw his dear face and crooked smile, I ran to Gregory and threw myself into his warm arms. I pictured covering him with wild kisses, but I pulled myself back. After all, I had just been thinking of David!

"My Gwyn," he said, and I thought I saw moisture glisten in his eye. "What a heavenly delight to see you again, so beautiful…." His voice choked a little and he smiled broadly, showing all his crowded teeth.

"Oh, Gregory!" We found ourselves at a loss for words, and that seemed fine.

We were just inside the front door holding each other's elbows. Mother came up to us. "Mother, this is Gregory. Gregory, our mother."

"Mrs. Rhys, I am so pleased to meet you and to know that you all survived. What a strong and clever family you all are." He bowed to Mother and took her hand in a courtly manner as if to kiss it. She was beaming at him. Happily, I remembered how contagious his good humor had always been.

"Thank you, Mr. Smythe, we still have difficulties to face, but they are as nothing since we are together."

"I can understand that," he said. "I regret that you come to the city whilst we are suffering this yellow fever, only to find that your fortune has been stolen."

I looked up to see James, with Ardath close behind him, watching us from the front doorway. Somehow, I knew that he was going to add a further complication to our situation, but he didn't speak immediately.

Mrs. Perry appeared with a pitcher of lemonade which she had made with the lemons and sugar Mother had brought from Charles Town. "Will everyone please come to the hearth room for refreshment?" she asked, seeing that we had James, Ardath, Smythe, Mother and myself already gathered. This we did, and sitting at our table drinking cool liquid was wonderfully refreshing. My temperature had risen upon seeing Gregory.

James sighed. I turned to him. "What is it that you need to tell us, James?" I asked. It didn't even surprise him anymore that I knew something was happening with him. He sighed again.

"While we are all gathered, I must report that my father is ill and my mother requires my presence in England. I deeply regret that I must respect her request if the colonel is able to spare me. I would much rather be here with all of you."

The gathered company sat in shocked silence. Mother watched Ardath, who tipped her head up to Mother. "It's all as it should be, Mother. He has responsibilities with his family, as much as we would love to have him here for the birth of his son," said Ardath.

"Oh, son is it?" said James, whose eyes glittered at Ardath. He squeezed her to him playfully. She laughed. All of us felt lightened by this exchange.

"We will take good care of Ardath while you are gone, James," said Mother.

"That is the thing that reassures me most," James said in a warm voice.

"And please don't be concerned that you ladies will be penniless," Smythe was saying, when I had really started to listen. "Are there immediate concerns that we need to see to, either financial or legal?"

Ardath answered. "I know we will need meat for the winter, especially if it is as bad as the last one was. I haven't looked at what has been, or can be, put up for vegetables." She looked at Mrs. Perry.

"My dears, knowing that your main finances have been taken, we have planted and preserved many things, including things that fill the stomach well, like the beans we have dried. We have jars of every vegetable you could wish, including leeks," she said, smiling at me. She knew leeks were my favorite.

"Well, that is a relief," said Ardath. "Thank you for managing that, Mrs. P."

"The chickens have done very well. They lay so well that we have pickled many of their eggs. If the winter is frigid, they could come into the animal room. We didn't buy other animals, since most of the money was gone," said Mrs. Perry.

Here Smythe picked up the story. "If you wish to buy stock before winter, you will find there are plenty for sale. The fever has killed so many people that their animals sometimes wander the streets looking for food. I can have agents find likely pigs and cows for a pittance."

"And a goat, please, if you can, Mr. Smythe," said Mother.

Ardath looked at James. "I think that's a good idea," said

James. "Fresh meat may be hard to come by since I'll not be here to hunt, and hunters may be staying away from the city because they fear the fever." Ardath nodded.

"Very well, I'll pursue the animals you want. They can be fattened through the fall. The miller is still operating. I can get more flour and oats from him," said Smythe.

"We will definitely need more of both," said Mrs. Perry. "Our family is expanding in a happy way. There must be cakes to celebrate. We will have corn meal coming when the corn finishes."

"What about materials to build extra housing?" Ardath asked.

"I wouldn't advise that right now, unless you can use your own wood. Omar could build for you, of course, but unless you use logs, you would need time to dry the wood. There isn't enough coin to buy prepared materials. Labor is scarce also. Last time, Ahmed helped Omar with the heavier work," said Smythe.

He looked around the table at all of us. "On a more serious note, I must warn you all to stay here at your house, unless some dire circumstance compels you to go to town," said Smythe. "Especially rest and take plenty of liquids. Even I, who have been here throughout the disease, have closed my business except for the most needful services. I use agents to take papers about town as needed."

He turned to James. "If you wish, I can have an agent take your request to the colonel and look into transport to London for you."

"That would be excellent, Smythe and thank you! You must take care of yourself too. I'll go to write my letter to the colonel. If he permits, I can leave in two days' time." James went to the front room to rummage in his bag for paper.

"Meanwhile, Mrs. Perry," said Ardath, "while Smythe looks into meat for the winter, are there other provisions we need to make for the household or the baby?"

"Let me show you the storeroom," said Mrs. Perry. Then she and Ardath went to look at the jars already stored and to make a list of other needed things. "Potatoes, early apples, winter squashes, and corn are still to come," she said as they walked away.

Gregory smiled. "If you would excuse us, Mrs. Rhys, I would walk out with Gwyn," he said.

"Of course," Mother said, showing the little dimple in her cheek.

We were hardly out the back door before he swept me into his arms and kissed me through and through. "Oh Gwyn, it's been far too long. How I have yearned for you, and worried that you were lost."

"And it has been a close thing at times, believe me. Now I truly feel I am home and happy." Despite the heat, I couldn't quit hugging him to me. In fact, I felt close to tears as the truth of our hardships and close escapes came back to me. A little sob escaped me.

"You are with me. You are safe," he said, gently brushing straggles of my black hair back from my sweaty forehead. Gregory always seemed to know what I was feeling, especially my worries, almost before I knew them myself. I had never had that with anyone before, except my mother, of course. This was one of the comforting things I was learning about love.

Calm now, I pulled back and said to him, "Gregory, right now, I must know what life here has been like for you."

"Yes ma'am!" he said, grinning, then becoming more serious. "Well, until the fever came, I learned everything I could from Mr. Willingham, the solicitor whose house and office I shared. It has been a time of intense study and of learning the clients whose work he did. But then, when the fever came, Mr. Willingham and his wife contracted the disease. I'm afraid they will not live." He looked down and shook his head.

"Oh, no! I'm so sorry," I said. "It seems you had become very close with them."

"Indeed, they said I was like the son they'd never had. They forbade me to come to the house after they got the disease. I was warned that the bad air from the fever might be about in the house, so I have been staying with a friend named Randolph."

"Dear Gregory, you have been going through your own trials here."

"True, this cursed fever has wreaked havoc in the city. I can no longer assume clients with whom I worked are still alive. Most of my business has been finding and interpreting wills for those who have survived, at least for now."

"A time of great uncertainty." I said.

He sighed again.

"You must be very careful not to get the fever. We all must be. Ibrahim says there is no cure, and I believe him," I said.

"So do I," he said.

We walked on under the shade of the big oaks. I didn't broach the subject that flew into my mind. That is, if Smythe would ask again to marry me?

"I have to admit, I spent some time up here at the cabin hoping you would just appear some day," he said, tugging at his neck cloth.

"It is wonderful to be here, but—wait, tell me of others in

the town. What of Franklin and his family? What of my uncle and aunt?"

"Hmmm, the Franklins are well. Your uncle has bravely visited the sick throughout, but has been spared. Your aunt succumbed in the first wave, I hear."

"Oh." I paused. Later, I'd try to know how I felt about it. "Well, Uncle must have been very distressed."

"I think perhaps he is working too hard to address himself to his loss."

"Oh," I said. Gregory always had a tactful way of expressing things. In truth, it was likely my uncle was relieved by that mean woman's death.

Chapter 5

James

As it turned out, the colonel needed a man to take confidential information to our superior officer in London. Thus was my leave of absence from my duties in the Pennsylvania colony easily accommodated. I wondered what could be both so crucial and so private that it couldn't go by post or on a naval vessel, but that was not my business. Mainly, I was relieved it had happened naturally. I did not like the idea of forsaking my duty to the army, or of using my family's influence to gain a favor.

In our bedroom, I prepared my small bag of possessions. I would not wear my uniform, but would take it on my voyage to London. I would sail there, then make my way across England by horse. It was a slight further delay, but the best I could manage.

Ardath was all encouragement and efficiency. "You must wish me gone quickly since you are so much help to me," I said to her in jest.

"Arrgggghhh," she said, pulling me off balance with surprising strength. We fell on the bed together and were soon engrossed in each other.

"How I wish I could stay," I said.

"How I wish you could too," she whispered in my ear, making the hair on my arms stand up.

"Witch, you have ensorcelled me," I said, then realized that she had been called that in earnest on our Atlantic voyage. "Oh, sorry, my dear, not the best endearment for you, so sorry." Her face showed, what? her shock? Thank God she couldn't hide the grin which broke full out, or the giggles.

"No, if I were a true witch, I would have cast a spell which bound you here to me."

I gazed at her face, flushed from the heat and our exertions, the high cheekbones ablaze, the green eyes gleaming, the classical nose, full lips and strong chin, a face of great strength and beauty. How I would miss it and, well, the rest of her too.

We all said goodbye at the cabin I knew as home, rather than risk a trip for any but myself to the docks. Traveling light, I had no delay getting aboard at the last minute, with my bag and my satchel of papers.

I welcomed the breeze on the river and looked forward to being at sea. Fortunately, I had a stomach for rough sailing and planned to spend every moment possible on deck. Smythe had procured me the fastest vessel possible. The captain was congenial and I anticipated good conversations with him as we traveled.

It was an infinite pleasure to be at leisure with a good captain and reliable crew, so that I didn't have to relive the awful business of our first voyage from Liverpool to Pennsylvania, with its epidemic of the small pox, a threatened mutiny, shipwreck, and the death of most on board.

On the other hand, that was how I met Ardath and came

to love her. Well, after being an arrogant prick to her and justly receiving her contempt, that is. Thank God, Smythe talked me out of that, so I was finally able to see what a treasure she was.

As for her family, I had felt myself drawn into it in a way that was new to me. Like a weaving, the warp I had brought with me from England was dull pea green cords of family station, discipline, tight-lipped strength, loyalty, honor, and prejudice. The weft of her, now our, family, was many gay-colored strands, soft but strong, made of respect, love, joy, wit, kindness, and welcome, such as I had never known.

If I compared Ardath's mother Carys to my mother, "The Countess," it was as if womankind were cracked into two parts, one kind and reaching out to me, the other cruel and angry, or worse, simply uncaring. I had to brace myself to think of facing the mother who gave me birth. Surely, there must be something good about her. I would search to find it, not out of need any more, but so I didn't have to think of her as a true witch.

We made excellent time, the journey which might take as much as thirteen or more weeks, lasted only eight weeks for us. I departed in London, finding my way through its busy, stinking, filthy streets to the stockade, leaving my message there as quickly as possible. The general to whom I reported pressed me to stay and enjoy his hospitality, but understood when I explained my family's situation.

With relief, I left the choking air of the smoke, hiring a sturdy but fast horse and setting out across the English countryside, still in summer green but with harvest hurrying on. Ensleigh is in the Cotswolds, with its beautiful rolling hills and houses made of honey-colored limestone, a rich and prosperous land and well suited for sheep, which we raise on our estates. To torment my mother, Father used to say we were nothing but sheep farmers, which he knew assaulted her intense pride in our nobility.

I stayed in inns, not wishing to be an amiable guest at neighbors' estates, making small talk while so worried about what I might find at Ensleigh. My poor horse got little rest during the short nights as I pushed her long into the evening and rode out early in the morning. The closer I got the more my apprehension grew.

On the fourth day, I rode into the circular drive fronting the house. Despite some bad memories of our family life, I had to admire the light golden colored stone of the façade, with the turrets and the traceries for decoration. At least it appeared that Mother had not had time to ruin the house.

A groom ran to take my reins, bowing at my side. "Welcome home, sir!"

"Thank you, Michael. Please give her some oats and a good rubdown. Her name is Maude."

"Yes, sir. Right away," he said.

From the front door came a welcome sight, my younger sister Elizabeth, pink cheeks and blue eyes all alight to see me.

I found I couldn't speak without tears welling, so I just held her for long minutes. She was frankly crying, as women are allowed to do.

"My best girl, always," I said, stroking her blond curls. "I got here as fast as I could. How is Father?"

She pulled away. "Oh, Sam, he's not well at all, but he shall rally when he sees you!"

"What word of Stephen and Richard?"

"No word at all and it has been almost six months now. What if they have perished and you are the next earl?"

"We will find them yet, and I hope Father will be with us

longer than you think."

"You always make things right, Sam."

I raised my eyebrows at that. There were many things I could certainly not make right.

"And Mother?"

"Thankfully not back yet from the neighbors. Come take some wine and wash up. Father will want to see you as soon as possible."

I went to my old room, still decorated as I remembered it, with heavy maroon drapes and a dark Turkey rug, a decor which seemed to promise no light could live there. I washed and brushed the dust off my clothes.

Just as I finished that, a valet knocked. He appeared flustered, smoothing down his uniform and smiling nervously, while bowing. "So sorry, sir, I should have been here to help you with your clothes. I am Giles, sir."

"Thank you, Giles. I have tended to that, but if you like, you can see what costumes are in my trunk or armoire that I might wear to dinner. I assume the Countess wants us to dress for dinner?"

"Yes, sir. I will prepare your clothes. Will that be all?"

"Yes. Is my father in his old room?"

"He is in the southeast corner room, sir."

"Then that's where I'll be."

Elizabeth tapped on the door as I turned to go find Father. "Sam, you should see how he brightened when I told him you were here."

"I'm going there now." She took my arm as we walked the long corridors.

I braced myself for the sight of Father in bed when he had always been so active, but I wasn't prepared for how he had shrunken into himself, become such an old man.

"Father, I am so happy to see you," I said.

He gestured at me to come closer. I thought I saw tears in his eyes. "Samuel," he said in a strangled voice. "Elizabeth, please leave us."

"Of course, Father," she said.

"I thought you might not get here in time," he said. I didn't like the sound of that.

"I was on the frontier to negotiate with the Indians when Mother's note came to Philadelphia, so it was delayed in reaching me. After that, I came as fast as I could, but you know travel is slow. Anyway, I am here now and eager to help in any way I can, sir."

"You always were a good son." This worried me more and more. It wasn't the rule in our family to speak so openly of feelings, especially to give an unexpected compliment. "You must take your mother in hand, Samuel. She is beyond listening to me any more. You must convince her." He stopped to clear phlegm from his throat.

When he straightened up in bed, I asked, "Convince her?"

"She seems worried that there will be no one capable of running the estate when I die. She has given up on Stephen and Richard and presses your sister to marry forthwith."

"But, hasn't she pressed Elizabeth for some years now?" I sat down on a stool close to the bed.

"Not with the fury she shows now." He rubbed his chin. His eyes, so clear before, were bleary. His nose stood out in a wasted face. His large hands trembled.

"Hmmm. I believe Stephen and Richard might still be alive. There's no evidence of their death, is there?"

"No, but somehow we've all become sure of it. If they are,

you would be the natural one to inherit and run the estates." He looked at me with sympathy. "I know that's the last thing you want to do. Elizabeth reads some of your letters to me. They are full of adventure and of your family in the new world."

I couldn't believe how openly he spoke to me. Perhaps he thought we wouldn't have many chances to speak in private. I decided to be equally candid.

"It isn't always possible to tell with Mother, but why does she not think me capable of running the estates?" I asked.

"I don't know, Samuel, but I suspect she looks down on you for marrying a commoner, a colonist, no less, and Welsh to boot!"

This shouldn't have surprised me about my mother. "But do you think the same about my marriage?" I asked with some trepidation.

"I do not. Have you listened to what I just said to you? You are the natural heir, if we have lost your brothers. In my case, I believe I'd be saddling you with something you don't want. Is that true?"

"Well, yes, but I am prepared to do my duty. As for Elizabeth, it is much better that I help her find a husband, than someone chosen by Mother, someone Elizabeth doesn't want to marry."

"Women have their duty too. This estate must not be lost at any cost. I do agree with your mother on that."

"Father, I understand. Can you tell me what ails you, that I find you here in bed?"

"Oh those doctors haven't the slightest idea, though they come and hem and haw and try to bleed and cup me. I've been in bed for some months now. I'll admit that having your brothers disappear has sunk me lower."

"I can imagine it has. When did you know they were missing?"

"Several weeks after they were to have arrived in Bruges to negotiate the wool sale, we received word that they had never arrived there. Of course, they were going to Paris first and we sent word to our agent there. He had not heard from them either, and had sent a message to that effect, but the message had not reached us."

"So, they went missing after they left here and before Paris."

"And the ship they took to France?"

"Has not been heard from." He rubbed his forehead and sighed.

"Father, this is tiring you. Rest now. I will begin to follow this mystery down right away."

He nodded and sank onto his pillow, closing his eyes.

Elizabeth was waiting on a bench in the hall. She rose, her pale skirts ballooning out, her eyes never leaving my face. "Now you know, Sam. What do you think?"

"Hmm, I don't have enough information yet. Let's have some food and drink while you tell me more."

"He's awfully diminished, isn't he?" she asked as we walked towards the drawing room.

I nodded, my lips tight. My thoughts were on our Welsh nursemaid Elen, who had been dismissed long years ago for warning that my brothers should not take to sea, or disaster would strike. I would never repeat this, of course, but it didn't lead to a sanguine outlook.

Chapter 6

Ardath

James was gone again. I had encouraged him to go, but truly I hated it. It was good that we were home and I had Mother and Gwyn here. Two stronger and more capable women would be hard to find, so I wasn't worried about my baby coming, with their help.

What I couldn't get out of my mind was Ahmed disappearing with our gold and silver coins. It rankled with me so badly that I lost sleep, tossing and turning, even though I knew it wasn't good for me. It was maddening that someone we had always tried to help had turned against us, and that our best hope of finding him was off to England, looking for his brothers.

Mother and Gwyn seemed mostly unaffected by Ahmed's betrayal, which just irritated me to no end. Without our money and without James to hunt for us and protect us, they focused on the fact that we should have all we needed for the winter. I hoped that we were relatively safe here, provided the yellow fever didn't slink up our hillside to kill us.

Smythe was our connection with the community that we sheltered from. He came the day after James left, to see Gwyn and to talk about the theft. At least, I insisted that he talk about it. I rushed out the back door when I heard him talking to

Gwyn.

"Greg, I need to know everything you can tell me about the theft and what investigation there has been since. No one here seems to care or to know what to do about it," I said

"Ah, well, I wish there were more to say. As your agent, I told the high constable about the missing coins as soon as Omar told me. He promised to contact the constables of surrounding towns. He actually knew Ahmed and the two others already, since they had been disturbing the peace very often, so he gave out their descriptions all around. He reported to me that he had done that. His constables were so burdened by trying to keep down thievery and grave desecrations that there was no one to send out after them, even had we known which way to send. Further, the Proprietor shut down the town, in fear that infected people might spread the fever from here."

"So we know nothing," I said. It was an effort to keep from yelling at poor Smythe, who was only trying to help in difficult circumstances.

"That's not entirely true," he said, scuffing his foot on the wet ground, for we were still in the yard. After our journey in the wilderness, houses sometimes felt confining. "We do know their descriptions. The other two were English, from Cheapside in London, so their speech would mark them. One had a distinctive scar running down his face from eye to chin. The other was short and wiry with a twisted back. Those would be marks very difficult to hide. If they spend only silver, they might not look too suspicious, but if they venture to pull out the gold, they will be seen as thieves."

"Hmmm, I suppose that should help. But there must be something else we can do. What can we do?"

Greg shook his head, his mouth grim. "I'm sorry Ardath,

but it is best while the fever rages to do what we can do to make your family comfortable and well provided for. I will make sure you don't suffer financially. The further search will have to wait."

Gwyn said, "Before you are off, how goes the town?"

He smiled at her. "I'm glad to say the fever cases seem to be decreasing, which gives us hope. Also I want you both to know that I have found animals for you. Two milking cows, a fat sow, and a she-goat."

"I'll tell Omar to prepare for them," I said. "When will they arrive?"

"Tomorrow, if possible."

"Yes, we'll be ready then," I said, starting off, then turned, remembering to thank Smythe, who bowed.

I hurried across the yard to Omar, who had already measured out a space for the animal shelter and cut some trees for lumber. "Ah, Miss Ardat'. Good day to you," he said. He wiped the sweat from his face with a gray cloth. "What can I do for you?"

"Smythe says he will have animals delivered tomorrow. There will be two cows, a goat, and a large pig, all of which will need to be confined." I had full confidence that Omar would understand and help me. All the Africans had learned English very well in the short time we had known them, whereas we had given up on learning Mandinka.

"Ah," he said. I saw him surveying the ground. "De cows we can put on ropes over dere." He pointed to a spot with some shade and reasonable grass. "De pig needs a pen. I can make dat today, furder from de house, so's not to stink too much. De goat can eat dos weeds." He pointed to a part of the garden that had not been cleaned after the beans were harvested. "I have iron stakes to tie dah ropes to."

He fell silent. I knew Ahmed had probably provided those stakes to us. Omar avoided anything that reminded him of his son.

"Thank you, Omar. For the winter shelter, we will now need at least two stalls."

"Maybe more, doh," he said. "Will you have horses again?"

"I don't know," I said. So much was unknowable to us, so much out of our control. When James returned—but when would that be? Would he want a horse? Would the contagion subside? Would I be hale and hearty after the baby came? Would the baby be healthy? Could Ahmed be found at a later date? When would we be able to move freely to look for him? All the unanswered questions banged around in my head.

Isa came into the garden then. She greeted me quietly. Her old exuberance had disappeared. I resented Ahmed for stealing away his parents' happiness along with our coin. I wanted to keep reassuring them that they weren't to blame, but that only seemed to make them feel worse.

"Isa, I was telling Omar that we will have animals coming tomorrow. The goat can clean up the old bean patch for you and any other weedy spots."

She nodded. "Dis is good. Den I put in greens for fall."

I told her about the other animals as well.

"I save manure for de garden. Omar and I can not butcher de pig for you," she said, "so sorry, but we know someone who can." I assumed this was a prohibition of their Moslem religion, so I nodded.

"I would be most grateful for that. I've never done it before."

"Not good luck for woman with child to do it!" she declared.

"Thank you, Isa," I said as I marched back to the house. Well, at least we could prepare for some things.

Mother was playing with Dougie who was learning to run after a ball. "Mother, can we talk?"

"Of course. Dougie, please go to check on the chickens. Then play outside."

He nodded and tore off. Isa would watch him. Everybody loved him well.

"I wonder if my child will be as happy as Dougie," I said.

She smiled at me. "A child who is well cared-for is usually happy."

"Hmmm. Where is that great peacefulness I am supposed to have with pregnancy?"

She cocked her head to one side. "Ardath what is it, really?" she asked, hands on hips.

"It's Ahmed stealing our coins. I had things I wanted to do with them, expand our business here, set up a trading post in the south." I tried not to gnash my teeth.

"I wonder if this is the time to do these things? We can't go about the city during the fever, and according to James, as a soldier, he is likely to be sent north, not south again. It seems it is a time for strengthening what we have here and a time for waiting."

"Waiting!" My brain boiled at the idea.

"Or, better yet, it is a time to beat the rug in my bedroom. I'll get it down for you," she said, smiling.

I soon found myself at the shady part of the clothesline, beating the rug to within an inch of its life, and venting my fury with Ahmed on every stroke.

Chapter 7

James

Elizabeth and I were in the informal, small drawing room, which had only one gold sofa and two cream-colored chairs, a quiet place where we could talk freely. Light streamed in through the semi-circular windows. I had opened one to let in the flower scents and birdsong. We could sit quietly with our tea, to speak of our father, Ardath, the babe to come, and the ridiculous suitors that Mother had paraded through the house to inspect my sister. At least these last provided some levity to our honest talk, since she felt protected by my presence.

From her seat on the sofa, Elizabeth said, "Sam, maybe it is just having been so confined here, but I dream of going to the colonies, perhaps to have a chance to make my own way there, although what that way would be I don't know. I dread any marriage because I'll be found out then. Perhaps that would not be as big a scandal as it would here, or there I could claim to be a widow and no one would know."

"What do you mean? You are a lovely, highly eligible woman; anyone would say so."

She began to sob quietly, tears leaking through her lashes. "I've never told anyone, but I must tell you. I am spoiled. I had relations with a boy from the town in Wales. I thought I loved him, or something, I don't know…." She twisted her handkerchief in her lap.

I groaned inwardly. "Oh, I see. You are afraid that your husband will discover you are not a virgin." I knew my eyebrows were raised and hoped she didn't take that for judgment.

"Worse, he will see that I have born a babe. I have stretch marks from the birth."

"Ah." Thank goodness I now had enough experience from real life to not reject her as I once would have. I rose to sit beside her on the sofa.

Her face flushed deep pink with shame. She wiped her nose. She couldn't look at me.   "It was about a year and a half ago. We kept it a secret, saying I was 'indisposed' and you know how we are much more isolated at Glenmorgan. Even Father didn't know."

"What happened to the babe?"

"I don't really know. I heard Mother tell the two men who brought the midwife to 'get rid of the baby'. I hope they didn't kill him. He was pink and plump and healthy." Here she began to sob uncontrollably. I had not known all she had suffered while I was gone. I could only imagine how dreadful Mother would have been in this circumstance, having Lizzie's sin to hold against her. I folded her shaking body into mine and held her there until the sobs slowed down.

She pulled back from me. "Now perhaps you will shun me too. I was stupid. I deserve to suffer."

I shook my head, intending to tell her she was human, when the door slammed back against the wainscoting. Mother entered like one of the Furies, ginger hair flying, face blood-red, and contorted mouth showing teeth prepared to bite. I leapt up to protect Elizabeth.

Mother threw her arms in the air. "So, the little bitch hopes to get sympathy for her weakness, her disregard for our family name, her selfish, idiotic actions! Not in this house she won't. Get away from her, Samuel. Can't you at least show better judgment?" she spit out.

"Mother, cease this railing! We are all adults here. I'll have you show me and Elizabeth the proper respect."

"Respect is earned and I don't see anyone here who has earned mine," she said. "You are a nothing in this world, reduced to being a vulgar soldier, of no account as a gentleman, someone who has married so far beneath us that I am embarrassed in front of my friends, that they might find out. And your sister, how dare you tell her it's all right to wallow in the hay with a lowly peasant and produce a child who has to be hidden and done away with?"

"Mother, did you have the child killed?" I said as calmly as I could with my heart pounding.

"I don't know what happened to the child, better off dead, I'd say." She turned her head away. It chilled me to the bone. I knew then that she had had him killed.

"Mother that is murder!"

"No, it is a mercy and that is all."

I stared at her in horror. I felt a wave of sickness rise within me. There was nothing more to say to her. I wanted to depart the house that instant, but I couldn't leave Father and Elizabeth in the hands of a monster, for now I saw that she was a monster indeed, and that my resolution to find something positive in her was going to fail. I could take control of the situation, though. Father was still the head of the household. I would go to him and ask him to confine her before she did more damage.

"Lizzie, come with me." I took her hand and we left the

drawing room with Mother standing there glaring at us.

When we stood outside, the day was warm and dry. We walked hand in hand towards the gardens, then past hedges until we were far away, almost to the stables. I breathed a sigh of relief.

"Lizzie, I'm so sorry for how she has treated you." She shrugged her shoulders, as if to say she was used to it. "How has she been with Father?"

"She berates him for staying abed. She won't accept that he is unwell."

Worse and worse! "And what is happening on the estates?" I asked.

"You must talk with Appleton. She ordered him not to shear the sheep when it was time, saying he should wait until Stephen returned. That was months ago. The wool would have been ruined. I sneaked Appleton to Father's room and of course, Father ordered him to continue with the shearing. But, oh Sam, if Father dies before we can find Stephen or Richard, I don't know what will happen. She has told me she won't recognize you as the heir, and I really believe her."

I shook my head, appalled at what she said. "Thank you for telling me all this. I need to see Appleton and then Father's solicitor to make sure we have legal documents to confirm Father's wishes."

"Of course. I am so used to feeling I have no power to keep her in check, I forget what a man can do so easily. What a relief!" She even showed me a broad, if shaky, smile.

"My sweet sister," I said. "If you feel ready to go about your day, I'll go to Appleton now," I said.

"I'm fine, now you're here. And believe me, I know how to avoid Mother."

◇◇◇◇◇◇◇◇◇◇

I found Appleton in his office near the stables. He looked so much older than when I had last seen him, I almost didn't recognize him. When he stood and smiled, though, I saw the same bright eyes and upright stance I knew.

"Master Samuel, how good to see you home."

"It's good to see you too, Appleton."

"I'm sorry your Father has been unwell," he said.

"Yes, it's hard to see him laid low, but he's still in there, though his body betrays him."

"True. I have tended the estates as best I could without much supervision since your brothers have been gone. I hope I have done an adequate job of it, but I am relieved that you are here to take over, or so I assume." He looked at me somewhat askance and I wondered what my mother had said to him about my place here.

"That is indeed my father's wish, although you will need to give me much guidance about what must be done. First of all, we need the estate solicitor here as soon as possible. Do we have a reliable messenger to reach him in London?"

"Yes, Jackie is a swift rider with a sharp mind. I'll send him to Crowquill forthwith."

"Do you have paper here? I'll send a note with him."

"Yes, but your mother has the earl's seal and I know not where."

"I'll not bother with that this time, though we must find it soon." My head began to ache.

I hastened to write about the urgency of our situation to our long-time solicitor. I felt sure he would understand the need to get here quickly. Appleton had Jackie saddled and supplied with an extra horse before I even left the office. Thank God Appleton had been here all these years, and even more so in the past months.

I found myself both animated and weary. I sat by the slow-winding river. When I took off my boots and dandled my feet in the cool water, I began to listen to bird calls, the silvery slide of a thrush, the rustling of the trees, to see fish in the clear water, to smell the earthy smells, to feel the rock steady beneath me. It was as if I were a child again, as this had often been my refuge then.

I was no longer on the sea, thank the Lord. I'd never make a navy man. I really did love the land, this one and the wilder one in the colonies. This musing led me to think of Ardath. How would she feel if I had to come here, take over the title, and manage the estates? She would have to face my mother; I foresaw a stunning explosion there. And what would happen to Elizabeth if I couldn't take her to the colonies and help her start a new life? In any case, I had to address the current situation first. I rose to return and speak to Father about my ideas.

Chapter 8

James

When Crowquill appeared, Elizabeth, Father, and I had our plan in place. Father left his bed so that we all could meet in his library. I guided his tottering footsteps there. Elizabeth and Mother's lady's maid Mary brought our mother there in good time.

Father sat in a chair behind his desk, supported by pillows that kept him upright. He opened the meeting in a stronger voice than I had thought possible. "We are here to discuss the situation that now confronts us. I have asked Mr. Crowquill to draw up documents to make my wishes legal and binding. Here they are: In the event that Stephen and Richard do not return to us, I bequeath my title and estates to my son Samuel Booth James. Whether or not her brothers return, in the event of Elizabeth's marriage, she will have sufficient moneys to make her comfortable for life, regardless of the estate of the person whom she marries. Elizabeth will choose her own husband with Samuel's advice. His consent is not necessary."

Here Father stopped to clear his throat. I glanced at Mother, whose general fiery glare had intensified. Her face was a mottled purple as if she might explode. Her hands clenched in her lap looking as though she would like to choke her husband.

Father took a sip of wine and began again. "As to my wife of many years, I require that she go to our house in Wales for some well-needed rest until either I or Samuel recall her to Ensleigh. She will be accompanied by her lady's maid Mary and two footmen who will see to her every comfort, as well as the staff there, of course. Now I am tired and wish you all to leave me. There will be no naysaying or argument of any kind. Thank you all."

With that, we were certainly dismissed. As planned, I turned to Mother and led her from the room.

She fought me. She bit at me like a mad dog, but I was so much stronger than she and fully determined too. I had no respect left for her. Her once red hair flared around her head in gray sprigs. Her anger had heated her body to an unnatural temperature. She spat venomous words at me.

"Traitor—your own mother. You'll pay for this. I'll not have it! You'll pay!"

I gave no real attention to her, but almost dragged her to her room. I placed her inside it none too gently. We had had a lock made for it during the morning. This I locked securely. We were on the third floor, so there was no need to lock the windows.

I leaned towards the door. "I'll have a footman bring you supper soon. Try to calm yourself."

With that, I checked back at the office. Father had been returned to his room. Elizabeth still sat there, seeming stunned.

"Elizabeth, are you all right?" I asked.

She turned to me. "Well, yes, but I still feel overwhelmed. Can it really be true that I am out from under her schemes, her cruelty now?"

"Yes, it is all spelled out legally now. I will make sure all is done to your good."

"Oh, Sam, how incredible it is to hear this is true." Tears sprang to her eyes and she jumped up to hug me. We stood there for a long time, finding comfort in each other.

"I'm afraid this has tired Father out very badly," she said.

"I agree. I asked him to let Crowquill and me tell her, but he insisted we do it this way. I'll go check on him, if you are feeling all right now."

"Yes, yes, go to him. I'll be in the morning room."

I was alarmed when I saw how drained Father looked. His eyes were open, so I asked him how I could help.

"You could get me some brandy please, and pour yourself one."

I returned from his cabinet with two glasses.

"You need to rest, Father."

"Hah, I'll soon have plenty of rest. It's not very Christian of me to feel triumph over an old woman, but she has tormented me so long. Why didn't I get rid of her long ago? We should toast to all we have accomplished here today."

"I admit to some surprise in hearing you say this," I said, not able to prevent a smile from curling catlike around my mouth.

"Pah! That 'Earl and his Countess' image had me imprisoned far too long."

I smiled. Father had avoided confronting Mother, perhaps because she was such a vicious fighter, but he had a rather sly glee in besting her.

"Well, I think we shocked her. When she leaves, we can get down to business."

"True, but first I want you to go to my bureau and open the top drawer."

"What am I looking for?" I asked.

"Under the bottom on the left-hand side, you'll find a false bottom. There you'll see a leather pouch. Bring it here."

"This is intriguing."

When I had passed it into his hands, he smiled at me. "Thinking that you would be left with nothing at my death by English law, I have been saving this for years to give it to you in person. That said, I must ask you not to look into it yet.

"It was given to me by a friend who worked in India for the East India Company for many years. When he returned, he feared for his life in England. He never told me why, but asked me to keep the pouch safe for him. I had been his closest friend in England, helped him along the way, so I agreed. In the event of his untimely death, it was to be left to me. Later I heard he had indeed been killed. I want you to have it, regardless of what we find about Stephen and Richard. I never told you, but I see you as a man of the highest character."

He slumped back on his pillows. The glass dropped from his hand. I thought the worst had happened then, just as he had told me what I had always wanted to hear, that he had a lasting regard for me.

When I reached over, I could hear that he was snoring softly. I cannot say what a relief it was that he was still alive! I gently removed the pouch from his loose hand, then mopped up the few drops of spilled brandy. I watched him for a few moments, making sure he truly was alive, sighing with the knowledge that I had been esteemed all these years when Mother had dominated the family and Father seemed remote and unfeeling. I was stunned.

When I left Father's room, I found myself needing solitude. I walked downstairs and out to the river again to sit on my rock.

I saw that I still carried the pouch in my hand. Its contents felt heavy on my knee and rustled softly around inside. It wasn't just one object, that was certain. Of course, I was curious about what it contained, but Father trusted me not to look.

My mind returned to the astounding words I had just heard from my father. They implied that all those years, as he groomed my brothers to be his heir, he had noticed me too. Tears rose in my eyes. This knowledge made me even more determined to make good on my promises to him, to do anything I could to honor the title and make prosper the estates. Perhaps I would someday have the same heartfelt mission as my father, to train a son to become an earl.

Which led me right back to Ardath and her teasing about having a boy. She couldn't know of course, but someday I would like a child to carry my name, a name I no longer felt I must shun. I could have some pride in my heritage now, not because I might be an earl. I cared nothing for the status that would bring in the eyes of others, but because I was claimed and appreciated. Yet I wished to be with my American family. They of all people would understand how my father's affection had given me strength and heart to do what I must. In truth, I ached to be among them again.

Chapter 9

Gwyn

I should have quit writing to my cousin David, but did I? I did not. I worried for him and thought about him frequently, and his dear boys. I couldn't forget the passionate feelings we had in North Carolina. He had wanted me to stay with him, but the longer we settled into Philadelphia, the more I saw the impossibility of returning to that colony. David was committed to his plantation there. My real family was here, and there was a long distance between us. Had he lived in Philadelphia, I don't know what could have happened. I hoped that didn't make me shallow and forgetful of what we had shared, or disloyal to Gregory. If anyone came near me while I was writing to him, or reading his, I hid it quickly.

Mrs. Perry had continued her mantua making, although several of her clients had died before she finished their dresses. She seemed to take this in stride, asking, "What else can I do but keep on with my work? Perhaps I can make them over for other ladies." I began to help her sew again, and Mother sometimes joined us in companionable silence.

Ibrahim sent notes to us with addresses of those women who might enter labor soon. Mother was determined to attend them in their hour of need, though she wore a face mask against contagion the few times she was called out.

Mother and I gathered herbs together, but didn't stray far from our own property. She had established her dispensary in a corner of her room, where herbs, especially those associated with childbirth, hung drying. We really needed more room in the house, though.

I missed seeing Ibrahim, but since his work took him among the sickest people in town, I understood why we couldn't meet. He didn't let Isa come near him either, so she had begun to help Omar with his building work. At that time they were living in one of our tents. The log framework for the animal shed was rising swiftly. Fortunately, Omar had saved some planks from when he built the floor of the house. These had aged well and could be used as siding for the shed.

When the animals came, I had to greet them and name those who would not be slaughtered. The cows were Butterscotch, for her creamy caramel coat, and Dapple, for her black and white spots. The goat, named by Ardath, was Goatrude, but we just called her Trude. The sow was just "pig." I was determined that I wouldn't feel close to her or be there when she was killed and her meat slowly smoked over a low fire.

The animals provided a distraction and more work for all of us, but a good kind of work. Dougie was delighted to see the goat, who reminded him of his animal friend from Jamaica. Trude tolerated his attentions well, that is, she ignored him and chewed away on anything in sight. Mother and Dougie set up a cooling box in the stream, bounded by larger rocks on the downstream side, which kept our milk products well. One of the best was the goat's cheese, which, when blended with our garden herbs, was my favorite.

Mrs. Perry helped organize us for other chores the animals brought. She set Ardath up at the churn, so that we could make our own butter and cheese. Churning could take up large portions of the day and left Ardath tired and somehow calmer. With both cows and the goat giving lots of milk, we would have plenty of butter and cheese without having to buy in town, not to speak of Mrs. Perry's delicious custards. We had not had domestic creatures in Wales, so Mother and I had to learn to milk them. It was surprisingly difficult, but I could see that it would strengthen our hands.

Ardath looked at the bigger issues. "We really need a full barn, for animal fodder, tools, and if we are even thinking about horses, more stalls. Already I see that the shed will not be enough," said Ardath.

Just thinking about a large project made her happier.

Regardless of her churning and her urging Omar to make the shed into a full barn, Ardath continued to be restless and could not get her mind off Ahmed. I wondered if she thought of this rather than speculate what had happened with James or think too much about childbirth. Although she was very healthy, it was never sure what that could bring.

We had to find things for her to do that didn't involve lifting heavy logs with Omar.   At times we could hear him shout, "No, no, Miss Ardat', not do dat."

Finally, I asked her what might help her restlessness. We were walking around the outside loop of our property, surrounded by woods. "Would we be able to buy a horse, do you think? Then you could ride out into the woods, perhaps even hunt."

"I don't think Mother will let me ride at this point, and I have to inquire of Gregory how our money stands now. I don't think we can afford a horse. I wouldn't want just any horse.

What are you thinking? One horse for all of us?"

"Well, yes, for a start. It might help us feel less confined."

She lifted her eyebrows and rolled her eyes. "Confinement is a good word for it, in my case."

"Oh, don't feel so sorry for yourself. There's many a woman who would be aloft with excitement to have a husband and a babe to come." I gazed up at the still-summery sky.

"Hmm. I have an idea for you as well," she said.

"And what would that be?"

"Let's set up a butt and practice our archery."

"I do like that idea. We must have a bunch of hay, and some white and red cloth for a bull's eye target."

We scurried around various places where Omar stored things and found the straw in "the animal room" under the larger bedroom. Omar carried the straw out for us. White sheeting and scraps of red cloth came from Mrs. Perry's stores.

We were able to set up a butt fairly easily. Unfortunately, Ardath's swelling abdomen got in the way of the bow and threw off her aim, which made her swear in a most unladylike way. Instead she took to hurling long knives at the butt. Her aim was just as good as it had been when she practiced on the ship, after the mutineers had attacked her.

During this time, my head was full of Gregory. I trusted him, though he didn't speak of marriage, to have my best interests at heart.

As we began to notice a few red leaves in the trees, a milky blue color to the sky, and occasionally a breeze that didn't stifle us, Gregory came to see us.

My heart banged against my ribs as I saw him walking steadily up the hill towards us. Please let him have good news, I thought.

His smile warmed me. "My dear Gwyn, I am so happy, as always, to see you. Are the others around?"

"What now, you don't wish some time alone with me?"

In answer, he kissed me until my knees turned to water and I had to hold onto him. "Silly girl! Don't distract me from my excellent news. But I'll have a gathering to tell it."

Into the house we went, finding Mother with Dougie, Ardath at the churn, and Mrs. Perry pressing water from the cheese.

"Ladies," said Gregory, bowing.

"More like working women, I'd say," said Mrs. Perry, as she wiped her hands and her perspiring forehead on a towel.

"No, always 'ladies' to me," said Gregory.

"What news?" asked Ardath suddenly. She had stood up from the churn and was wringing her hands repeatedly.

"Right to the point then," he said. Reaching into his pocket, he pulled out a letter. "Ahem, your husband, Ardath, is acting as head of his family estates. But here, read for yourself." He handed it to her.

"Oh, it is addressed to us all," she said. She bent her head over the paper. "He is well. His father is rallying somewhat and his sister is feeling better. His brothers have not come home and the family is spending all efforts to find them. We are not to worry, but he may still be some time there. He hopes to bring his sister back with him, and asks that we look for a suitable house for her."

She looked up. "Well, he seems fine," she said. "Was there any other letter?"

Gregory grinned, "Yes, one for you alone." He handed Ardath a letter, which she almost snatched from his hand. She ran from the room.

"Well, this is good news, in that James has made the journey successfully. But who knows what the situation is currently? When did he send it?" I asked.

"Six weeks ago, so the ship made good time in getting it to us," said Gregory. "There is even better local news, however, as the cases of yellow fever seem to be slowing. Perhaps the cooler weather will truly make a difference."

"What a blessing that would be," said Mother.

As usual, Gregory and I slipped away as soon as we could. We walked out under the trees. Rain had ceased altogether for some days now, so the dust was powdery under our feet.

"I have never been so eager to see what fall may bring," I said.

"Yes, I can almost feel the town holding its breath in hope, when I am on the street," he said. "It has been such a strange time, maybe even stranger as it passes. I'm afraid I shall be inundated with work when I open my office again."

He sighed, twisting his hat in his hand.

"What is it, Gregory?"

"The Willinghams have died. You know I had read law under him and lodged with them as well. They were so kind to me in life and even more so in death. They have left me everything they had, the law practice, their coin, and the house."

"Gregory, you must be crushed. They gave you everything to get started when we first arrived in Philadelphia and they continued both considerate and generous to you."

"They left a note saying that they had viewed me as the son they never had. I am disconsolate. I can't stay there, because the fever may still persist in the house, but have been boarding with my friend Randolph.

"I dread having to clean up the house. I don't know how to ensure that the disease doesn't linger there. Perhaps I should burn the drapes and bedding as we would when dealing with the small pox. No one knows how the fever spreads."

"I guess that would be safest thing to do. Some of the bedding could probably be well cleaned with a good washing, though not anything of brocade or satin. Would it be the destruction of many precious things?"

His brow lightened. "Actually, it would not. Most of the cloth furnishings are many years old and frayed or faded. In the last few years, the Willinghams didn't care about society much and they never spent their money on fancy decoration or collections. I rather like their simple taste in silver and furniture, and these are all of good quality. The house itself is very well built, with roof and floors in excellent condition. In that way, they used the house lightly."

"That sounds as if a renovation could make the place more your own without too much financial outlay. The furniture is highly polished? If so, I believe we could wipe it down with vinegar, and make it safe to use." I stopped abruptly, realizing that I had said "we" as if I would be the mistress of this house. I flushed with embarrassment, but Gregory was staring at the ground and didn't seem to notice.

"Well, these are problems for another day, but I wonder if I wasn't happier when I was a poor student reading law, without such responsibilities. That was such a short time ago. I didn't expect to have money, a house, and a business so suddenly."

He grinned at me. "Am I getting wrinkles?" he asked.

"You will if you continue to worry about things that you are either capable of doing yourself, given time, or that you can pay someone else to do. Despite your loss of these good friends, I believe they would want you to enjoy what they left for you. It is really quite a windfall."

"Ah, perspective! Honestly, I have spent too much time alone while you and James were gone. Now he is gone once more."

He grimaced at me as if angry. "As for you, I command you not to go roaming about the country ever again."

"But I have gotten quite a taste for it now. I might dash away at any time," I said, pressing my lips against a smile.

"Oh, no! I shall tie you to this tree here," he said, spinning me around and pushing me gently towards it.

"No, no, kind sir. I forbid…" Then his mouth was on mine shutting out words and the world.

Chapter 10

Gwyn

Now that we were supplied for winter, had shelter for our animals because of Omar's quick work, had gathered in and preserved or dried our vegetables, sewed winter clothes for Dougie and Mother, and prayed for frost, it seemed that we were settling into Philadelphia again. The yellow fever wasn't gone, but we hoped to see its end soon.

Our link to the outside was still Gregory, who brought news of the town and the epidemic and more rarely, letters from James. One week, though, we hadn't seen him for many days and I began to worry.

"Mother," I said. We were sitting in the shade of the house as the sun moved to the west.

"Umm," she said, laying down the knitting she worked on.

"I'm worried about Gregory. You know I'm a worrier anyway, but wasn't it Monday that we saw him last?"

"Yes, that's right. Are you having a 'seeing' or more of a 'thinking?'"

I blushed. "Just thinking about him. You know he told me about inheriting the Willingham house, but hasn't asked me to marry him. Previously, I thought it was his lack of income that made him hesitate."

"What do you think now?"

"Well, maybe he doesn't want to rush me, since I said I wasn't ready when Ardath and I left for North Carolina, or maybe he wants to wait until after the fever leaves, or maybe he isn't sure he wants me any more."

She replied with a purse of her mouth. "Honestly, he doesn't seem to me to have lost interest in you." She raised her eyebrows. "Does he seem uninterested to you?"

I thought of our passionate embraces when we were alone under the trees. "Uh, no, not really." I shuffled my feet on the stones beneath us. Now I was truly embarrassed.

"I wonder when I'll ever get over such an inclination toward worry," I said.

She had no answer to that. As far as I knew, I had always worried.

The next day, some of my worries didn't seem so foolish. A messenger arrived with a note from the friend with whom Gregory was staying. I will never forget where I was when I received it. Dougie and I had just finished feeding his "dickies" in their pen. He loved to scream when they ran at his feet to get to the old corn we put out.

"Miss Gwyn Rhys?" asked the messenger boy.

"Yes?" I steered Dougie out of the pen.

"Message for you." He held out the letter in one hand and an open palm for payment in the other.

"Oh, yes." I felt in my apron pocket for a small coin. He took it and ran away.

My chest tightened with foreboding. I opened the note with a little shake in my hand. I saw it was from Greg's friend Randolph. It read:

Miss Rhys, I am sorry to tell you that Mr. Smythe has taken ill with the fever. I cannot risk infection of my elderly parents who live with me and have had to remove him to the Willingham house. I'm afraid he is quite ill.

Yours responsibly, Randolph.

I took Dougie's hand and pulled him inside. "Mother, where are you?"

She came from the preserves room. "Is everything all right?" she asked.

"Gregory has the fever. He is alone in the Willingham house. I must go see to him," I said.

She didn't argue with me. There was no one else we could ask to go. "Let me get some herbs to bring down the fever so he won't feel so terrible," she said. She clattered up the stairs while I donned my coolest gown and pulled up some sturdy boots. I ran to get fresh water from the stream in a bottle. Mother packed some food and insisted that I wear a cloth over my face in hopes that I might not get the contagion.

She said, "Don't hesitate to send word if you need me." We hugged briefly, then I flew down the street to the Willingham house, my basket banging against my hip as I ran.

It was still shuttered and looked abandoned from the street. I tried the door nearest Gregory's office. I supposed it was where Randolph might leave him. Thank goodness it was unlocked. Once inside I listened for Gregory. I heard labored breathing and followed the sound to the parlor, where Randolph had left Gregory on a lounge.

"Gregory, I'm here, dear one." He didn't stir. He was burning up with fever. I could feel the waves of it coming off him. I loosened all his clothing and opened a window to let in some fresher air, as the room was stifling. I tried to give him water but it ran down his chin. Soaking one of the clean cloths Mother had put in my basket, I bathed his face and chest with it. His feet were already bare; I cooled those too.

Although I had never seen a case of the fever, I knew the features of the disease. His eyes were quite yellow when I lifted his lids to see them. Even his skin had turned a yellowish hue. I knew that he might vomit and ran to get a basin for him. The hearth needed to be lit so that I could make him some herbal tea, but since he wasn't taking water, I left tea-making until later. I cooled him as best I could with the damp cloths, even putting some under him. I had found a large fan in Mrs. Willingham's bedchamber and waved it over him.

Toward evening, his fever seemed to rage less, making me hopeful. I never stopped cooling him. As well, he took some water, not enough, but a sip.

I had rolled the rug as far away as I could get it from the lounge. I spread out some rags underneath the basin prepared for his vomit.

I was exhausted; I had to prepare a place to lie down while I could still stand up. Taking the small rug from his office, I bundled it and repaired to the sitting room, took clean linens from the maid's closet, and made myself a pallet from which I could see his face in the night. I'd had nothing to eat and needed to keep my strength up, so I fumbled in the basket to reach the cheese and bread Mother had packed for me. I'd already made a fire in the kitchen hearth and steaming water for tea awaited me. I steeped the herbal tea for Gregory as well.

After eating, I checked Gregory again. His forehead was cooler. He took a little tea. I flopped down on the pallet with a deep sigh. I knew I'd hear if he so much as shifted in the night.

I awoke to the dreadful sound and the acrid smell of his retching. I groped for my candle, which had guttered out, and shuffled to the hearth area to light it with a spill. What he endured was no small thing; his whole body tried to expel everything in him. I held his head as the black vomit, like ground coffee, spewed from his mouth. Just when I felt I couldn't stand his suffering any longer, he moaned and lay back on the lounge. I wet the cloths, wiped his mouth, and began to cool him again, as he tossed his head and groaned. After a short while, he went back to sleep. I lifted my candlestick. Then picking up the basin and the rags soiled with his vomit, I threw the nasty stuff into a far corner of the yard. The night air seemed fresh and revived me somewhat. I washed both the basin and my hands thoroughly at the pump outside before returning to Gregory. All night we went through this same torment again and again until he only brought up a slimy bile.

Between bouts, he lay and shook with a fierce intensity. I feared for his life; how could anyone live after such agony?

In the morning, though, a miracle. He saw and recognized me. "No, no, Gwyn, you shouldn't be here! Go away. I have the fever. You mustn't catch it, dear Gwyn."

"It's all right. Be calm. I'm here to help you and I am fine."

He continued to shake his head until he sighed and fell back on the pillow, spent. I tipped a cup of the herbal tea into his mouth. He was able to swallow if I gave him small sips.

Blearing yellow eyes stared up at me. "Gwyn, please go into the office. I left a message for you there. You must read it now, then go." He choked. "I love you."

"All right," I said as his eyes closed again. I hoped he'd sleep now.

Then I rose and stretched my aching back. Trudging down

to his office, I looked at his desk, which was characteristically neat. One envelope with my name on it lay unopened in the middle of his writing table. I took it in hand, feeling the thick richness of legal paper.

When I opened it, I found his will. I skipped through the legal terms to find the meat of it. He had made me his executor and left all his worldly goods to me. I cried then. It was dated some weeks back; he had prepared the will just in case he died from the fever, a fever he had hoped never to have, but just in case…. And only yesterday I had questioned his attachment to me!

I was touched by his generosity, but of course, it wouldn't be necessary. It couldn't be. He must live.

Chapter 11

James

Thank God Mother was quickly sent on her way to Glenmorgan. Two stalwart footmen helped with her trunks. Her maid Mary stood close by her as they entered the carriage.

"Farewell, children," she said with false gaiety to Elizabeth and me waiting in the gravel drive. "Wales is so lovely this time of year. Do come and see me."

The carriage had crunched its way to the end of the drive before we spoke.

"Is she completely mad?" Elizabeth wondered.

I held my head. "Honestly, I don't know. I can't even guess. She is so used to living a contrived life that she has decided life will be what she makes it. Perhaps insanity is her last refuge." I shook my head in confusion. "I don't know. I'm just grateful she decided to make it seem her choice that she was going away. It prevented the nasty scene I had feared."

"Oh, I feel so free," said Elizabeth, twirling around and holding out her light blue gown, grinning at me. I had to laugh.

"You are free and we will make sure it stays that way!"

We sighed together, smiling some more.

"Sam, what is next?"

"Lizzie, do you think you would be comfortable staying

with Father alone here? I need to trace our brothers' steps to see what has happened to them. I may have to go to France. It could take a long time."

Her lip trembled a little. "But if he dies…."

"I have spoken with him, and with Crowquill and the Reverend Wilson. The papers have been signed, and Wilson knows what Father wants to happen. Wilson would guide you. The butler knows how to handle the body." She blanched at this, but I kept talking. "You can do this, if it should happen. You are stronger than you think you are."

"I know I have been a weakling up till now."

"No, not a weakling, but perhaps badly bullied by Mother. You will learn your strength. But I believe Father has rallied. He wants me to find the truth. He knows it must be I who goes. I believe he has to know what has happened before he can find some peace."

"I understand. I will miss you awfully, though."

"And I, you," I said, holding her to me with a sigh.

I had to return to the smoke of London, to the shipping dock whence Stephen and Richard had set sail for France. Appleton had supplied me with plenty of bank notes and some coin to use for bribes as needed. I was dressed in my dullest gray gentleman's clothes. Though I was going to France, where gaudy clothing was high fashion, I'd be in the rural areas for most of the trip and wanted to blend in with the local people.

"Good day to you," I said to the ship owner. "I am Samuel James, son of the Earl of Redfern."

"Yes, sir, I have had enquiries from your father concerning

your brothers. I regret to say I have no more news for you. I'm so sorry. We have no news from France, where they were to land at Calais. It is as if the ocean swallowed them up. Oh, dear, not a good term. But no word of any wreckage either, I hasten to say."

"Hmmm. Could you show me the route they were to have taken?"

"Of course, it is subject to the vagaries of tides, currents, and weather, but here is the route." He traced it on the map with a worn finger.

"Hmm, have other vessels gone by the same route since then?"

"Yes, sir, but as I said, no trace."

"Are there likely beaches where remnants may have washed up?"

"Well, if they were wrecked it could have been near any of the beaches here." He traced a large portion of the coast of France.

"What about farther south, towards Spain, for example?"

"Yes, certainly possible there too."

"Farther south than Spain?"

"Very unlikely, sir."

"But not to the north of Calais, I assume."

"Not the way the winds blew during those days."

I sighed.

"Very sorry, sir. Will you be needing a ship to take you to France?"

"If you have one going to Calais, I do."

"Yes sir, the Marylebone leaves with the morning tide. Best to be here by half six."

"Very well, then, I shall take it."

I went to a nearby tavern where I took some ale and stew and slept for a few hours, reporting to the ship before dawn. It was a sturdy vessel, and in good order, with clean decks that smoked as the sun rose.

Skies were clear, the trip uneventful. I couldn't help scanning the seas around me, but of course there was nothing to be seen there. What hope I had seemed dim, but I had to try.

"Entering Calais harbor soon, sir," said the captain.

"Thank you."

I took up my traveling bag. We docked neatly. The harbor area roiled with men as usual, crying out in many languages, loading and unloading wares, with others shouting over the turmoil. I was compelled to elbow my way through the crowd while holding tight to my bag. My height and heavy shoulders aided my passage.

"Monsieur, a coach?" called a ragged man who gripped my arm.

"Oui, lead me there," I said, hoping he wasn't planning to take me to some alley to be robbed. I never went out without a dagger in my boot, always ready to fight if need be. In the event, he really had a coach waiting in a nearby street. The driver looked respectable, so I asked him to take me to a livery stable.

When this was accomplished, I felt more at ease, for I knew how to judge horses, so I'd not be cheated there. I chose a bay gelding, "le Whisky," who looked well able to keep a steady pace for many miles. The stableman recommended decent lodgings and the horse clomped down narrow streets to one we English would call the "Harbor Light."

The inn was at least clean, though an unremarkable place otherwise. The stables offered good fodder for my horse and a guard throughout the night. I had a room to myself upstairs and generous propositions from the filles de joie who came to lean over me as I ordered my wine. They only reminded me of the absence of Ardath, to whom they couldn't hold a candle. In truth, I preferred the cool shade of a chestnut tree in the courtyard, where I could make my plans for the trip.

I planned to ride south from Calais through small and large towns, speaking with gendarmes and local people near the shorelines where survivors might have washed up. I realized this was probably a hopeless journey. If Stephen or Richard, or both, had survived, they would have had time to write to Father and ask for help or let us know they were alive. I shook my head. I had to go and to find out all I could about what had happened.

I wished for a companion right then, thinking how Ardath would have willingly ridden with me anywhere just for the adventure of it. I found myself smiling about her spirit and prayed she and all in our little Philadelphia cabin were well.

Grateful that we were not yet at war with France, I proceeded south down the coast. Generally, people were kind and patient with my detailed enquiries. Everywhere I showed the miniatures of Stephen and Richard, they gazed carefully and shook their heads. I had to be careful how I phrased my questions, to emphasize that I wasn't enquiring about goods that might have washed ashore. Like Englishmen on our own coasts, they probably benefitted from wrecks in the treacherous waters.

The coast alternated between marvelous white cliffs and sandy or shingle beaches. It was a scene of beauty I could hardly appreciate, nor did I fully appreciate the food I was served, well-prepared in even the lowliest tavern.

Mont St. Michel rose in mist before me. I was almost at the end of the territory I had planned to travel and almost at the end of my hope for any information. I entered the small village and proceeded to the tavern above the shore.

When I had dismounted and given Whisky to a dark-haired lad, who led him away to the stable, I entered the courtyard of the inn.

"Bonjour, Monsieur," a stocky tavern keeper greeted me, wiping his hands on an almost clean apron. He looked more closely at me. "You are English?"

"Yes, you are very perceptive! You speak very good English yourself."

"Thank you." He leaned closer to me as if it were a tremendous secret. "In fact, my mother was actually English, but she came to a better land!"

I smiled at him. I could feel how baggy my eyes were. I was ready for food and a rest. "Have you a room then?" I asked.

"Oh yes sir, only the best for an English cousin. You will see the sun set over the water, most dramatic." He hurried through the cool stone building and up some stairs to a room which did indeed look over the water, with a pink sunset just beginning to show. I sank to the bed to watch in weary amazement as the sky turned orange and a deep rose.

"Please settle yourself. Then join us for supper and some of the best wine you have tasted. I am Hugo."

After splashing water on my face, I straightened and brushed off my clothes and went downstairs.

The tavern keeper beamed at me and ushered me to a table in the courtyard. The last rays of the sun poked through the tree under which I enjoyed some hearty red wine. The landlord lit torches around the yard, which attracted huge fluttering moths. As family groups and convivial men gathered to laugh and eat, I again felt lonely and ready for home. Perhaps I could find a ship to take me and Whisky back to Calais, where I could be bound for Ensleigh, sadly having failed in my undertaking.

The next morning, I asked my question of the innkeeper Hugo, seeing once again a regretful shaking head. Then he brightened. "But sir, I believe Claude might know of someone who saw wreckage nearby. Claude lives in the next village over. Claude," he shouted.

It seemed that Claude was the young boy who had taken Whisky the day before. He came at a run to the courtyard. "Claude, what do you know about a ship's wreckage that might have been found a few months ago?" Hugo asked in French.

"Oh sir, a few planks only came ashore, no treasure."

"Ahem, were there any survivors or dead men found?"

"Two dead men and one lunatic," said Claude.

I blessed my stars that I knew French well and had followed the conversation. "Where were the bodies taken and where is the lunatic?" I asked. My heart was pounding to think I might have some answers, though none of them good.

"The bodies were buried in the churchyard by Father Guillaume. The lunatic, I don't know where he is," he said earnestly, as if he might be blamed for admitting he knew no more.

"I will reward you if you can take me to the priest," I said.

He looked at Hugo, who nodded his permission.

Claude saddled Whisky, who carried us both to the nearby village, hardly a few small houses, but with a pleasant small church and a churchyard behind.

"The Father lives here," said Claude, pointing to a very modest home next to the church. "I must get back to work."

I gave him some coins, at which he beamed. He ran off clutching them in his hand.

Dread lay heavy on my chest as I turned toward the house.

Chapter 12

Ardath

How misfortune seemed to enwrap us! Mother reported that she had gone to check on Gwyn, who insisted on staying with a very ill Gregory. She left food for Gwyn, who then shooed her out of his house. Everyone except Gregory who had lived there before was now dead. His illness was a sobering reminder that the community still wasn't free of the fever.

Try as I might, I found I could not leave behind my own kind of fever. The frustration of losing our fortune, after all that we had been through to get back to our peaceful home, burned like a brand within my chest. Betrayal felt all too familiar because of our father's abandonment. At least his silver had been some compensation for that. But I had never forgiven him for leaving us as small children and I'd never forgive Ahmed for his thievery. Of course, I hid my anger from Isa and Omar.

On a slightly cooler day than most, restless, I determined to walk out from our house. No one protested, as I was going away from the city. I strode along, almost as fast as I could in "the old days" when I wasn't so pregnant. My destination was the corral where we had bought our horses for the trip along the Wagon Road to North Carolina. Of course, I was sweating like a dockworker by the time I got there, but I was no lady who would complain of the moisture.

An eerie silence surrounded the stables. I heard neither horses nor men. I almost tiptoed up to the stalls. No one was there. In the tack room, I found the body of Mr. Graham, curled on the bed. I felt for a pulse, but he was cold; I could smell that he was thoroughly dead. The black vomit dried on the floor confirmed that the yellow fever had killed him.

When I heard a nicker, I searched the nearby field. Several horses were there, gathered around a watering trough which stank of mold and gleamed green with slime. The grass was cropped to the roots. They were lean and hungry animals, but they had survived. I had brought old carrots from our stores at home to give them a treat, but these were gobbled from my hand, as they pushed at each other to get to the food. When they calmed, I patted each on the neck. Soft lips nuzzled my hands, hoping for more. Two of them were mares, a chestnut with whom I immediately fell in love, and a dun, quite beautiful, tan with a black mane and stripe down her back. Her forelocks were a dusty black also. The other was a magnificent black gelding. These must have been Graham's finest animals, now in desperate need.

In the stables I found oats, not exactly fresh, but edible. I threw these out on the ground in the pasture, but they wouldn't last long. I could not find a pitchfork to pull down hay from the loft; I needed aid.

I hurried straight to Omar when I arrived home. He was working on the barn that would shelter our animals for the winter.

"Omar, I need your help."

"Yes, Mrs. Ardat', what can I do?" He gave me a warm smile. He seemed even more fond of us since we had not blamed him for his son's betrayal.

"There is a tragedy at Mr. Graham's stable. Mr. Graham has died from the fever and no one is there to bury him. I have found three horses at the stable who have no one to care for them. We must help them. They have nothing to eat and no decent water and I can't get down the hay to give them. You will need to take a pitchfork."

"Ah, not good! Poor Mr. Graham. Do you wish to care for dem dere, or bring dem here?"

"Will we have enough room to stable them in winter?"

He looked at the structure he was building. "Hmmm, I could make dis longer before da snow starts. We need hay and oats for food, doh. Not enough grass here."

"There is a fair amount of hay there at the stables."

"Dat's good. What if I go feed dem and water dem today. I will see what dey need and what is dere. Den we can make better plan, yes?"

Suddenly, I was exhausted and glad to turn it over to Omar. I gave him directions. He could take Isa with him to care for the horses.

"And," I sighed. "Omar, he's beyond our help, but Mr. Graham lies in the tack room."

"Oh, I should bury him, if no one's dere to do it."

"Yes, please. Be careful. Don't touch the body. Take a cloth to wrap him in." He got a long horse blanket, a shovel, and a pitchfork and walked off to get Isa.

I needed to talk this over with Mother and Mrs. Perry, who were in the hearth room working on vegetables.

"Mother, Mrs. P, I walked to the old horse stables. Mr. Graham has died, probably of the fever. The horses haven't been fed for a while. Omar and Isa have gone over to help them, poor things, and to bury Mr. Graham."

"Oh, my, I thought I heard Gwyn for a moment there," Mother said. "But why has no one tended to Mr. Graham?" she asked.

"I don't know. He must not have family and I don't know where the stable boy has got to."

"Horses, eh? You'll not be bringing the great beasts into the animal room, will you?" Mrs. P eyed me with downturned mouth. She referred to the dirt-floored room under my bedroom, which I had briefly used for our horses before our trip down the wagon road.

I sighed. "Aside from poor Mr. Graham, this is a fortuitous happening. We can't afford to buy horses and now we will have them for the price of their care."

"And can we afford the price of their care?" said Mrs. Perry.

"Yes, we must. We can borrow from Smythe or Franklin, surely. For now we have grass they can graze."

"Well, they can't be abandoned," said Mother. "But someone must own them. Did you say Graham didn't have a family?"

"I don't know. There was no sign that anyone had been there to check on him, but I never met him other than at the stables," I said.

"When the fever abates, we will need to find his relations. Even the land office must know something. By the by, Ardath, what do you plan to use them for?" Mother gave me her most direct stare.

I could hardly meet her gaze. "Well, they are valuable animals. If no one claims them, and they are revived by good care, we could sell them."

Mother narrowed her eyes. "You shouldn't be riding this late in pregnancy," she said, while Mrs. Perry shook her head.

Since I had returned to Philadelphia pregnant, Mrs. Perry waxed judgmental about any activity for me.

"Hmf!" said Mrs. Perry. She thumped a burlap bag of potatoes on the table.

"Oh, no, they couldn't be ridden now anyway," I said. But soon, I thought…

"Get busy. There are potatoes to be peeled," said Mrs. P, but she smiled.

I pulled out a chair and eased myself down into it. I couldn't get as close to the table as I used to. Mother handed me an apron that spread over my former lap.

I might be here peeling potatoes, but my mind travelled widely. Where might Ahmed be, I wondered. If I were he, I'd have gone north. We had told all the Africans of the slavery rampant south of here, and how even here they must carry their manumission papers everywhere. He was a smart man; he had surely taken his papers. He was cautious of the Indians to our west and the river would discourage the three robbers from going east. With Omar along I could use horses and a wagon to visit the small communities where they might have passed through, just as James was doing along the coast of France as he looked for his brothers.

With a pang, I pictured James's lonely ride. How I wished to be with him. How I wished I could talk to him for only one minute of time. Tears threatened.

"Please leave some potato for us," said Mrs. Perry.

I glanced at my hand. Where a robust potato had lain, a tiny crooked shape remained. All the rest had come off with the peel.

I'm not only restless; I'm truly useless, I thought. "Excuse me," I said to Mother and Mrs. Perry. "I think I need to rest."

This was my excuse to continue my brooding while lying on the bed staring at the rafters. I couldn't get a rational thought in my head, though. My elation at rescuing the horses ran together with my agitation about James being gone for an indefinite time and the helplessness of being pregnant, as well as my burning anger at Ahmed. While these feelings whirled around in me, my mind couldn't work in a straight line.

Finally, I fell asleep. When I woke, it was late in the day. I splashed water on my face and went out, finding Omar at the barn.

"Mrs. Ardat', we're back. Dos horses are lucky you found dem. So hungry! Dey ate like no tomorrow."

A smile broke over my face. "I am delighted. I suppose you left them with plenty of hay."

"Yes. Also found some oats, but only gave dem a little of dat. Not wanting to make dem sick."

"That's wise. Omar, I don't know what we would do without you."

His wide grin told me of his pleasure in helping the poor creatures, and us as well. "Well, you know, dere's no work for me in de city. It's good to be useful here." He shifted his feet. "Dere's a good wagon dere, too. And we cleaned out dere trough. Dat was a shameful mess."

"Everyone has been afraid to go out with the fever raging, but it does seem that someone should have found Mr. Graham before I did. I wonder what happened to the stable boy he had?"

He wiped sweat from the back of his neck with an old cloth.

"Don't know. We saw no sign anyone had been dere. So many people dying, maybe…."

That was a grim explanation, but in these strange times, could be true. "It will be cooler in the morning. I'll go over and see to them."

"Would you like me to come?" Omar asked.

"No, thank you. Did you see a wheelbarrow there?"

"Yes, a good one. Also good rakes and shovels. Everyt'ing looks good. Except for Mr. Graham. I marked his grave wit' a cross. I hope dat is best."

"Yes, That's good," I said.

I wandered through the yard, thinking, distracted. What would I name them, I thought with amusement. I was like Gwyn with a new pet. This led to the guilty realization that I hadn't wondered today how she was doing in her brave fight against Gregory's fever.

When I returned to the house, Mother was there, having just come back from Gregory's house.

"Oh Ardath, good. I was about to find you and Mrs. Perry."

As if on cue, Mrs. Perry came in red-faced from stooping in the garden.

"Whew, I look forward to fall weather, for so many reasons," said Mrs. P. "Here, sit, I have cool ale."

"Wonderful," said Mother. "Well, Gregory suffers, but Gwyn is a good nurse, as you can imagine," she continued after we sat and drank. "I believe she is getting to sleep more. She shows no sign of the fever, but I worry. She won't let me in to see Gregory, in case I might get infected. At least I can take her food. She stays by his bed night and day."

There were few times when Mother looked her age; she seemed worn now, every wrinkle deeper.

"Mother, please rest. I wish I could go down there for you. I worry for you. You must take care of yourself." I smiled. "After all, we went to a lot of trouble to find you."

Her eyes twinkled; she looked younger.

"It's time you enjoyed that hammock under the oak, Mother. Remember, you were the one who brought it to us."

She finished her ale and nodded. At that moment, Dougie awoke from a nap, calling for her from the front room.

"I'm coming, Dougie," I called quickly, before she could answer. I shooed her out the back door.

Dougie's little face was rosy and creased from sleeping hard on his pillow. "Arda, where's Mama?"

"She's taking a rest, just like you did. Would you like to hear about the horses I found yesterday?"

"Yes, oh yes!"

"Let's go to the necessary. Then we can have a drink and sit to talk out on the front porch."

I was trying to get to know Dougie better in preparation for my own child, though I could hardly imagine what that would be like. At least I'd have lots of women caretakers to help me. There might be more, as well. James's letters revealed that he might bring his sister back with him when he came. Our burgeoning household threatened to become its own little community.

After Dougie and I talked, he ran off to play. Immediately, my mind returned to the horses and what they might mean to us. If I didn't tell Mother what was happening and got Omar to agree, I thought I could leave in a few days to pursue Ahmed and his fellows. I located the saddlebags which we had used on our trip from North Carolina back to Philadelphia. I began to stuff in an extra gown. I'd need foodstuffs that would not spoil on the road. Of course, if we had a wagon….

The next day, I took some early apples in hand to walk to Graham's place. The black gelding greeted me eagerly, first to the fence. The other two were close behind. I believed they looked better already, which I guess could be true, if it was only that their faith in mankind had been restored. Omar had done a wonderful job here with cleaning their area and feeding them. I enjoyed rubbing their noses, talking to them, and looking for any problems I could find. They seemed healthy, thank the Goddess!

I ventured into the field, with the horses following my every step. Did I imagine the black gelding looked more robust than the mares?

I walked across the field, hoping to find another area where they could graze, but to no avail. The stable was in good shape. I wished we could leave the horses and tend to them here, but that was too difficult, the distance too great, with no way to supervise them if trouble arose. The wagon would do for our trip, though we needed some sailcloth to cover its bed. I poked around in the storeroom, finding such a cover folded under other equipment in a dusty corner. I shook it out. With a hearty sneeze, I left it to air on a stall's wall. Saddles and bridles hung on pegs in the tack room, hardly dirty, ready for quick use. I wished I could ride now.

My next task was to talk with Omar. I found him, as usual, working on the barn. I looked around to be sure there was no one nearby.

"Ah, Mrs. Ardat', good day to you. May I help?"

"Yes, please, Omar, but this must be our secret."

"Oh yes. You know I would do anyt'ing for you."

"Well, I do need your help. I am determined to find Ahmed and our coins."

His eyes were downcast. "It is a shame," he said quietly. "I would be most glad to do so, but how? We have found no way to know where dey are."

"I'm sure they have gone north. Now that we have horses, as soon as they recover, we could take the wagon."

"Ah, Mrs. Ardat', what would your mother and Mrs. Perry t'ink?"

"That is why it must be our secret, Omar. Promise me!"

"We must not let you be hurt." He glanced at my belly.

"Omar, you know how strong I can be. Did I not pull you out of your prison on the ship?"

"Yes, but…."

"Then it is settled. Tell no one but Isa," I warned. "I will leave a note."

His wide lips pressed together. I knew he didn't like it.

I went to the house to collect more of what we would need. It had to be done in little corners of time. This house was not big enough for secrets. Luckily, Omar and I had been on the road before. We knew what was needed and what could be left behind.

Omar brought the wagon over, parking it and the three horses under the barn roof. The black gelding was too large to yoke with a mare. We would leave him there with Isa to care for. The dun and the chestnut would work as a team for the wagon.

We fed and groomed the horses and walked them around for exercise. Within a few days, the mares seemed ready to pull. The gelding had become frisky and pranced around.

I wrote to Mother the night before we were to leave, explaining the need to go after Ahmed. Isa was in on the secret as we needed her to take care of the other animals while we were gone. She was no more pleased about me making the trip than Omar was. I felt some guilt at roping these two into my scheme.

In the moonlight, long before the real dawn, we set out on the north road with a crude map in hand. The woods were all around us as we left the city. Traces of red and yellow leaves adorned the trees, looking dull in the moonlight. We'd soon be in a real fall; we had not a moment to lose. In the back we had oats and hay for the horses and plenty of food for us on the trail. I had James's brace of pistols under the seat, loaded and ready, and a set of long knives with which I had been practicing. Omar had brought both a long knife and a double-pronged pitchfork.

This was a more settled road than the one we had to North Carolina. Almost immediately we were in farmlands. We soon passed the estates of many Quakers who bought them from William Penn in days long gone, prosperous farms and well-established. Small villages had grown up along the way.

We followed wagons to market that morning. One town even had a small constable's office. After three steps up to the clapboard structure, we knocked on the door. We found him in, luckily, as he was on his way to the market.

"Good day, Constable, my name is Ardath James. My freedman and I are looking for three fugitives who stole our coin and probably came in this direction, about six weeks ago."

A rotund man, he looked unready to run after thieves. He bowed slightly, but eyed my stomach with seeming horror. "Madame, surely you are not traveling the roads in your condition!"

I cleared my throat. "Sir, I have descriptions of the three."

I proceeded to describe Ahmed, a tall and well-muscled young freedman with brown skin and eyes, and his cohorts, two white men, one small with a limp and a crooked nose, one tall with a long scar on the left side of his face, while the constable strove to move his eyes up to mine.

"Hmmm. I think we received a notice about this theft some time back." He shuffled through some papers on a rather messy desk. "Yes, here we are, ahem. No one saw them come through here, but we are still very close to Philadelphia. They could have hidden in the woods hereabouts. Sorry to have no news for you. You must surely return to Philadelphia now."

"There is still terrible fever there, as you may have heard. We will go north for our health now, and perhaps find some news of them." I had decided that I would meet less opposition if we pretended to be fleeing a pestilent city as well as searching for the miscreants.

"Well, then, best of luck to you," said the constable. "I must be off to the market before the drinking starts." He started out the door, but paused. "I must warn you that the roads north are not safe from rough men, especially at night. Do not be caught out."

"Thank you, Constable," I said.

We decided to push on. According to our map, the next town of any size could be reached before dark. That trip was uneventful, although my bottom was sore from the jostling of the wagon on a rough road. As dark began to fall, we found ourselves outside a fairly respectable-looking tavern.

Chapter 13

James

Finally I had come to a place where I might have some answers. After the small French boy disappeared, I turned to the church. It was open and I went to pray that I would find some end to my quest. If two bodies had washed up, were they both my brothers? Or just some of the crew? Or had one of them survived, only to become a lunatic, whatever Claude meant by that. Or was all this from another wreck? I breathed to calm myself until I was able to question the priest.

As if he had been called, the priest appeared in the aisle near me. "My son, may I help you? I am Father Guillaume." I saw why he had such a small church, as his face was remarkably disfigured, but his voice was kind.

"Thank you, Father. I am Samuel James. I am looking for my brothers, who may have been shipwrecked near here. The boy Claude told me there were two bodies and a 'lunatic.'"

"Ah, well he is correct in the main."

"I have brought likenesses of them. The one with the blonde curls is Stephen and the one with the darker hair is Richard."

"Hmmm," he said as he tapped on Richard's picture. "Well, this one might be the survivor. Was it some time back?"

"Yes, months now."

"That would fit. I'm sorry to say that I believe one of the bodies may be this one," he said, pointing to Stephen. "The water had, excuse me, changed their faces, but he had blonde hair."

I sighed. I hadn't given up on either brother until now. Stephen appeared in my mind as he had always been, a strapping, energetic figure. I missed him now, or at least the idea of him.

"I'm sorry, my son."

I looked at the priest blankly. Stirring myself, I asked, "And the other man, where is he now?"

"Madame Poschette has taken him in as a mission from God. He works in her garden and she feeds him. He seems simple, but it is hard to tell where his mind goes."

"Ah, well perhaps you could show me where she lives, then."

"Better, I will take you there," he said and stepped toward the sanctuary door.

As soon as we were outside, Father Guillaume pointed in the direction I had come. Up the slight hill in the direction of the inn, I saw a house larger than any in the small village. It was gray stone and looked as if it had been there a long time. All around it bloomed the most riotous beds of flowers in every color.

I took a breath. The priest followed a stone path through some shrubbery with me close behind him. He paused often to catch his breath. I curbed my impatience, as it seemed he had more injuries than showed on his face. When we arrived at the front walk, he straightened and knocked loudly on the door.

An ancient lady answered the door. Her countenance was wreathed in wrinkles, but blue eyes sparkled at us. "Why, Father, how good to see you! And you have brought me a handsome young man to brighten my day."

I bowed and introduced myself.

"Well, then please come in to have a glass of champagne with me."

"Delighted," said Father Guillaume.

It seemed to me a strange drink for almost midday, but at her age, she could do as she wished. We went through a large hall of dark wood to an outside terrace. I did appreciate how the French made use of the outside in pleasant weather, which they seemed to have more of than we in the English countryside. Her back gardens were as riotous as her front. They stretched as far as we could clearly see, only parted by a green lawn between.

When she returned with elegant slim glasses and poured the bubbly drink for us, it was wonderfully cool and had a taste that matched her lively ways.

"What can I do for you?" she asked, turning to me.

"Father Guillaume has explained to me that some wreckage and bodies appeared on your shore several months back, and that you graciously took in the survivor from the beach."

"Oh yes, the poor man. He couldn't remember who he was; we have called him Joseph. I thought to ask him to work in the gardens; that is calming and absorbing work. Why do you ask?"

"I am looking for my two brothers. I have miniatures of them here." I showed her my pictures.

She reached around her to a table on which stood some round-rimmed spectacles. After hooking them carefully over her ears, she spoke. I leaned far forward in my chair to hear her.

"Hmmm, this one I do not know," she said, handing me back the portrait of Stephen. "But this one, could it be our Joseph?" She looked at the priest as she said this.

"We came to see if it could be his brother," he said.

"Oh, oh, well, I must call for him, of course," she said. "Marie," she said to the maid who entered the room, "please find Joseph and bring him here. He may be at his shed now."

As the maid left, she looked at me. "How did you think to look here for your brothers?"

I smiled, feeling weary. "I have traveled from Calais, where the ship was to sail. This was my last hope."

"Ah," she said. "Then we must pray for you." She and the priest bowed heads and sat quietly. I could feel their good wishes for me, which was comforting.

Soon Marie came back to us over the lawn. She curtsied. "He is coming."

I watched as a lone figure came from the trees beyond the flower beds on our left. He was dressed in faded blue peasant clothes; he slumped along staring at the ground, his head covered by a broad straw hat. This didn't look promising, but I rose from my chair and couldn't stop myself going to him.

"Joseph, how are you? I am Samuel Booth James. Do you know me?" I asked in English.

He lifted his eyes to my face. "Please speak French, Monsieur," he said.

I repeated it in French. He looked at me. "I work in the gardens here," he said.

Could this beaten man be our Richard? His slack expression was so unlike anything I had seen from Richard, the family joker and its most light-hearted member. I actually hadn't seen my brothers in several years and found I remembered their mannerisms more than their features. This man also had grown a beard and mustache. The hair was as dark as I remembered. He showed absolutely no recognition of me.

"Please come and sit with us, Joseph," said Madame Poschette. She was very gentle with him. I thought it might be best if she tried to explain to him. "This man is looking for his brothers who may have suffered a shipwreck near our beach. Do you remember anything about a shipwreck, or being on the beach here?"

"On the beach," he said, pointing to Father Guillaume.

"Yes, I came to the beach to help you," said the priest.

"Yes, I remember that," Joseph said. He straightened up a little. "Very kind people." He waved to include Madame and the priest.

"Joseph, can you remember how you came to be on the beach?" asked Madame.

"DEAD MEN!" he shouted in English. We all started. He began to rock in his chair.

"Oh, dear, I was afraid this might happen," said Madame.

I moved my chair closer to him. I sang a song our nurse Elen used to sing to us in Wales. "Dinogad's coat was speckled, speckled, made from the hair of martens, martens." His eyes cleared and lifted to mine. Right then I knew him to be my brother Richard. "Everything is all right now. I'm here. Sammy is here. You are safe with me."

He began to cry, reaching out for me. I held him and murmured to him until his sobs stopped. Tears glinted on his dark lashes. He rubbed his nose with his arm like a child. The room was still, witnessing a remarkable wakening. Yet, watching his eyes, I saw that it was the wakening of a child, not Richard the grown man.

I sighed. I had no idea what I should do.

"Going back to the garden," he said. "I work in the gardens here."

I nodded, watching him go with a terrible sadness. Any disturbance of his current identity as a gardener seemed to threaten his sanity, such as it was. The priest and Madame Poschette seemed sad as well.

"I'm afraid to press him with his real identity."

"Yes, I have seen this in men returned from battle. It can take years to return to any memory of themselves," said Father Guillaume.

I addressed Madame, " My father lies dying in England. If my brother Stephen is dead, Richard is the heir to vast estates, yet I cannot see this man coping with a role of such complexity."

She smiled sadly at me. "I cannot see him getting on a ship after what he has experienced, can you?"

I shook my head. What was I to do? Well, the next thing was to discover if Stephen were truly the man buried in the graveyard here.

I rose. "Thank you, Madame, for your kindness to him. May I leave him here with you while I sort this out?" I said through a clotted throat.

"Of course, I am prepared to take care of him as long as he shall need it."

I kissed her hand. "Thank you."

Father Guillaume and I made our slow way down to the church again. As we approached the graveyard, I broached the gruesome subject at hand.

"Father, I must know if the man from the beach is truly my other brother, Stephen."

"Yes, I know," he said.

"Did you undress the body, or prepare it in any way?"

"I apologize to you. We did not. The body was in such shape that it needed immediate burial, so we laid it in a shroud and put it with other shipwreck victims that the tides have brought us here. Here is their resting ground," he said, gesturing to an area of the burial grounds slightly set off from the rest.

"Father, I must ask your permission to unearth the blonde man to understand if it is my brother."

He managed not to look shocked, but slowly shook his head. "It is not our custom to disturb the rest of the dead."

"Believe me, I don't want to do this, but I owe my father as much certainty as I can give him about his children."

"That I do understand, but how could you know him, as the body is so disintegrated by now?"

"He had a very large dark wine colored stain on his back and two broken fingers on his left hand. If those are still there, I will know for sure."

"I cannot ask my grave diggers to do this. They believe they would be haunted by the ghost, you understand?"

"Yes, I will do it and in the dark of night, if you will loan me a lantern and a shovel."

He crossed himself, shaking his head as if he had made a deal with the devil.

"Yes, then, if you must. This one is his spot."

"Thank you. I will be respectful," I said.

Chapter 14

James

A day of awful sadness had left me tired, and I stretched my neck to ease the ache. The leather bag Father had given me thudded against my chest. I took it off for the digging, laying it on my coat in a grassy spot. The graveyard for victims of shipwreck lay before me, gray and nondescript. The moon had risen, giving me an eerie half-light to see the plot where I must dig. I sighed. At least, being behind the church, I was sheltered from unwanted watchers.

The soil was blessedly sandy, since we were not far from the ocean. I pitched in with an energy I didn't feel, working through a ground not yet compacted. In my mind I tried to prepare myself for what I might see. Years of discipline helped me think of this as a job of work.

In no time at all, for it was a shallow grave, I was through the dirt and found the shroud, still shining a whitish color in the moonlight. The church here couldn't afford coffins. The unknown shipwreck victims got a decent burial and that was it. I lit the lantern with my flint. It spluttered, almost dying out. Finally, a golden glow swelled from it.

Lengthening the hole so that I could descend into it took the last of my strength. I lowered myself down at the head. The body had slewed sideways as I dug, making it easier to lift, but also belching out the smell of corruption. I tied a handkerchief around my nose.

I slit the shroud down to the waist using my long knife. I hoped I wasn't hooking the flesh with it. Looking in, I saw an unrecognizable pallid greenish face with a halo of blond curls.

The next part was the most grisly. I wore gloves but still it seemed awful to turn this body, knowing it might be the remains of Stephen. I took hold of the whole shroud to rotate the body. Again, I ripped the cloth to the waist, gazing at the man's back. It was pale in the bloated skin, but there was a dull darker area that covered him from his waist almost to his shoulders, his birthmark showing, pasty, but there. I checked his hands, finding the two broken fingers on his left hand, where the flesh fell off in strings.

Apparently, I had still had some hopes despite my efforts to dispel them, for I cried aloud. This was my brother, Stephen, heir to the earldom of Redford, a stinking, corrupted mass of flesh.

I turned the body face up, settled the shroud around it. Then I dragged myself out of the hole. A torrential rain started as I pushed the gritty dirt back into the grave. Maybe someday I could bring him back to his native land. For now, I'd order a wooden coffin and a bronze plaque made with his name on it. I was beyond sadness and exhaustion. I trudged up the small hill to the inn.

The owner exclaimed when he saw me, my clothes dripping with mud and water.

"Sir, oh, sir, let me heat some water for you to wash with. You've been caught in this rain. I'll have it sent to your room." He handed me a towel with which I scrubbed at my hair. "I'll bring brandy with it."

"Yes, thank you. That would be very much appreciated," I said. With legs of lead I climbed those stairs into a world I could hardly bear, a world without my brothers in it, one in which I could not yet face what that meant for me, for our whole family.

When I had sloughed off the worst of the sand, mud, and rain, I sank briefly into the tub of water. Then I took to my bed and knew no more.

The morning dawned bright, the world washed and fresh. I was happy until I remembered what the day before had brought. After I had breakfasted, I needed to talk to someone. I chose the priest, since he impressed me as being world-weary enough to understand my situation. Walking down the path to the church, I saw the sea, a clean blue expanse of seeming benevolence. Sparkling water rushed green to the beach, which glistened with the froth of white as the waves broke and retreated. Little pert birds on long legs scurried around looking for food in the sand. The world continued on, regardless of us mere humans.

Father Guillaume must have been waiting for me. As I entered the church, he rose from his prayers at the altar.

"My friend, God bless you. How do you fare?" he asked.

"I ask your listening ear," I said.

He nodded. "Shall we sit out in the arbor?" Next to his little house was a grape arbor pungent with the smells of burst purple grapes.

"Yes, that is good." Bees buzzed around us but showed no interest in us. Just like the sea, Nature's life went on.

I took a deep breath.

"At your own pace, Samuel. We have as much time as you need," Guillaume said.

"You are very kind," I said, wondering where to start. After a pause, "It was Stephen in that grave and it is Richard on the hill. My father will be heart-broken."

"And what of you?"

"I suppose I am heart-broken too—yes, I am. Hmmm." I sat there feeling a vast emptiness for a long while.

"The bigger question for me now is what to do. I'll try to get Richard at least used to seeing me, if I can. If his capabilities don't improve, then I feel I must return to England. I worry about my father and my sister, who are at the estate there. My mother, she's, hmmm, she's not entirely sane. She can be tyrannical, especially to my sister. I would like to take my sister to the American colonies where she can get a fresh start. My wife is there, in Philadelphia. She is expecting our child soon. I love her and her family is precious to me. I feel I belong there more than in England. My father would have me run the estates, if Stephen and Richard were both dead, but Richard is in a kind of limbo. Should I ask my father, if he still lives, to give the title to Richard and let me run the estates? Have we a hope that Richard might improve over time? Could I ever get back to the colonies, or should I ask my wife to leave everything she loves there and live with me in England? How could I do that to her?"

"You do have many decisions before you. If Richard is incapable, is there someone else who could run the estates for you?"

"Well, the present estate manager certainly knows what to do, though he is getting older, so that might not be a permanent solution."

"Might that at least give you time to get back to the colonies and your family there, taking your sister with you? You might have to return to England later, but that would be another day. Meanwhile, you can be assured that Madame Poshcette and I will look after Richard and keep close contact with you if he recovers himself. As far as running an estate, even a farm, he couldn't do it now, we know."

"But my mother—I honestly don't know what can be done about her. I am afraid she will try to ruin the estate out of vengeance or simple ignorance."

"Surely, your family must be very wealthy if your father is an earl?"

"Yes, that is true. Right now, Mother is at a remote estate in Wales, being looked after by her lady's maid and some burly footmen."

He nodded. "Could that situation be continued indefinitely?"

"Well, unless she takes it in mind to steal a horse and ride off."

"It seems that she must be watched at all times. Are these footmen capable of standing watch at all hours?"

"I told them to, but I would have to ascertain that they are doing so. That's another reason for me to return as soon as possible. I'm not easy in my mind about her."

"You are a man with many responsibilities."

"Yes, in addition, I am on leave from the army to help with my family affairs."

"Samuel, I don't see how you can remain with the army given that two families on two separate continents are depending on you."

"Hmmm, I may have to travel the Atlantic numerous times, it's true. I have no other income, though."

"Unless your father gives it to you, or you become earl."

I shuddered. That was how much I didn't want to be the earl.

Father Guillaume nodded wisely. With a touch of humor, he remarked. "I notice the idea of becoming earl makes you shudder."

I had to laugh. "You have read me well!"

"What if your sister, that is, I gather she isn't married?"

"That's right," I said.

"Could her husband, when she marries, be in charge of the estates?"

"I don't know. Until all this came about, I never paid attention to the rules of succession. I supposed that if Richard is incapable, I would have to assume the title after my father dies. I know that's what Father wants. My wife would not want to move to England though; of that, I'm certain."

"So you are torn between the needs of one family and another."

I nodded. "Exactly." My hunched shoulders sank down a bit. It was a relief to talk this out.

"The wedding vows tell you to cling to your wife, forsaking all others, as long as you both shall live."

"Yes, that would be so much easier if my original family didn't bear so much responsibility to our nation and the people on our estates, as they have for the last 300 years or so."

"Once again, I say in the kindest way I can, 'forsaking all others.' I do understand that you are a very responsible man. I find it admirable. Now we come to the question of what you want."

"I don't think that has much to do with this situation."

"Perhaps it will not influence what you decide to do. Still it is important to know what hopes you have, since desire will inevitably show its head at some point."

"I want my father to live forever and Richard to regain himself and eventually take over the title and Elizabeth, my sister, to find a good marriage. I want to be with my wife, to live in America, to have a son." I lapsed into silence. "Well, you didn't ask me what was possible, only what I wanted."

"Do you want to be an army major or general?"

"Want? No, not really." I was amazed to hear this from my own lips. Had I always told myself I wanted to be in the army because that was the logical place for me? "I felt I must do my duty," I mused.

"Well, so far you have told me that you want to return to England soon, sell your commission, make sure your mother is safe, as are the people around her, put the estate agent in charge of running the business aspects, take your sister to America, return to your wife, pray for a boy."

I laughed out loud. "Guillaume, you are exceeding perspicacious!"

He tilted his head, raising his eyebrows. "Those, at least, are the things you may be able to manage. Over many things we have no choice, but be careful that you do not assume no control where you indeed do have some!"

I arranged for a coffin and a plaque for Stephen's grave. Then I called on Mrs. Poschette each day, over several days. I saw Richard and spent time with him in the gardens, where he seemed most at ease. If I told him of our family and things I remembered from childhood, he occasionally showed interest, but not recognition. I appeared to be a peculiar stranger to him.

His little house displayed Mrs. Poschette's loving touch as it was cozy and clean, yet simple. He seemed very happy there and saw it as his home.

With great reluctance, I took my leave of Richard, Mrs. Poschette, and Father Guillaume. I gave the good father a bank draft for Richard's expenses. We exchanged addresses and promised to keep in touch. He would let me know of any change in Richard's state. I would always let him know where to find me.

I took ship for England from the nearest port. The harbor-master would arrange to return Whiskey to Calais for me.

Chapter 15

Gwyn

I gazed at Gregory, lying peaceful for that moment. I hadn't marked down the days that I nursed him through his fever. The agony of that time seemed to stretch forever, behind and before me. Outside beckoned me, some small respite from the stuffy room.

I leaned against the back door breathing fresh air. Several minutes later, I saw two figures come in through the back gate. They were a young couple, each with black hair pulled away from their faces and dark eyes, dressed in worn but clean gray workers' clothes and standing with hands clasped in front of them. The man was wiry, the girl slight but erect.

"What may I do for you?" I asked them, trying not to show how startled I was at seeing strangers. I hardly felt presentable. I knew my hair must straggle and my clothes were not fresh, but they answered quickly.

"Mistress, we were lately the servants of Mr. and Mrs. Willingham. We nursed them until they died, then returned home to our mother. We are Mary and Robert Evans and we seek work, if mayhap, you are living here now and could make use of us," said the young woman, smiling and executing a curtsy.

"Aye, Mistress, I know I may seem young, but I am strong,

can work both outside and in, if you wish," said Robert.

Hat in hand, with earnest face, he seemed to plead with me. I thought they looked thinner than they should, so my heart went out to them.

"I could certainly use some help, but I have no coin to pay you. For now, I can feed you; that is about all I could do," I said.

"May we shelter here as well? Our mother's house is crowded with those who have lost their positions because of the fever. My sister and I could stay in the shed there," he said, pointing to a rather dilapidated building in the far corner of the back garden. "I know it looks rundown, but I remember the structure is sound and water-tight."

"My betrothed has the fever and lies in the sitting room. Do you not fear that you will catch it if you come inside?"

Robert looked at his sister. "Mistress, we stayed here in the house with Mr. and Mrs. Willingham until the last. We are more afeared of starving, to say the plain truth."

"I understand. Do you know my betrothed, Gregory Smythe?"

Robert smiled. "Oh yes, Mr. Gregory. He went to live with a friend. He is a good man." His face blanched. "Is it he who lies within?"

"Yes." I held back a sob, finally realizing just how exhausted I was.

"May we see him then?" said Mary.

"Of course. Come in."

We found Gregory somewhat awake when we entered. "Gwyn," he croaked.

"Mr. Gregory, let me get you some water," said Mary, who moved to the next room to pump some fresh water from the sink.

Gregory struggled to get more upright, helped gently by Robert. "Robert, why are you here?" he asked.

"Why, we thought we might help, sir," Robert replied.

"Good," said Gregory. "Not afraid?"

"No, sir, we're not," said Robert, while Mary put a cup to Gregory's lips.

After he drank some, Gregory went back to sleep.

Mary turned to me. "Mistress, where do you sleep?" She glanced at the pallet I had made on the floor near Gregory's lounge. She drew in a sharp breath. "Not here, surely."

"Well, of course, I have needed to be very close to him," I said.

"Hmm, we are here now. I will make you up a fresh bed in the best room upstairs."

In the meantime, I wrote a note to Mother letting her know of the Evans' arrival and asking for more food to be sent back. Mary returned in no time from upstairs.

I explained where to find our house. Giving her the note for Mother, I sat down with a deep sigh.

Mary said to Robert. "I have put her in the south bedroom. Help her there, then bathe Mr. Gregory please." Then she left the house.

With great care, Robert helped me up the stairs. I fell into the real bed with fresh sheets and a breeze making its way through two open windows, and thanked God I now had some help.

After I woke, it was getting toward evening, the sky glowing with orange and crimson clouds. I refreshed myself with a splash of water over my hot face. I wanted so much to return to bed, but I needed to be with Gregory. I clattered down the stairs to find him awake and sitting up more than I had seen him since the fever struck. His dear face was still yellowish around the edges, but I thought his true colors were returning.

I'll excuse myself," said Mary, leaving the room.

"Gwyn. How long have I been down with this fever?"

It was more than he had said in all the time I had nursed him.

"Weeks. I'm not sure how long it was before Randolph notified us."

"I think I was at his house. I don't remember well."

"He brought you here. I have been here since," I said.

He struggled up on the lounge some more. "No, you shouldn't have come here."

"Gregory, I would never leave you to be nursed by another," I said. "However, today the Evans have come asking for work, so I engaged them to help us. I think they are close to starving." I could say this because I had heard Robert and Mary working on the shelter outside.

"Gwyn, always so caring of others," he mumbled as he went back to sleep.

I began to sleep in a bed each night. It definitely helped me regain my strength. One of the Evans was always available to sleep next to Gregory. They knew how to do the nursing. If his fever sprang up again, they bathed him as well as I could have.

I even took time one day to go to the apothecary shop. Ibrahim answered the door. This time he let me in. We embraced a long time, then had tea together. It was like old times, very old times.

"Gwyn, first tell me of your family. Have they escaped the

contagion? I haven't had a chance to visit yet."

"Yes, we all have been fortunate, but Smythe is very ill. I've been nursing him at the Willingham house, where he has lived and had his office."

"Would you wish for me to come examine him?"

"Oh, yes, please."

"I know what a good healer you are and I doubt there's anything more I can do, but if you wish…."

"Ibrahim, it would settle my mind greatly."

"Then shall we go now?"

"Yes, please. The Willinghams' former servants are there to help now, Robert and Mary."

"I have met them. I'm glad you have help."

He picked up his bag, closed the doors behind us, and we went down still-empty streets to Gregory's house. I explained that the Willinghams had left it to Gregory.

"Have I told you that our mother has an adopted child? And James has left for England as his father is very ill. Ardath is due to deliver before Christmas and we have small hope that James will be back by then. Gregory promised to look after us but we got word that he was ill. You must have heard that Ahmed stole all our coin and we have little left in capital."

"Yes, I had heard about Ahmed. A grievous shame all around! As for the rest, I look forward to seeing everyone in the next few days. I pray that life will become sweet once again, and soon." He smiled at me. "You look tired, but still hopeful, as I am also."

I was hopeful, if only because I walked next to one of the most kind and talented men I had ever met, turban and all.

Ibrahim saw Gregory and approved all we had done for him. "I think he will recover, but this fever can return again when you least expect it. In any case, he will have a long slow recovery afterwards."

Somehow having his crisp evaluation made me feel so much better, as it had seemed that the fever would be the same forever, that I would be stuck in wondering and dreading forever. I felt my shoulders relaxing down from my neck. Mother had said it was best not to doctor people close to you, if there was an alternative. Now I saw why.

"Robert, can you stay with him longer? I want to walk Ibrahim to his home," I said.

"Thank you, but no," said Ibrahim. "For then you would be walking back by yourself in the dark. Come when I summon you. We will visit your cabin and I will meet your wonderful mother and the others."

"Of course, I will come. Thank you!" I said.

"Mary will be coming soon," said Robert. "Please go to bed now. You can rest tonight and then she will rest tomorrow."

"Yes, yes, I will," I said. Climbing the stairs, my legs felt like lead. I flopped on the bed. Such a luxury. I closed my eyes in relief.

It was as Ibrahim had said. Slowly dear Gregory began to waken for more of the day. He even ate the broths that Mary and I fixed for him, but he was exceedingly weak. We had to use a bedpan for his waste. Robert lifted him onto it and tended his cleansing afterward.

While awake he wanted some stimulation, so I read to him, or wrote down his letters to clients, even though we didn't know if they were living or dead.

What finally alerted us to the easing of the fever in the city were the sounds that poured through our open windows. We were close to the market area here. From Third Street we heard the sellers, hoarse from calling their wares, the bubbles of laughter and shouted conversations, the clop of horse hooves on the cobbles, the grunting of pigs and squawks of geese, the clucks of chickens. The city lived again. It spoke of its life after weeks of eerie silence.

"I think I hear the market, Gwyn," Gregory said one early morning. He lifted his head, scrunching up on his lounge to sit.

"In fact you do," I said, delighted. "The city awakes, thank God, in time for fall and preparations for the winter."

"I pray the winter will hold off long enough for me to become useful again," said Gregory. "I wish to begin getting off this couch and onto my feet. Lord above, either I or this couch smell foul. Perhaps we can throw away its accumulated filth soon, please?" he inclined his head toward me holding his nose.

"Robert, please come here," I called. Robert came running. "Gregory, Robert has been a veritable treasure to us. Though you have lost weight, you are still too heavy for me to lift."

"Ah, so you wish to rise, sir?" Robert said.

"Well, that must be a slow process," I said. "First, help him to sitting. Gregory, be aware that you will probably be dizzy."

Robert moved him to a sitting position, where he did indeed waver over the lounge, his head moving side to side as if his neck couldn't support it. He breathed deeply.

"Stay there, Gregory, please," I said. But he would not! He strained to rise, leaning heavily on Robert. He didn't fall, but swayed on his feet. I reached out to him, fear making my heart lurch.

He laughed at me, but sat down abruptly. "All right, nurse,

you win, but I do want to sit up a while, provided my beloved can bear to sit next to me." He again clamped his fingers over his nose.

I smiled too, sitting close to him. "What is that heavenly smell? It must be the bakery has fresh rolls today."

"Ah yes, that must be it." He smiled down at me. "Robert, thank you. Please leave us now." To me, "if you can stand me like this, imagine the joys of clean hair and a shaven chin, somewhere far from this couch."

"Let's get Robert to wash and shave you. He can bring down a fresh mattress also.

"Now that you are conscious, it is best if I leave you with Robert and Mary. Think of my reputation," I simpered, fluttering my hands as if I were a silly girl.

"Oh, my dear. I do think of your reputation. That is why, though I cannot yet bend a knee, I wish to be married to you as soon as you deem possible." He grinned at me, the old Gregory whom I loved so much.

"You know, I wasn't sure you would still want me after we took to the Wagon Road so suddenly. We were gone so long, I thought perhaps you weren't ready to settle for me when we returned."

"Oh my! Settle for you? Poor girl, you are a little daft, it's true…."

I poked him in his ribs, which stood out prominently.

"Do not harm the patient," he said with mock solemnity.

"Truly, I little knew how you would view marriage to me after all your adventures. I am serious. Even now, I wonder if you are just used to me," he said.

"Well, you could just be grateful that I nursed you," I said.

He shook his head. "Oh Gwyn, I have loved you since I first

saw you, on a ship in the middle of nowhere. How much more I love you now that I know you well. And I have the means now to support you and our children. My law practice is well established in the town, and I have ample money and this house left to me by the Willinghams. We will even have the means to help your family. I want you to transform this house into a home we can both enjoy, whatever that takes, and live here happily together."

"That means so much to me, Gregory, but I must warn you that I want to be a doctor, or as close to that as I can get. It will take much time away from the household to learn and to serve my patients. I wouldn't be as other women, who would always be at your beck and call or that of the children."

He nodded, considering this. "Did your time away from Philadelphia help you decide this?"

"Yes, very much so, while it convinced Ardath she wanted to live in the wilderness."

"Dear Gwyn, you'll not be a prisoner of this marriage, I swear it to you. We can hire help. The house is big enough for you to have an office here if you wish. This desire is part of you and your giving heart. I would not wish it otherwise."

"Then yes, a thousand times, let us be married!" I said.

Chapter 16

James

Father Guillaume had become a good friend. I missed him on the rough sea passage to London. We docked in an early morning. I stretched my limbs and hurried off the ship. After hiring a horse, I rode as fast as possible to Ensleigh, arriving two days later.

I dreaded finding out that Father had not survived in my absence. I dearly wanted to see him again. The news of my brothers' situations had to be delivered, though I feared it might be the final blow for my father. At least, I longed to see him again and to somehow ease that shock, if only by my presence. I alone could assure him that Ensleigh and the other estates would go on, that there was a potential heir coming as well.

Dear Elizabeth was out walking when I rode into the drive. I leapt from my horse to embrace her.

"Sorry, I must smell of horse!" I said, but she merely leaned into me more.

"Samuel, how very fine to see you!" she said. Her eyes shone with emotion. She smelled of lemons and honey.

"Father?" I asked.

"Still here and waiting for you."

"Thank God!"

"The news?"

"Not good," I said. "I couldn't put it in a letter."

"Tell me now. I am ready." She squared her shoulders.

After a pause to collect myself, I said, "There was a shipwreck. Stephen drowned."

She gasped, then nodded, with a firm chin. "And Richard?"

"He is alive, but he doesn't know himself, or me. He is living with a kind lady in France. He is happy working as a gardener."

"How very strange. Is there hope that he will come to himself?"

"That is hard to know, but the lady and the local priest are watching over him."

"It must have been a very hard time, finding out all this," she sighed and shook her head. "For us, it is not unexpected news, after so long." We walked on toward the house.

"Well, yes, but still, how have you been? Any word from Mother?"

"Nothing. Mary sends word that she is happy in Wales. They are watching her very carefully."

"I'm relieved to hear that, I must say."

We walked arm in arm back toward the stables, where a groom took my horse.

"I must wash before I see Father," I said.

"Yes, I'll go prepare him to see you. We have become closer without Mother to poison the bond between us."

"Father loves you, but for too long you have been in the middle of the fight between them."

"Oh, Sam, you do truly understand it!"

"I am determined, if it suit you, to take you out of this limbo and transport you to the American colonies, where we can make a good life for you."

"I couldn't leave Father now."

"Of course not, but how long do you think he can keep going?"

"I don't want to feel I am waiting for his death," she said, with anger.

"I understand; I do…. Let us say no more now."

When I had washed, thinking all the while that it was a miracle that Father still lived, I donned a fresh suit of clothes. They had been stored with lavender. Having servants do all these things still felt odd to me after life in the colonies.

Elizabeth knocked on my door. She smiled to see me clean and looking like a gentleman again. "Father is waiting to see you."

Father was propped up in bed. "Father, you are looking well," I said.

"Don't lie to me," he said with a growl, then smiled broadly.

It was perhaps unmanly of me, but I rushed to put my arms around him. He still felt slight to me, but his color seemed better than when I had left. "I'm not lying."

"Well, mayhap you have removed a thorn from my side," he said. I could only conclude he meant my mother! "Have some brandy."

I poured myself a glass, sitting down beside the bed.

"It can't be good news about your brothers, as I gather you returned alone," he said.

"There was a shipwreck," I said.

"Both are dead?" he replied without flinching.

"Stephen is gone. Richard lives but cannot remember who

he is and didn't recognize me. I had to leave him in the care of his friends in France. They will let us know if he returns to his senses."

"I don't know if this is the worst or not. I truly have thought them dead for months now," Father said. "I suppose I seem unfeeling, but I have mourned them all this time."

"I understand that well." I wanted him to talk about what this meant for the estates, but I left him time to digest the news.

Soon he began again. "You must bring Richard back so that we may care for him."

"I wanted to, Father, but I believed, as did his friends, that it would break his fragile spirit."

"Elizabeth, leave us please," he said.

"Of course, Father," she said.

After she closed the door quietly behind her, he straightened himself in the bed. "Samuel, I will need to revise my will. It should read that should my older sons die or become incapacitated, you would become my heir to title and estates, while making sure that my other children and your mother are well-cared for. Send for Crowquill at once."

"Father, I understand your urgency, but Richard might recover."

"True, then it must also say that 'having been incapacitated, if the older son makes a full recovery, he then becomes the heir.' 'Writing maketh an exact man.'"

"And this is how lawyers maketh their money," I said.

"Indeed."

"I will tend to it immediately." I restrained myself from saying that he seemed completely satisfied with the situation, a situation that left me with many dilemmas.

"Father, I must say, while this provides for the future, I trust you will live on for many years. None can fill your shoes here."

He smiled. "It is true I can rally for now, now that you are here and having got some relief from your mother's sharp tongue, but the fact of my failing body still remains."

My brow furrowed.

"Oh, I know you don't like to hear it, but we must face the truth. Tell me of this wife you miss so much."

"I worry for her, Father. She is due to give birth before Christmas…"

"Perhaps a boy?" he asked eagerly.

"Well, of course we don't know." I could see now where his thoughts were leading. He wanted his legacy secure. It mattered to him more than any person could, including me. I was disappointed by his selfishness, having thought him truly fond of me when I was last here. Perhaps he merely saw me as a competent and convenient solution. Despite my best self, my heart hardened toward him. I'd now be cautious how much I told him of my thoughts.

"The point is, I must return to my American family. Now that we know what has happened to Stephen and Richard, and with the legal process almost finished, I cannot leave them alone while I continue here."

"Hmmm, there is many a wife that must take a back seat to the responsibilities of the husband. That is the way of the world." He paused, his face clouded. "Or have you become so unmanned by this woman that you cannot see that?"

He spewed these last words at me, becoming quickly angry. Then I saw; he couldn't comprehend real love. He really only understood duty in the end. That was appalling to me. Again, I understood how much I had changed through the agency not only of Ardath, but of her family, who were poor but truly loved each other.

I could not convey this in any way to my father. Many of my dilemmas would remain incomprehensible to him. He would be horrified if I mentioned giving up my commission in the army to tend to family, here or in America. During the silence which followed his outburst, he had calmed himself.

"I must apologize for speaking as a blackguard rather than a gentleman," he said, raising shaggy eyebrows.

I endeavored to put it into his own terms. "I understand the desire to see the legacy of our family continue uninterrupted. However, that is not the only duty I have. If you wish for us to have an heir, I cannot leave my wife without my protection from the vagaries of our less-civilized colonies. It is not the calm and ordered existence you have here."

"Well, then, go and get her and her family if need be, and bring them here. We have dozens of empty bedrooms."

"That is a very generous offer, Father."

"And why not, you'll be the earl soon enough anyway. You should be here."

"Thank you," I said. "Ahem. If I may broach the subject without Mother's interference, I wonder what you think of Elizabeth's marriage prospects here."

"Why, none and nil, I'd say. Mayhap, if we could get her to Charlotte's house in London, she'd see some likely prospects."

"Mother tried that before without success, I believe. Since it might become my duty to see her wed…."

"Well, that is highly likely, I'd say," Father said.

"And since I must return to Philadelphia soon, the sooner to return here, what if I took her there with me? There are more likely bachelors there than here, and she has a great desire to see that part of the world before she returns to England. She doesn't want to leave you, though."

"Oh, for pity's sake! Why does everyone tippy-toe around me? Let her go. I shall be quite content here, in peace and quiet."

"I will broach it with her. She's not getting any younger and I feel I must get her wed sooner than later."

"You have my blessing on that. Now let's get on with adding that part to my will as we said."

"I'll ask the clerk to write it up for your signature, Father. You should rest now."

"Yes, yes, they're always saying that," he protested, but his eyes were closing as he spoke. I helped ease him down on his pillow.

I felt a pang of guilt. I was lying to my father in essence if not by word, but then he had maneuvered me also, into a position not of my own choosing. I left the room with resolve. I would write to Ardath, telling her I hoped to be home by Christmas and to bring Elizabeth with me. We would just have to see what time and fate wrought, not to speak of my own free choice, whatever of choice might be left to me.

Chapter 17

Carys

After Ibrahim left that early morning, I walked outside. Dougie was watching the chickens from inside the pen. I checked to see if he had fastened the door securely, and he had. My heart glowed with pride for him. He was safe with these calm chickens, known as Dominiques.

"Hello, Dougie, do you like these chickens?"

"Sof," he said, patting a hen gently.

"Yes, their feathers make our pillows soft."

"Red," he said, gesturing over his head to show he meant their short red combs.

"That's right." They were gray or black with white bands. Their flesh was tasty and they laid large brown eggs.

"In Jamaica, the only chickens we had were Red Junglefowl. They ran wild and pecked." I made a pecking motion with my hands.

"Yes, pecked," he said. Even in chickens, Dougie was getting quite the education at his young age.

"Here soft dickies," he said to me with satisfaction.

"Yes," I said, "they are."

"Ard?" he said, for this is how he named his sister.

"I haven't seen Ardath today."

He made his plump littlehands into a tent and inclined his head in the sign for sleep.

"Yes, she sleeps a lot, doesn't she?" I said. "But it's time she was awake and abroad."

"Yep," he said in a stout voice.

"I'm going to wake her."

"Stay here," said Dougie, pointing to himself.

"Good."

"Ardath," I called as I gathered my skirts to head upstairs. I heard nothing, not even a groan, as I went up. Suddenly, I was overtaken by a great fear, running the last steps in my haste. Her bed was made and hardly mussed at all. She wasn't here and I hadn't heard her rise.

"Mrs. Perry," I shouted, tripping over my skirts and clutching the rail as I ran down.

"What, my dear Mrs. Rhys?" she said from the storage room.

"I can't find Ardath. Have you seen her this morning?"

"Why no, I haven't. Could she be with the horses, mayhap?"

I spoke no more to her, but ran for the stable, shouting for Omar. He didn't reply. Soon I was at the door to the unfinished structure. No answer there either. Just peaceful sounds from the goat who hadn't been tethered outside. Then I noticed two horses were gone. The black one, Rascal, was still in his stall. A note in Ardath's handwriting was tacked to the door.

Don't worry, Mother. Omar and I have gone in pursuit of Ahmed. We will be fine. We have the wagon and supplies. Back soon. Love, Ardath.

Mrs. Perry reached me, huffing and puffing. "Oh, no! That girl thinks she can do anything," she gasped as she read the note. "In her condition too!"

I pushed the hair from my brow, breathing deeply. I hated myself for it, but my first thought was to wonder what man we could call on for help. Omar and Ahmed gone, James on the sea, Smythe in bed, who was there to come to our aid? I had not yet met Franklin, though I was sure he would have some ideas, but the fever in town was keeping him within doors. There was only Ibrahim, and there was Isa, who was very strong.

"Mrs. Perry, can you go for Ibrahim, and find Isa if you can? I need to stay with Dougie."

"Of course, Mrs. Rhys." She had her boots on already, as she worked from morning to night, of her own desire. Removing her apron with a flourish, she hung it over the railing. She took off at a great pace, her elbows pumping away. How loyal were my daughters' friends! It seemed they would do anything for them. That loyalty must have been well-earned on their ocean voyage. I know they had given Mrs. Perry a home when she had none, after her husband died on the ship.

I searched for the wagon tracks leading away from the barn. They were faint, but were pointing to the north. Nobody really knew where Ahmed and his fellow thieves had gone. Ardath must have guessed at it. I had raised the girls to be sure of themselves, but Ardath could still surprise me with her rash decisions. I snatched up a switch from a willow bush and slapped it against the barn with increasing ferocity, until the green tip split. I was frankly furious with Ardath, as well as very worried about the dangers of the road she would be on towards New York.

Dougie was waiting for me by the back door when I returned . "Hungy," he said.

We proceeded to make and eat a simple breakfast of cheese, bread, and ale. Such simple tasks and Dougie's good humor calmed me. I returned to the barnyard soon after.

Ibrahim arrived with a young man I didn't know. Mrs. Rhys, this is Robert, who is working at Smythe's. He wants to help us find Ardath. Isa is tending the apothecary for me but she can come later if you want."

"Thank you both for coming so quickly." I said. "I looked for wagon tracks, which seem to be heading north." I noticed that the men looked at each other. Robert bit his bottom lip.

"Ma'am, this may mean they have taken the York Road towards New York. We had best be on our way, if so. I don't want to worry you, but that road is not safe in these times," Robert said.

"Can you ride?" I asked. He spoke well for a servant, but many servants had never been on a horse.

"Yes, Ma'am. Is there a horse?" he asked.

"Yes, but he's not easy to ride, quite headstrong I believe."

"I will try him. My father worked in a livery, so I've ridden all kinds."

My shoulders slumped in relief. I showed him to the black's stall and left him talking to the horse.

Ibrahim still stood outdoors. "I am not a rider," he said, tilting his head in regret.

"And we don't have another horse," I said. He nodded, with a slight smile.

"Mrs. Rhys," he began.

"Please call me Carys," I said. "After all that you and my daughters have been through together, you are part of our family."

"It is an honor," he said bowing his head. "If I may suggest it, I will give Robert the names of Franklin's post riders whom he may find on the road. Smythe sent information to them before, though none of them had seen Ahmed."

"That sounds good to me. Oh, Ardath!" I shook my head.

"Yes, she does things in her own way. She is a powerful person," he said.

"Thank you, Ibrahim."

We heard a mighty puffing as Mrs. Perry came across the yard from town, red of face and sweating profusely; the day was getting warmer. She waved to us all, as she gasped for breath.

"Mrs. Perry, thank you for summoning Ibrahim for us," I said.

"Aye, well, I'll go sit now. But first I must know the plan." She wiped her brow.

"If Robert, who has been helping at Smythe's house, can ride Rascal, he'll pursue them on the north road."

"Well, that'll be a fast horse if he can stay on him," she said.

"Please check on Dougie for me. We just had some breakfast."

"I will that; excuse me now," she said, turning toward the house.

"I gave Robert a detailed description of Omar and Ardath as we walked here," said Ibrahim. His quiet voice reassured me. I could imagine he was a great comfort to his patients.

"Thank you again."

"Ardath and Gwyn are like kinswomen to me," he said. "I would do anything I could for them. I admire both of them greatly."

I looked into his large brown eyes. They matched his long and solemn face, which could change in a trice, when he smiled, into a quite merry countenance.

"Thank you for looking after them on that journey across the Atlantic," I said.

"That was mutual. Many times they were of such help to me during the small pox epidemic, I couldn't have done without them. Then they rescued me from an uncertain future when we arrived here in the colonies, by buying and establishing the apothecary shop, so that I could have a place to live and continue my work."

"Um," I said. I had almost forgotten why we were standing by the stable, when suddenly, Robert and Rascal erupted from the stable door. I was startled, but Robert grinned broadly and expertly managed the reins of the frisky black gelding.

"He's got spirit, I'll say!" he said as the horse shifted his feet restlessly. He dismounted, tying the reins to a fencepost, still speaking to the horse in a soothing voice. "Ibrahim, I have your coins in case I need to stay overnight."

"Take this list of the mail riders' names," said Ibrahim.

"I'm afraid I don't read, sir," said Robert.

"Others can read it for you, if you ask for the post riders."

Just in time, Mrs. Perry arrived with a sack and leather water pouch in hand. "Here we go. I've got considerable trail food for you, young man," she said.

"Well, and thanks to all. I believe Rascal is ready to go. Don't worry. I'll find them," said Robert.

His confidence heartened us. We watched as he mounted and wheeled away on the gelding.

I breathed deeply. Mrs. Perry had already turned toward the house.

"Ibrahim, you must return to the shop. We will be fine."

"Of course." He paused to give us a reassuring look. "I believe Robert will find them soon," he said.

"I hope so." Meanwhile, I'd get nowhere by worrying. Mrs. Perry would help me find useful work, or Dougie would distract me from my worries. With the sun beating on my head, I hurried toward the cabin.

Chapter 18

James

After arranging for the changes to Father's will, I sought out Elizabeth again. She sat in the parlor working at her embroidery. She laid it down as I entered. Eyebrows arched, she smiled.

"Well, what secrets did you and Father discuss?"

"None. He just wanted to be sure that I succeed him as long as Richard is unable."

"Ah, that is very like him."

"Yes, it has been his main concern. I first took it as a sign of his affection for me, but now I think I am just a convenient way to maintain the family name."

Her lips twisted as did mine. "Maybe he and Mother are more alike than we thought," she said.

I nodded, pausing. "He seems in better health to me," I said.

"Yes, I think so too. If you will still have me, I will take up your offer of going to the American Colonies."

"Of course. I even got Father's approval." I began to pace the room. "We should go before the winter storms begin, in other words, as soon as we can. You will have packing to do, including fancy gowns, but work-a-day clothes will suit most of the time."

"Oh, Sam, I'm so excited and happy to be with you again! We'll have an adventure!"

"Enough of adventure. Let us just pray to have an uneventful journey."

I brought Mr. Appleton up to Father's room, where all plans were laid for him to manage the estates in my absence. Father looked quite healthy. I counted my trip here a success, and that was before Father instructed Mr. Appleton to give me bank notes and coin so that Elizabeth and I would have adequate resources to make the Philadelphia trip, set her up in good lodgings, and keep us until I could get back to England.

After the manager left and I retrieved the information to give to Mr. Crowquill, I asked, "Father, as you instructed, I have kept the leather bag with me, but what should I do with it now?"

"Open it in London. It is a gift for you to do with as you wish. You may wish to sell some in London, as I doubt there is much market for it in the colonies, but it's yours to decide."

"Thank you, Father. I appreciate your generosity to me."

"You will be the earl. You must get used to being a wealthy man."

Of course he didn't know that my deepest prayer was for Richard to recover.

Elizabeth came to see Father before we left. He pressed a miniature of himself as a younger man in her hand. "Don't forget me," he said to her. "And be sure to marry someone just like me."

"Oh Father, that may be beyond me, but I will try!" she said, a tear sliding down her face.

Our journey to London could not be swift, as we must take a coach to carry all the luggage. I had brought some more "gentleman" clothes from Ensleigh with me this time, to set us up with the gentry in Philadelphia. Elizabeth, the widow, must be presented in the best possible light.

We stayed with Aunt Charlotte in London. She was our best hope for a good story for Elizabeth. She also knew the real story.

We sat with her as the sun shone into her pleasant morning room. "Aunt Charlotte, do you know of an unmarried man, but of marriageable age, who has died in the last several years?" I asked.

Charlotte was a happy, and wealthy, gray-haired widow herself, having lost Mother's brother some years back. She clasped her pointed chin, staring at the floor.

"Hmmm, well there was poor Freddie Wilson, of course."

"Oh, I remember Freddie," said Elizabeth. "Rather sickly, wasn't he? But I think he did like me. All the girls thought he'd die before he could produce an heir, so he wasn't very popular."

"He sounds perfect to me," I said. "You took pity on his lonely plight and married him on his deathbed."

"No, first the marriage was consummated, so slightly before the deathbed," said Elizabeth. She bit her lip to stop a smile, then became serious. "In my sorrow, I lost the baby."

"Ah yes. Are any of his relatives or close friends in the colonies?" I asked Charlotte.

"No, I think not. They are not the adventuring sort," said Charlotte.

"Again, perfect," I said. I was practically rubbing my hands together. I could feel an evil grin creeping onto my face. "Poor Freddie."

"I will go to Pennsylvania as the widowed Mrs. Wilson, but I'll not make reference to Freddie or a child unless pressed to do so, just in case," said Elizabeth.

That evening in my room I unpacked the leather pouch. Why my father had told me to wait before opening it, I didn't know. Perhaps it was some test of my honesty or loyalty. I bounced it on my hand, again feeling a slight grating, as of rocks, inside. I drew a deep breath. Whatever it was might be a clue to the rest of my life. With care I emptied the contents onto a white shirt. First the packing of many cotton balls fell out. Then, in the light from several candles, I saw the jewels, intense, dazzling gleams. Before me lay a necklace of sapphires and diamonds, with matching earrings of the same brilliance. They were made for the neck and ears of a beautiful young woman. Because of her rosy complexion, they would be perfect for Elizabeth. She should have a gown of deep blue to show them off.

I was so overcome by my impressions of the necklace, I hardly noticed the rest of the jewels at first. They were unset, but beautifully cut, aquamarine, rubies, emeralds, star opals, and many more sapphires, all probably from India. A large teardrop shaped emerald would make a fine pendant for Ardath. The sapphire necklace alone would be worth thousands and thousands of guineas. The rest, I couldn't begin to calculate.

Another story must be forthcoming, of how my father had bought these from a friend who had made his fortune in India. In reality, his friend had probably gotten them illegally and been killed for it. There was, however, no way to know to whom they actually belonged, or to make restitution for them. No one must ever see them all together, or the story might not hold. I would sell several of the sapphires in London and take the rest with me to the colonies.

With Charlotte's advice I went to a jeweler in London. He was eager to buy two sapphires and wanted more "if I should come across them." I asked for payment in raw gold. I'd use that for having jewelry made for my American family.

After securing us passage on a ship to Philadelphia, I donned my uniform and went to the commander of the London barracks. With a strong sense of apprehension, I asked him to reimburse me or help me sell my commission as Major, since my responsibilities as the next earl did not allow me time to pursue an army career.

"Why, sir, I quite understand, although your colonel will be disappointed." He cleared his throat. "You are in luck, as Lieutenant Smathers has requested this rank when it became available. Excuse me, sir." He left the room, returning quickly while I was still taking deep breaths over this decision.

"Major James has had a tragedy in his family and now will be his father the earl's heir," he was saying, as he was trailed by a very slight man with pock marks on his face.

"Major James, may I present Lieutenant Smathers? If you both agree, we can formalize the exchange over a sherry."

Smathers stood at attention, saluting me crisply. "Sir!" he said. "I am prepared to hand you the usual sum for such an honor."

"Thank you, Smathers, now Major Smathers," I said, returning his salute.

With the handover of a substantial amount, we drank to our new status, he as a major and I as, what? A wealthier civilian? The whole meeting seemed fraught with irony. Had I been as green and useless as this man who was now a major because he had money? I hoped not, but it was water under the bridge.

I did feel somewhat naked at the thought of never wearing my uniform again.

My last visit was to Crowquill, who was as competent and cordial as ever. He well understood the conditions Father had specified and promised to get the completed papers to Ensleigh as quickly as possible. He congratulated me on my future as earl and promised to serve the family as he always had. He was much more excited than I was about my future.

When I returned to Elizabeth, she was packed and ready to go. "I have completed my business here. The ship leaves at first light on the day after tomorrow," I said.

All she said was "good." We nodded to each other.

"I admit I'm ready to get out of the city, " I said. It was October, the winter winds would soon blow, but we would have hope of reaching Philadelphia before Christmas.

Our ship, the Margaret Allen, was a finely appointed vessel. We each had a cabin to ourselves, though these were as tiny as could be. The captain was a tall, somber man with black hair and matching beard, neatly trimmed, who seemed to lack humor of any sort. Nevertheless, we would dine with him each evening. I didn't look forward to conversing with him. Another reason to hope the voyage was done quickly!

Now my thoughts could fully turn to Ardath and the rest of my new family. I wondered how she was enduring her confinement, as she was truly not a creature who would be pleased by it. How were Smythe and Gwyn progressing with their courtship, if at all? It would please me greatly if those two married. Had Mrs. Rhys met with her brother-in-law yet, and had she met Ibrahim?

So many things depended on the yellow fever that raged when I left. In fact the horrible realization again presented itself that I didn't know who had survived it. Ardath's vitality had led me to assume she would be waiting for me, but several times I dreamed that she and my child had succumbed to the fever. I awoke drenched with sweat and filled with foreboding.

As I broke fast with Elizabeth after one of those nights, she turned to face me. "Sam, you are hardly speaking to me lately. Your eyes are red as if you do not sleep well. What troubles your soul?"

"Ah, Elizabeth, I hate to reveal the weakness of my mind, but you always could read my face."

"Well, you certainly have plenty of responsibilities on your mind, but I cannot agree to any weakness there. No, you must tell me. Perhaps it will lighten your burden."

"It isn't the responsibilities that cause me to worry, but the things I cannot control. The yellow fever was sweeping through Philadelphia when I left my family there. I have dreams that my wife and child have died while I took up the problems in England."

"But you have heard from Ardath several times before we left England. She certainly sounded healthy in the passages you read to me."

"I don't say that the dreams show what has actually happened. Perhaps they merely show my worries."

"Umm, I can see that." She tilted her head to the side, nodding, blue eyes sympathetic.

"In so many ways, I have made steps to create more security for both my families, but illness, accidents, and death can happen suddenly."

"And there is nothing you can do about that."

"Hence the dreams."

"Well," I said. I feel blessed that I have you. I admit to sometimes having dreams that Father has died or will die, while I am away."

"I'm sorry for that. Do you regret coming with me?"

"No. I felt in some ways it was my duty to stay with him, but I also need to get on with my life."

"Don't worry, he wanted you to go for that very reason."

"Sam, I could never say this to anyone else and you may disapprove of it…"

Her voice caught in her throat. If I turned on her, she had no one.

"You may say it. I promise it will not break us apart." I laid my hand on hers.

"I…I have felt such anger toward Mother."

"Understandable!"

"But, toward Father too." She rushed on. "He professed to be concerned about me, yet I really never felt his heart was in it. It was just something he should feel about a daughter, protective or … I don't know."

"Believe me, Lizzy. I lived in some confusion too, only I was quite sure that he didn't care at all about me. And Mother, well, you heard her outburst. Where all that scorn came from, I can't guess, but I took it to heart when I was younger. You will understand when you are out in the world for a while that they can't see us clearly. They wear the blinders of their own viewpoint. How they see you should not overly concern you. You are your own person and very worthy of respect and love."

"I believe you have saved me. I'm not going to feel guilty." She smiled at me. I put my arm around her shoulders. Father hadn't protected her, but I would.

Chapter 19

Gwyn

"Are we serious, Gregory?"

"Absolutely! Never more so," he said, grinning at me, gaunt, yellowed cheeks notwithstanding. "In fact, don't delay. Rush to your uncle's house and ask him to read the banns."

"Oh. I will not stop until I get there, oh my," I said. I flung on my hat and went into the growing warmth of the late morning. Uncle's house wasn't far away. I didn't pause to think what a momentous step this was. Honestly, I was tired of being so wishy-washy about my future.

I tried not to beat on the rectory door, but to knock demurely. The door opened with an unexpected jerk, leaving me to practically fall through it, but not into my uncle's arms. I braced myself against the door and gazed with astonishment into the dark eyes of my cousin from North Carolina, David, whom I had left at his plantation, though he wanted me to stay, wed him, and be a mother to his three winsome sons.

"Gwyn, my dear, I was just coming to look for you."

My mouth hung open; I closed it with a conscious effort. "David, how come you to be here? Where are the boys?"

But he pulled me into his embrace, closing the door behind me. With his usual intensity, he gazed at me, then held me tightly to him. I felt his black curls fall soft over my face. He kissed me and I was melting into him, as if we hadn't been apart all these weeks.

When the kiss ended, we were reeling in the hallway. David took my hand. Still breathless, I followed him into the parlor. We sat together on the sofa.

"Gwyn, how I have longed for you."

"But David, how could you leave your crops? Your boys, are, are they with you?"

"My sons are with a neighbor who will watch over them until I return. My tobacco crop is in and I am wealthy from it. I don't have to be there, when all I want is to be with you."

"But," I said, "you know I made the decision to be here, to learn from my mother and Ibrahim, to be a doctor, or something close to that."

"Yes, I know. I haven't forgotten a word you said to me," he said, taking hold of my hand. Leaning forward from the waist, as if to press his point, he appeared both earnest and surprisingly young. "But don't you see? I don't have to stay in North Carolina. I can sell my farm for a good profit, come to Philadelphia, and start a new endeavor here."

"What would you do here?" I asked, to allow time to steel myself against the deluge of sentiment that flowed from him.

"Why, I don't know yet, a business of some kind, I suppose. I would have to be here longer to see what is needed in the city."

I sat in silence, overcome with confusion, then spoke slowly. "Dear David, this is so unexpected. Please don't think of jeopardizing your future to be with me. You went to North Carolina for the opportunity you saw, where there is a great frontier to be explored and fortunes to be made."

"Ah, I was afraid you wouldn't see it as I do." He sighed. "All

I have been able to do is to think of you."

"Oh," I said. His arm was around my shoulder. I could feel the melting start again. I so wanted to let it happen, to be swept away in his passion. Just to let him take over and give in without constraint.

But with an electrical knowing, I heard my mother calling for help. Something disastrous was happening at the cabin. I was needed there immediately.

"I'm sorry David, I have to go. Something is terribly wrong at home."

I left him standing in the parlor and rushed for the door, flinging it aside in my haste. Up I went through the dusty street, with never a look backward. I passed Gregory's house at speed. I would have to tend to my confusion and make decisions later, no time now.

Chapter 20

Ardath

After a fairly comfortable night in the inn, I felt ready to attack the road again. No one had seen any of the three thieves so far, along the York Road, but it had been some time since they would have traveled through these settlements. I refused to be discouraged.

"Omar, have you eaten?" I asked as I found him at the stables. He was petting and feeding the horses. Though he was a freedman, I was uncertain whether he would be served food from the inn.

"Yes, Mrs. Ardat'. Have you?"

"I have and I'm ready to go on."

"De horses ate well. Dey got some oats," he said, smiling sweetly at me.

It was, after all, a lovely morning, with sun and a breeze ruffling my hair. The cooler air caused the horses to move restlessly in their stalls.

"I'll soon have dem sorted and on de road."

When Omar had the wagon attached, we mounted to the seat. He flicked the reins and we were off. The horses trotted with heads high. We were leaving the last settlement in Pennsylvania. We were going farther north; I believed we would hear something soon.

There was a certain tedium to following the dusty main road, brushing away the flies that the horses attracted. I began to think there was an advantage to wearing a veil in such situations, although I knew that I must remain vigilant for highwaymen. I checked my pistols. They were clean. I left the box unfastened in order to retrieve them faster. I loosened the sheaves my knives lived in. I wore one of them on my hip always.

When the sun rose high enough to blister down on us, I said to Omar, "Let's pull aside on that path next to the stream. It should be cooler in the shade and we can water the horses."

"Yes, Mrs. Ardat," he said. He steered them over some surprisingly lumpy ground, then loosened their traces so that they could get their heads down to drink. I spread a blanket on the grass, closing my eyes to rest.

I thought of Omar and what this trip meant to him. He was hunting his own son, after all. My anger at Ahmed had made me blind to what Omar might suffer, whether finding Ahmed or having to conclude we never would find him. I resolved to be more sensitive to Omar, to talk with him about it.

Thank goodness I didn't fall asleep as I had done so regularly on the Wagon Road, because….

Someone was crunching stealthily through the undergrowth near us. A low voice said, "We cud really use that wagon." His voice broke off as if someone were silencing him. I reared up as fast as I could. Omar was by the stream and couldn't hear small sounds over its rushing.

"Omar!" I shouted. "Get your knife!"

He heard me, right enough, but so had the men creeping up.

I fled behind the wagon, grabbing both pistols and my extra knife. Omar rushed to crouch next to me.

We didn't speak. He carefully lifted the pitchfork from the wagon bed.

We waited in silence, tension crawling up my arms. We could hear nothing now, which was somehow more ominous. Had they slipped away when I called out? Or were they now coming from another direction?

If they had been watching, they would know that we couldn't get out of there quickly, as there wasn't enough room to turn the horses, much less time to tighten them in the traces.

I turned my head to listen from the direction of the road and from the direction of the bushes. Nothing.

Finally, I whispered to Omar, "You go get the horses ready. I'll keep watch from here. I think they are less likely to attack on the road."

Omar nodded. He moved so quietly that I couldn't hear him tighten the traces, while I swiveled my head in all directions. Nothing.

He turned the horses, leading them toward the road. I walked beside the wagon, still on high alert as it bumped over the ground.

We reached the road, staying on the farther side of the wagon. "What do you think we should do, Omar?" I whispered.

He shook his head. "Did you hear horses?" he asked.

"No. Does that mean we could outrun them in the wagon?"

"At first, maybe, but den dey maybe catch up," he said over his shoulder.

I climbed cautiously into the bed of the wagon, while Omar slid up into the driver's bench, keeping his head bent.

"Well, we can't stay here. Spur on the horses!"

Without reply, Omar called out "Hey-yah" and slapped the

reins hard.

I fired my pistol into the air to let the thieves know we were armed, as I gripped the wagon side. The usual cloud of smoke and the smell of rotten eggs somehow surprised me this time. I needed to practice more.

Our team jumped down the road at top speed, wagon swaying and dust flying. We rocked along our way, I on my knees, looking backward, with my other pistol cocked.

The horses tired more quickly than I had hoped, but we were some way down the road and I hadn't seen sign of pursuit.

Omar and I were puffing almost as hard as the horses. We drew in long breaths, daring to smile at each other. It was early in the day, but I thought we should find an inn.

Omar agreed, so after resting the horses, we rolled at a stately pace toward the next settlement. It was a very small town. The inn was dilapidated and horribly dirty.

"I think this is the kind of place where highwaymen might gather," I said. "I'd rather push on to the next town, if you think the horses can do it."

"Dis not looking like a good place," Omar agreed.

We asked the innkeeper how far the next town was. "Oh, not far. You can make it, no trouble, by tonight." He belched a big whiskey breath, running a filthy hand over the stubble on his chin.

We gratefully got back on the road, eating some hard bread and cheese that we had packed.

"Whew!" I said, while Omar grinned widely.

"Hmm, I t'ought all white men smelled good," he said.

"Oh, yes, of course." I laughed.

The day wore on. We relaxed in the belief that all was well. However, as daylight began to fade with no town in sight, I became worried again.

"I think maybe that innkeeper was lying to us, or just too stewed in alcohol to know the truth," I said.

"Umm," said Omar. "We can push on some more, but de horses are tired."

We did go on further, but there was not so much as a farmhouse in sight.

"Omar, I think we have to stop." In the waning light, I looked around us and listened hard, but heard nothing.

We made camp in a small grassy area beside the road. We brushed the horses down, then harnessed them again. We kept our weapons close to us. When I finally lay down, even that old wagon bed felt good. Omar lay under the wagon, next to his pitchfork.

I woke suddenly, hearing a muffled clatter from the road behind us. A pale moon gave us little light.

"Omar," I hissed.

"I hear it," he whispered. He slid on his back from under the wagon while I bunched up my pallet in front of me.

The light was dim, but as I stared, I saw two figures creeping towards us. It was two white men with slouch hats shading their faces in the starlight. Their silence was eerie, yet it might mean they had not seen us move and hoped to surprise us.

My heart pounded. It was too dark to make an accurate shot. And what if they were innocent parties? Then I couldn't just shoot them. I waited in an agony of indecision.

They were almost upon us when Omar dashed into the road, yelling "Halt!"

The men stopped. "Don't shoot us, please! We are just travellers like you."

"Why you creeping down de road, den?" asked Omar.

"Not creeping, just wore out, moving slow, is all," the taller one said. "Didn't see you there."

I relaxed a bit. Thieves would probably have run away. Maybe these men were harmless.

The sun edged up on the gray eastern horizon; the starlight faded. I was still staring intently at the men, my guns ready.

The taller man spoke, "We'll just be on our way, then." He turned back down the road in the direction from which they had come.

"But, Charlie," said the small, wiry man.

"Hush now," said Charlie.

We watched the two men until they were out of sight to the south, then broke camp and resumed our trip north. But I could tell something was bothering Omar. Our efforts soon seemed futile, as we encountered no one, and saw only a few scattered small farms. We eventually stopped for an early lunch, cooling both ourselves and the horses by a pleasant stream.

Omar finally spoke up, shaking his head, a hard look on his face. "Miss Ardat', I t'ink dose were two of dem we seeking. I've seen dem in town, and dey trouble-makers."

With that prompt from Omar, I realized that the smaller man had walked as if his back hurt him. "Omar, did the taller man have a scar down his face?"

"Light was bad, but I t'ink so."

I felt like slapping myself awake. I couldn't believe how witless I had been. But if these were the men, where was Ahmed? Perhaps they thought he would make them stand out. Perhaps he was hiding in the woods. In any event, they had turned back the wrong way, which was suspicious in itself.

I made up my mind — it was time to turn back, and hopefully get a better look at those two men. Omar turned the team, and we headed south, becoming especially watchful after we passed the previous night's camping spot and the town with the questionable inn. But we did not see the men, nor had the few people with whom we spoke. As dusk fell we found a spot well off the road for our camp. We remained on alert, but the night passed uneventfully.

After a quick breakfast, Omar hitched the team and I climbed aboard, berating myself for our missed opportunities. My self-doubt and frustration grew, and after the first miles I was blaming myself for turning back too soon. But then those two men jumped out from the woods at each side of the road.

"Git down. We need your wagon!" said the taller man, Charlie, who was on my right.

In an instant, I had my pistol pointed at his scarred face. He stopped.

His compatriot was on the left side, running at Omar. Omar moved fast, scooping up the pitchfork from the floor in front of him. Before I knew it, that fork swooshed through the air. A scream broke from the other thief, but I kept my eyes glued on my quarry.

"Sit down in the road, now," I said. "I'm a good shot."

"Now little lady, you aren't going to shoot me. We mean you no harm. Just give us your wagon and we'll be on our way."

He actually took off his hat, like a supplicant, but he made the mistake of taking one step closer. I wanted his information, so I shot him in the right shoulder. Both his arms jerked back. In his right hand he had held a knife. He landed in the dust of the road, whimpering in pain, red spreading out from his wound.

I hopped from the wagon, grabbed the rope from its bed, and tied his arms behind his back, causing him to writhe in pain.

"Omar, how are you?" I called out.

"Good, Miss Ardat', but he bleeding fast," he said about his prisoner.

My man wasn't going anywhere, so I got my healing bag from the wagon, hurrying to kneel beside Omar.

"What is your name?" I asked, while examining the wound on his thigh.

"Name of Will," he groaned.

"All right, Will, I'm going to help you, but you must answer all my questions truthfully."

"Yes, yes ma'am" he cried.

"Omar, remove the fork quickly, when I say to."

"Yes, Miss Ardath."

When I had all the bandages and washing elements ready, I said, "Now!"

Out came the fork, with gouts of blood, which was good. The first part of the cleaning was done by the blood, which wasn't spurting, so the weapon had not hit an artery. Next I washed with juice of garlic, made by combining garlic powder and warm water, then put ground yarrow into the wound to help with the clotting. I sewed him up and finished with a poultice of comfrey and a clean bandage. I was grateful I didn't have to seal it with fire, as I never liked the smell of burning flesh.

"Now to you," I said to Charlie. He lay, helpless, on his left side. "I will give you the same deal as I gave Will. I will help you, but you must answer every question truthfully."

He had the temerity to snarl at me. He even eyed the knife I held.

"Very well, then. I shall leave you as you are. The bullet and cloth will remain inside you, festering and paining you. Finally, it will suppurate and then turn black. Poison will reach your heart and you will die in agony." I was making up some of this as I went, but eventually he would be in bad shape without help.

He still looked rebellious, but nodded at me, with sour downturned mouth. I washed out his wound. The bullet had actually passed through the flesh. It wasn't really a terrible wound, but the bullet had deposited cloth in his body, which I picked out, then cleansed and bound the wound.

He struggled to his feet. Omar stood next to me, so Charlie wasn't inclined to lunge at me.

"Get up in de wagon," said Omar, giving him a shove. He stumbled, catching himself on the tailgate. Omar hurried him into the wagon bed. Charlie was clumsy with his hands tied behind him, but he got in. Omar then tied his legs together and attached his good arm to the wagon slats.

"What can we do with Will, Omar?"

"It's gonna hurt him, but in he goes," Omar said rather cheerfully. He pulled Will out of the dust. Will leaned heavily on Omar's side and went into the wagon with his help, wailing all the way. Omar tied him into the slats with Will's hands bound behind him.

"Shut up, will you?" said Charlie.

Will subsided into snuffling.

I brought the water jug, first drinking and offering it to Omar. "Dusty work," I said. He nodded.

Despite their hostile looks, we let our prisoners drink too.

"Now then," I said, " Charlie, I want the whole story, starting with where my coins are now."

He looked at me in surprise.

"Don't bother to lie. You and Will here, and my former friend, Ahmed, dug up my coins, both gold and silver and ran north. Where have you stashed them?"

He looked at me, sullen. I reached forward and pressed my thumb into his wound. He couldn't stop himself from crying out.

"Let me be, woman!"

"I'll be glad to stop once you are ready to talk," I said, renewing my torture.

He screamed then, but couldn't twist away. "All right, all right!" he cried. "All our money is just back down the road a little way. We was going to fetch it when you attacked. We need the wagon to carry it 'cause it's heavy."

He still saw things from his own perspective.

"I think you mean my money, " I said. "We will drive back slowly and do not try to deceive us. Call out when we are near it."

We had not gone far when Will said, "It's here. Look under that hollow log there." He pointed to a huge hollow log beside the road. Omar jumped down from the driver's seat while I remained there with my guns trained on the thieves.

"I found it, Miss Ardat'!" he shouted, hefting the stout leather bag in which I had buried the money. He clambered onto the wagon seat. The bag felt almost as heavy in my hand as when I had buried it.

Charlie said, "Now, some of that there is ours, fair and square, what we got for the Negro."

My heart chilled. "What do you mean?" I asked. "And tell me quickly!"

"That black boy, he did us wrong. He carried the gold and hid it and then he said we should take all the coin back, so we tore up his papers and sold him."

Omar's face went gray.

"Where did you sell him?' I asked.

"Why when we got to New York and he kept saying we should go back, take the money back, well that made no sense! So we told him to give us the gold right then, but it turned out he was carrying rocks, said he had hidden the gold along the Kinkanny Creek, all the way back to Philadelphia almost."

"Whom did you sell him to?"

"Why, a planter, name of, what was it Will? Miller or something. He's long gone to South Carolina now. Man needed a slave to work his forge. I reckon he's a sober man now, our Negro!"

"We're all too sober now, Charlie! Man's name was Melton from the Albermarle in North Carolina, least that's what he said. Got us a good price in silver too," said Will.

Poor Omar. He leaned against the wagon, apparently overcome at this information.

"Omar, Ahmed regretted what he did. He was foolish, but not so wicked as we thought," I said, laying my hand on his arm.

"T'ank you, Miss Ardat'. He's gone Sout', doh, and we'll never see him again. Isa, it will break her heart some more."

"I am sorry," I said, and I was. "Omar, I think we should take these men to the constable in the next town south of here. There's no point in going farther north now."

He nodded. He got back in the driver's seat slowly, his spirit flown away.

I checked the bag as we rode. It was full of silver, but not a piece of gold.

Chapter 21

Gwyn

As I ran up the street, I could feel my mother's heart burning like a flame, drawing me forward. Normally, she moved inside a stillness I could only hope to inhabit, some day far in the future. But now the stillness had shattered. I had not felt her in such turmoil since we were reunited in Wilmington in the summer. Today, someone or something had caused her great pain.

When I ran into the yard, silence greeted me, more ominous than wailing. I jerked open the back door, finding Mother in the hearth area with Dougie. "What is it?" I panted.

She rose from the table where Dougie sat playing with his wood blocks. Her expression was guarded. "Dougie, I'll be outside with Gwyn," she said. Her voice was calm for him; he didn't look up at her.

Once we were outside and away from the door, I grabbed her arms. "Mother?"

"Oh Gwyn! It's Ardath. I'm angry, ashamed of her, afraid for her."

"What?" I asked.

"She's left here last night, going after the thieves, alone, well, with Omar, but, in a wagon over rough roads said to be full of highwaymen. I'm afraid for the babies." Every line in her beautiful face stood out in pain.

"Oh Ardath. How stupid can she be? Mother, you must not let this upset you so. Ardath somehow escapes the worst of consequences when she does something on impulse. I saw that when we traveled." I shook my head, thinking of how Ardath could have been swept to her death in that raging river as we traveled down the Wagon Road. "But, you said 'babies?'"

"Yes. She's much larger than she should be. I haven't listened to her womb yet. I was going to do that today, but something tells me she could be carrying twins."

"She should be in bed. I understand," I said. I shook my head again. Despair, aggravation!

"I should have curbed her more, not let her be such a wild spirit over the years. Why didn't I?"

"Mother, I don't think anyone could curb her. I worry for James, in fact," I admitted.

Tears had streaked her face. I had never seen my mother cry, but she had endured many shocks in the last years, which would have worn anyone down.

I hugged her to me, though she was the taller of us. Her head settled on my shoulder. "I truly believe this will be all right. For one thing, I haven't had any premonitions about her being in danger, though I wouldn't always know."

She sighed deeply. "That does comfort me. Goddess! How could she be so careless? The money means nothing. We are fine without it. Is it just the revenge she wants?"

"The money represents something to her that I don't fully understand. Something about her independence, her security, and her plans. I know she wants to be an equal to James in their marriage. Perhaps money means she can still feel that self-reliance, especially if he becomes an earl."

"Well, and she has seen me forced to be self-reliant after your father left."

"She's never forgiven him for that, and she's never trusted others to help. She can be secretive. And I think revenge would be sweet to her also."

"Hmm," Mother said. "I should have noticed how much it was bothering her."

"We can feel guilty forever, or we can know that this is just how Ardath will be until the world teaches her otherwise," I said.

We stood apart, gazing at one another. I realized that we had spoken as two equals, rather than as mother and daughter.

"Dear Gwyn, you are quite a woman," she said.

"Until I examine my own life, that is," I said.

"Oh dear, is it your turn to say your doubts?" she asked.

"First, let me ask what you have done about Ardath's problems."

"I spoke to Ibrahim. We have sent Smythe's servant Robert after her on Rascal. Apparently, he's a good horseman and Ibrahim trusts him to find her and Omar. The wagon tracks indicated they were going to the north road."

"I see. I will need to get back to the Willingham house soon, if it is only Mary there to tend Gregory."

"Do you need any herbs or food? How is he doing?"

"I think we are fine. Mary works constantly, so she keeps things in order. Gregory is better too and needs less physical help."

I found I was looking at my shoes, where I scuffed my toe in the dirt.

"Gwyn, what is it?"

"After we agreed to get married. I went to Uncle's house to

ask him to post the banns. Uncle wasn't there but David was."

"David? But what was he doing here? I thought he was in North Carolina." She touched her hand to mine.

"I think he came to see me, mainly." I raised my eyes to Mother's face. I felt as hard and hollow as a gourd.

"Oh Gwyn!"

"Yes, he kissed me and said we should be together. He's thinking of moving back here."

Now it was Mother's turn to shake her head. "What did you say?"

"I was so astonished, I could not reply to him. Then I felt your distress, excused myself, and ran right here."

"What will you do?" she asked, tilting her head.

"I shall return to Gregory and tell him I did not find Uncle at home!" I said. "That is, if you are all right here."

"I'll be thinking of you, of course, but I'm not alone. Mrs. Perry and Dougie will help me keep my mind off of Ardath."

"You'll let me know if there's any word?"

"Of course. We can't do anything but wait now."

"I know, but I hate it."

"As do I," said Mother. "But, Gwyn, I need to tell you that I married your father because of his charm, the intensity of his love for me. It's similar to what you say attracts you to David. We had some happiness for a few years and of course, I wouldn't trade anything for the two daughters that we had together. But I do wish I had had a friend to marry, such as you have with Gregory. I believe that would have been a better marriage for both of us in the end. And, dare I say it, David is your first cousin. I believe that is a too close a blood relationship to be wholesome. I know Ibrahim also thinks that, as a doctor."

I walked "home" to the Willingham house, thinking about

what Mother had said about marriage. I also wished I could tell Ardath how I felt about her actions, but that was frankly not my main concern. Gregory was such a good confidant that I wanted to ask him what I could do about my situation with him and David. That was ridiculous. It is not in my nature to be devious, but I would have to hide from Gregory what David had said to me. My stomach turned at the thought. I needed time to sort my feelings out.

I let myself in at the back door. Gregory was sitting up on the new bed that Robert had brought into the sitting room for him.

"Gregory, my dear, where is Mary?" The room smelled suspiciously of vomit.

"She's out looking for some eggs. I felt hungry and I am well enough to be alone. Have you convinced your uncle to read the banns?" He smiled up at me and took my hands in his, but he looked more worried than happy.

"My uncle wasn't at home." I sighed.

"Gwyn, what is it?"

"Oh, I thought you might have heard from Ibrahim, or Robert." I sat down beside him.

"Robert hasn't been here today." He put his arm around my shoulder. I leaned into him.

"Oh, well, my mother is distraught. Ardath decided that she would go after Ahmed and the thieves."

"What? By herself?" He leaned away to see my face better.

"No, she went in a wagon with Omar. They sneaked off in the night. Robert has gone after them on our biggest horse, Rascal."

"Robert is a smart man. He'll find them."

"I'm so tired. I don't want to talk about it any more."

Gregory nodded slowly. "Let's sit together in the large chair."

I took off my hat. Gregory rose and crept to the chair. He walked somewhat hunched, like a much older man. He really wasn't as well as he claimed to be. I nestled in with him, feeling his prominent bones.

"Are you very disappointed that I wasn't able to talk to my uncle?" I asked him.

He sighed. "No, I think it is better, my dear one. I was carried away with delight at the thought of you as my wife, but I don't feel well enough to get married yet. I hope that doesn't disappoint you. It doesn't mean I don't want to marry you as soon as I am more able. Please know that!"

"I do know that. Don't worry about me. I trust you and I want you to feel better too."

"And, well, please take this in the right way, I think you should return to the cabin. I seriosly worry about your reputation with folk moving about the city more. And we have Robert and Mary to care for me. I want you to be not my nurse, but my beloved."

As always, he really wanted what was best for me. One thing I knew then. I couldn't hurt him. At the same time, my mouth still had the feel of David's lips on it.

Mary returned with eggs in hand and offered to make them up for me as well as Gregory.

"I know that your mother is worried about Ardath and has sent Robert after her," she said.

"Thank you, Mary. Since you are here, I believe I should return to my cabin to be with my mother until we can hear news about Ardath."

I smiled at Gregory to let him know the other reason I was leaving.

"I am well enough so that she shouldn't stay here," he said.

She grinned at that. "Of course. Life returns to the customary as the fever retreats!" she said.

I nodded. I rose slowly; Gregory kissed my hand and I withdrew it reluctantly.

Walking to the shade of the nearest square, I had to contemplate my mother's thoughts on my dilemma. It struck me as true; my love for Gregory had started as a friendship and continued as a deep sympathy between us. He had really known me over time, which David had not. Nor had I known David over time. I understood that I had a profound trust in Gregory, whereas David's behavior surrounding his wife's death, though understandable, revealed some weaknesses with which I could not feel secure. Choosing a medical life, as a woman, I would have enough challenges without a husband who might be passionate, but also impulsive. Perhaps Mother thought the close blood relationship wouldn't bother me, but it did. Suppose I passed on Ardath's impulsiveness, and David passed on the same characteristic to our children. It didn't bear thinking about.

Chapter 22

Ardath

It seemed to take forever to get back to the town where we had talked to a constable on our way north. The thieves moaned and groaned as we bumped along the road. I had no sympathy for them, but I felt every bump too. It was as if the suspension in my sides had given way as we traveled. My middle ached worse with every mile. I could practically hear my mother and Mrs. Perry saying "I told you so." Mother had told me not to ride a horse, but I'm not sure the wagon ride was any better.

As we entered the area north of Philadelphia, I heard a whispered conversation from the wagon bed. I showed no reaction, as Will said to Charlie, "Isn't this where we camped near that creek, the Kinkaky?"

"Hush." Charlie hissed. "Don't say nothing about it. When we get free again, we'll look around some more. That gold couldn't be too far from here."

Ah ha, so the thieves thought Ahmed had left the gold hidden near here. If they hadn't found it quickly, I doubted we would either. I looked at Omar, whose twisted mouth showed he was thinking something similar.

I had to be satisfied for now with a plump bag of silver, because I wasn't feeling very well. I thought I might be coming down with an ague. All I wanted now was to crawl into a bed, preferably mine.

I was near to panting when we rolled into the little town. Thankfully, the constable was in his office and immediately took charge of the thieves, while I stayed on the wagon seat.

"Are you Mrs. Ardath James?" he asked.

"Yes, I am," I said between gritted teeth.

"There's a young man here looking for you. Says his name is Robert. Your mother sent him."

I looked at Omar. "Robert?"

"I believe he's da man working for Miss Gwyn," he said.

"Oh, where is he, exactly?" I asked the constable.

The constable spit into the dust while his deputy steered Will and Charlie past us into the gaol. "Here he comes now."

I turned my head too quickly. Black dots spread before my eyes.

When I awoke, I found Omar and Robert had laid me on a pallet in the wagon. I was aware of shade, dusty yellow leaves above me, and blue sky beyond.

"Mrs. Ardat', you all right?" came Omar's call.

"Yes, yes, I'm fine," I said, embarrassed to have fainted like a weakling woman.

Robert put a respectful, but firm, hand on my shoulder when I tried to sit up. "I think you should rest awhile, Mrs. James," he said. He was short, but very strong, a Welshman, with dark hair and an air of authority.

I breathed deeply. "You are working for my sister Gwyn?" I asked.

"Yes, ma'am. I take care of Mr. Gregory's house. Everyone was worried about you. I rode Rascal to find you, but I wasn't been successful for the last three days. Somehow, I kept missing you. But looks like you caught the thieves."

I put my hands on my chest. "Yes, we did. Omar, does the constable have all the facts he needs to lock these men up?"

"Yes, ma'am. He'll have dem patched up some more, den sent down to de city to stand trial."

And I would have to convince some man to testify for me, some white man. That idea made me steam. A woman couldn't testify in court and I doubted that a black man could. All this trouble for me and Omar when the thieves were the guilty party.

Omar and Robert sat on the edge of the wagon. "We will take you to the inn here to rest until tomorrow," said Robert. "I'll ride back to your mother's house and let them know I have found you."

"No, I don't want to stay here. We could get home today, couldn't we, Omar?"

"I t'ink it's better we rest here," he said.

"Omar, you have always said that you would do anything for me, haven't you?"

"Yes, ma'am, but—"

"I can rest as well in the wagon; take me home."

Omar and Robert looked at each other. Omar's lips tightened. "Mrs. Rhys won't like it," he said.

"I'll speak with her. I'm not getting out of this wagon," I said.

Robert tipped his hat to me. He led Rascal out to the road and galloped away.

"Omar, don't look so wretched. I'm fine. Let's go." He fixed my pallet carefully under me, shaking his head.

In truth, I wasn't fine, but if I was becoming ill, I'd rather be with the two best healers I knew, Mother and Ibrahim. If they thought it was yellow fever, I could stay in the barn away from anyone.

First, I made sure I had the leather bag of silver tucked next to me, then nodded to Omar. He mounted to the wagon seat, clucked to the mares, and off we went.

It was a very long trip home. I felt even more beaten and battered as we jolted down the road. Omar drove carefully, but it was still taxing. However, pulling into the yard at our house was a full reward for the pain.

Mother was at my side right away. I am ashamed to say that I cried when I saw her. That was probably the only thing that saved me from a severe tongue lashing.

"Oh Ardath, where does it hurt?" she asked.

"Everywhere!" I said, between sobs. Then I saw that Ibrahim had come also. "Do I have the yellow fever?" I asked.

His hands passed over my body. He peered into my eyes. He felt my forehead. "I don't see any signs of it. Have you felt feverish? Chills?"

"Not much, just aching, especially my sides."

He and my mother exchanged glances. She couldn't stop herself. "Did you ride a horse?"

"No, Mother, you said I shouldn't." I could see her thinking that her advice hadn't stopped me from doing stupid things in the past.

"I t'inking the wagon bumped around too much," said Omar. "I'm sorry."

"Omar, this isn't your fault and don't you think it was," I said. "You are not to feel responsible."

"Yes, ma'am," he said.

"You must go to bed and stay there," said Ibrahim. I had never heard him speak to a patient so sternly.

"Her bed is ready. Do you think you and Omar could get her up the stairs?" Mother asked Ibrahim.

They both nodded. They lifted me, pallet and all, and trundled me up the stairs to my room, gently rolling me out onto the soft, clean sheets. "I'll take it from here," said Mother. "Thank you."

To Omar she said, "Please go and rest. Robert has rubbed down Rascal and told Gwyn that Ardath was coming home. "

"T'ank you, Mrs. Rhys. I was sorry to take her away."

"Don't worry. I know that Ardath can be hard to refuse."

I heard the two men hurry down the stairs.

I finally let myself relax and feel glad I hadn't brought yellow fever to the house. Mother and Mrs. Perry soon had my clothes off and bathed me with warm water, afterwards slipping my nightgown over my head. Next, they brought herb tea and then custard. I didn't protest that I still could chew. I just appreciated every loving deed.

After Mrs. Perry left to prepare a late supper, Mother asked how I was feeling.

"I am feeling grateful and at ease, but my body seems awfully sore. Mother, have I hurt my baby?" I gazed into her eyes, feeling guilt about my carelessness. What would I say to James if I had harmed our child?

"I don't think so, but I would like to examine you more thoroughly and listen to your womb. You may have stretched the muscles holding the womb in place. Also, I found blood on your skirts. That's why bed rest is so important."

My chin began to tremble. "Blood? Could I be miscarrying? Look now, please."

She pulled out her delivery bag. Inside was that strange wooden instrument sometimes called an ear trumpet, which helped her hear what was happening in the womb. I had never heard of anyone else using it this way, but my mother was very clever. She put this on my abdomen, pressing very gently, her ear on the other end of the tube.

I found I was holding my breath.

"Breathe," Mother said.

She moved the tube around here and there. Suddenly I felt a big thump on the inside.

"He doesn't like to be pressed on," my mother said with a smile.

"Is he kicking?" I asked.

"Yes, that's what you feel."

Suddenly it was real. I was having a baby, and he was alive, regardless of my bad behavior. Tears rolled down my cheeks again.

"Stay still now," Mother said. She continued to move the tube around on my stomach. "Hmmm, that's interesting."

"What?"

She stood up, nodding at me. "I hear two heart beats. You are having two babies."

"But the blood! What if…Oh God! I'm never leaving this bed 'til they come, am I?" I asked.

"No, oh no, indeed. I will put a cloth on for you. If there is more blood, we will revisit their condition," said Mother.

"Oh, pray that they are all right! With two babies, James

would be so excited." I said. I hardly dared hope that they would be healthy.

"Don't worry too much yet. It could just be normal spotting." She hugged me to her, then left me to rest. The bag of silver lay beside me in the bed. I pushed it onto the floor, wondering whatever had possessed me to risk myself and my babies for it. I was disgusted with myself, and haunted by the fear I could lose them.

Chapter 23

Gwyn

Four days passed, during which we had worried and waited to hear what had happened to Ardath and Omar. When Robert finally returned with the news that they were safe and on their way home, I hugged Mother and left to do some badly needed shopping.

Of course, I hadn't just worried, but had continued to talk with Mother about my situation with Greg and David, becoming ever more certain that I would be happiest choosing Greg. David had not come to see us, as his father counseled him to leave us alone until Ardath was settled.

Though I wasn't prepared, I chanced upon David at the market. He was chatting with a man of business there, one I scarcely knew. He broke off when he saw me and came to my side, so close that he made my gown rustle. I was relieved that we were not alone together.

"Gwyn, I have been thinking of you, as always," he said, black eyes studying my face.

"Ah, how are your business inquiries going?" We began to

walk along together to a patch of shade.

"Not well so far. I can find nothing in which I would invest."

"I suppose you are missing your plantation and your boys too."

"Well, of course, but you are here."

I swung around to face him. "David, please don't move here for me," I urged. "I don't want to hurt you and I…I'm afraid I have led you on in some ways."

"What do you mean?" he asked. "You cannot deny our passion for each other." He scrubbed his hand through his dark hair.

"No," I said, through trembling lips. "I cannot deny that, but passion is not all in life. Oh, this is so hard!"

He pulled back from me, brow creased in pain. "You have found someone else, someone you love more than me."

"I have found someone to whom I am more suited, an old friend who is already established here." I cringed within my heart to tell him this.

"You are settling for him, then."

"No, I love him deeply too. It is just different. And I admit that our close consanguinity has worried me."

He sighed from deep in his chest. "That I cannot argue." His head lowered on his shoulders.

He seemed to be giving up on us, a little, which should have made me relieved.

"I will stay longer. Perhaps you will change your mind," he said, looking up.

"No, I will not, David. Please don't waste your precious time pursuing me."

I strode away as quickly as I could, my heart breaking within, knowing I had caused him pain and realizing that I had slammed a door behind me. I made it around the first corner, which was thankfully uninhabited, before I shamefully broke into tears and leaned against the warm, tall, brick wall of someone's garden, shaken by my sobs, my throat closed and aching with pain.

Chapter 24

Carys

Goddess, protect us! My daughter had endangered her babies in order to go after the thieves. As usual, Ardath had accomplished what she set out to do, but at what cost? And Gwyn's situation was worrisome too.

As I thought on these things the next day, Ibrahim came by to check on us. He bowed to me in the front doorway.

"Mrs. Rhys, how are you?" His warm brown eyes gazed into mine.

"Much concerned for my daughters," I replied. Glancing toward the stairs, I spoke in a low voice.

"Perhaps we can speak outdoors," he said.

We stood on the porch. A breeze blew birdsong and scents of the forest to us. Ibrahim smelled of an exotic spice that somehow said "Africa."

"Please tell me of your concerns if you wish to."

I was grateful to him for his palpable kindness, and I told him my worries.

He listened very carefully before he said, "You have always been the strong one, but you are not alone any more." A gentle smile creased his face. "I will be happy to help you, either as one who hears you, or to talk with your daughters if you wish. In effect, they have become my family too. And you have a young boy to raise as well."

"Whom I need to look for now, in fact. Thank you for your kind offer. I am very grateful and I readily accept. A heavy weight is now much easier to bear."

"It is the least I can do," he said. He nodded. "May I go to see Ardath?"

"Yes, yes, of course, please do."

He rose and bowed to me, went through the cabin door, and proceeded quietly to the back stairs. I stayed on the front steps, musing. There truly was a larger family here, which included Mrs. Perry, Ibrahim, Smythe, Omar, Isa, and once, Ahmed, and of course, James. They had all forged relationships on their ship and worked for the common good. They now enfolded Dougie and me. I had felt alone for a moment, but I wasn't really, as Ibrahim had showed me.

However, as Dougie and I, and now others, joined the original "family," sleeping space was getting tight. When James returned, we would have three beds to hold six people. Omar and Isa couldn't stay in their tent, but they could return to the apothecary with Ibrahim, as winter came on. If Gwen married Smythe, she would move to his house, but that was far from decided. In the present, I might contribute best by planning how to house more of "the family."

As I came back inside, Ibrahim was leaving. "Mrs. Rhys, I believe that Ardath is prepared to respect our admonition that she must stay in bed."

"Thank you for telling her again," I said. "I'll call for you if her condition worsens, but I think we can handle it from here. And thank you, in general, for looking out for all of us."

"It is my pleasure to help where I can," he said.

Dougie was nowhere to be seen, so I continued through the back door. I found him playing with rocks in the stream. He grinned up at me. "Mama!"

"I see what you have done to build a dam and make a pool. Very good."

"Good, fun," he said.

"Are you hungry?" I asked.

"No, stay here," he said, pointing to himself.

"That's good. I am going to the barn to talk with Omar."

He nodded, again absorbed in his enterprise.

I noticed Omar hard at work on timbers outside the shed. "Omar, do you have a moment to talk?"

"Of course, ma'am," he said.

"I want to thank you for looking out for my daughters," I started.

"Oh, ma'am, we look out for each ot'er."

"I see that you do. It's quite wonderful!"

"Yes, ma'am. It is Allah's will."

"I feel very disturbed to hear from Ardath that Ahmed has been sold as a slave."

Now he looked at the ground, pain creasing his face. "Isa cries at night."

"If you agree, I would like to write to some officials about his plight. Perhaps we could still find him."

"If you t'ink it could help, we would be most grateful," he said. He looked up toward the sky. "Children can bring much pain," he said.

"Yes, they can. Our lives are never the same after we are

parents."

"Dat is right! How is Miss Ardat'?"

"I believe she will recover in time. I will speak with Mr. Smythe as soon as he is able. He will know what can be done to look for Ahmed."

"We t'ank you. Isa will be most grateful too."

"You are welcome. Could you please show me how the barn is coming along?"

"Yes ma'am." He showed me inside, where the stalls were being used for the three horses. Another area could shelter the goat and pig. There was even a spot for the chickens, if the weather became too chill for their outside roosts.

"Omar, I know you aren't finished with the barn yet, but when you are, I believe the animals will be safe and warm. You build very well."

"T'ank you, ma'am. I am happy I can help. It is very cold here in winter, much snow also." He shuddered. "My homeland was never so cold as dis."

I nodded. "I will have to get used to that too."

We walked out into the yard. "Omar, is there room on this property for another house?"

He looked around, considering the boundaries of the land Ardath had bought. "No ma'am, not if we are to have dese animals and de garden."

"Hmm, yes we need those, surely. Thank you, Omar. I won't keep you any longer."

He returned to work and I returned to the house, after checking on Dougie, still having fun in the stream, as he had done so often when we were in Jamaica. He should enjoy it now. Soon he wouldn't be able to play as much outside. He had never known cold or snow before in his short life. I felt a twinge of homesickness for that warm and wonderful land in the Caribbean.

I asked Mrs. Perry to bring Dougie in shortly. When I reached Ardath's room, I found her propped up in bed on several pillows. "Have you had any more bleeding?" I asked.

"Oh, no, Mother, thank goodness," she said. "I'm so bored. Tell me what is happening around 'the estate.'"

We laughed together. "I'm happy to see that you are rested enough to be bored," I said. "And preparing to become a countess of an actual estate, as well."

"To be truthful, I am terrified at the thought. I know James never wanted to be an earl, either. Both of us are unprepared." She raised her eyebrows. "Not to be too coarse, but the money would be nice. James has never seen a penny of his own from that estate."

"Primogeniture is a strange system, but I guess it keeps property from being divided into diminishing shares."

"Speaking of money," I said, "we should count the silver I retrieved. I'm wondering if it's enough to buy more land around here. I have a thought that Philadelphia may be poised to see rising land values."

"I know you relied on Smythe to look into such business for you. With all the time spent traveling to North Carolina and back, and then the yellow fever epidemic, we can't know much about how the city will develop currently. It's odd that I was talking in the barn with Omar just now about land. Not enough room to build more here."

"We did rely on Smythe. Do you think he will be able to work again?"

"In all likelihood, I'd say yes, but I don't know how soon."

"Mother, is Gwyn going to marry him?" Her voice and eyebrows rose high.

"I don't know, but you sound dubious."

"Do I? He's a good man, but he doesn't seem very strong, at least physically."

"Of course he isn't right now, but I hope he can regain strength. Not everyone can have, or indeed needs, great physical power."

"True. Mother, would you do something for me? Would you ask Mrs. Perry to keep Dougie and go see Gwyn? I just need to know how she's doing,"

"Of course, I will."

"Just set the silver up here on my tray and I will count it out."

"Of course. I'll bring pencil and paper too." For they had shown me the pencils Franklin sold, which would be much easier for her to use in bed than quill and ink.

When I had arranged things at home, I walked down to the Willingham house. Mary answered the door. Gregory and Gwyn were in the sitting room, heads together in a large chair.

"Mother, how wonderful to see you! I'll put on the kettle for tea," said Gwyn. While she rushed out to the kitchen, I viewed Gregory carefully from the corner of my eye. He looked very pale and bloodless.

"How are you, Gregory?"

"Tired and sick, but don't tell Gwyn. We hope to get the banns read when I feel better."

"You can readily tell me that it is none of my business, but please consider postponing the wedding until you are truly well. It's a serious step and you should be back to full strength before you undertake it," I said.

"I understand and I think you have a good point, but please have no doubt that I love her. I have loved her since we first met on that dreadful voyage across the Atlantic."

"I have no doubts about your love," I said.

"Well, thank you for that," he said, smiling. "How is Ardath?"

"She is bored. She is counting up the silver to see if we can afford to buy land. She is confined to her bed for the next few months though."

"Ah, I used to know about all business deals involving land, but currently I don't know even if the State Land Office is up to date because of the epidemic. I'm sure many estates in town are in limbo, with owners having passed away. There may be land out beyond yours which is not claimed, although it may have squatters on it. Our best bet would be to start with the Land Office and see what they know. Perhaps your brother, the Reverend Rhys, could enquire for you."

"They wouldn't sell to a widow with some silver to spend?" I asked.

"Uncertain. Even though you are a *feme sole*, capable of making legal arrangements for yourself, by law, most clerks prefer to deal with men, and may well ignore you without an escort."

"I understand. It's no different from England, though I might still have some credibility in Wales."

"It's certainly an argument against remarriage as far as having possessions in your own name."

"I don't think I have to worry about remarriage."

"Oh, I wouldn't be too sure about that," he said. He was

grinning at me in a most impish way, which made me realize one thing Gwyn loved about him.

"Well, I need to visit the Reverend Rhys anyway. Though we have been here for over a month now, some wise person warned us not to come to town, so I haven't seen him yet."

"I wish I could go with you or for you. Since I can't yet, I think Mr. Rhys would be a good start." He looked up. "Ah, here's our tea. Please let me know what you find out about property. I can advise you from there," he said.

"Thank you. In addition," I said to Gwyn and Gregory as Mary set out the tea dishes, "we need to find Ahmed. It turns out that he wanted to restore our money to us, so the thieves sold him into slavery, to a man from North Carolina."

"We know how to contact newspapers and agents in North Carolina, Mother. When Ardath recovers to some degree, she will remember where to send letters," Gwyn said. "I will help you both to get those sent out."

The three of us sighed. It always seemed that there was another situation to be dealt with.

Chapter 25

Carys

After the short visit at Smythe's, I followed his directions to the Reverend Rhys's house. I wore a cloth around my nose and mouth, since he lived near the church and close to the docks, where the yellow fever had been the most prevalent. It was a modest house, as most parsonages are, but sturdily built in brick and stone.

The Reverend Rhys opened the door himself. Though it had been many years since I had seen him, he looked familiar, enough like his brother, my late husband. He greeted me warmly. I pulled off my mask.

"Sister! I hoped to see you soon. Welcome," he said, pulling me into his arms for a heartfelt hug.

"Brother! Finally we meet again. So sorry for your loss of Priscilla," I replied.

"Thank you," he said.

We stood back from each other to look again. "We have seen many hard times, but you are as lovely as always," he said.

"Very kind of you to say, but, truly, I am lifted by the discovery that my daughters are alive, when I had thought them dead."

"Yes, alive and prospering, for the most part. What adventures they have endured! And you, also, I have heard, but I hope to hear more detail. For now, please come, sit down, have some tea with me."

"I'll enjoy your company, thank you, but I've just come from tea with Gwyn and Gregory," I said.

"Ah, in that case," he gestured to an upholstered chair in the sitting room.

After he sat on a straight chair, he said, "Thank you for your condolences for my wife. She perished in the first wave of illness and I've been very involved since in ministering to my flock. It seems that being busy helps with grieving."

"Yes, I'm convinced of that," I said. "Gwyn tells me that you have been kind to my daughters."

"Well, most of the time, I hope. My wife was not, but she had many flaws in this earthly life, I'm sad to say." He sighed.

"She also says that your son David is in town."

"That he is." He cleared his throat. "I believe he hopes to take Gwyn as his wife. They formed an attachment when they met in North Carolina."

"I have heard about that. Thomas, how do you feel about the idea?"

"Ah, well, there's no persuading young people when they are, hmm, attached, but I have my hesitations." He rubbed his chin.

"As do I. First cousins seem a close consanguinity," I said.

"I must agree. I know some among the nobility believe close relationship makes for the best marriages, as in, what could be better than more of the same noble blood, I suppose."

"Umm. Others might say it is too inbred."

"It certainly wouldn't be done with the best sheep, I believe," he said.

We smiled at each other.

"I will speak with David," he said.

"And I will continue to speak with Gwyn," I offered.

We went on to talk of the many changes in our lives since we had last been in one another's company. I found that my voyages from Wales to Philadelphia, cleaned up for his priestly ears, were utterly fascinating to him. I realized that I had seen much more of the world than he. He was a very attentive audience, groaning over my ill treatment on the slave ship, exclaiming over my time in Jamaica with Dougie and Alex Whitson, breathless over my extraordinary reunion with my daughters in Wilmington.

After a while, though, I changed the conversation to the main purpose for my visit. He knew the ins and outs of the city, so I ventured to ask him about property.

"Smythe advised me to ask you about property in the city. I know you have gone freely about town in your ministry and may know if the Land Office is open, or where property is being sold. Our little family will be growing and the cabin will not suffice for us soon. We have the silver that Ardath recovered. A house or land near the cabin would be ideal. Also, James has sent a letter saying a house may be needed for James's sister Elizabeth to let when they arrive, he hopes in December. Closer in to town would be best for that, as she will wish the society of others her age."

"I do know of several houses to be let. They should be available after first frost has cleared the area of the fever. They can then be cleaned with vinegar to further discourage infection. In two cases, I know the agents and can speak to them for you. Will Smythe go with you to the Land Office?"

"He is unable to go about at present. He suggested you might accompany me there, but I know you are very busy."

"Sister, it would be my pleasure to help the family in this way. The Land Office should be open by later this week. May I come to the cabin to visit your household and alert you to the possibilities? Then we can consult Ardath about her ideas as well. I know she would not like to be left out of this."

"Oh, no! You're correct about Ardath. I know she is interested in the lands of Mr. Graham, who died of the fever. She will also know how much we have in coin."

"And I have more money saved than I need. I would be pleased to loan it to you with no interest for as long as you need."

"Thank you, Brother." Despite my supposedly independent self, I felt tears come to my eyes.

"Be at peace, Sister. I know my younger brother didn't provide for you as he should have. I would like to do what I can to make up for that."

"Please do come to us as soon as you can. You are our only kin here," I said.

"I will," he said.

At that moment, as I rose to leave, we heard the front door open. David, for from Gwyn's description it could be no other, entered the parlor.

"Oh, so sorry to interrupt," he said.

I took in the black hair, black eyes, strong wiry frame, and personal intensity of a very handsome young man, as if through my breath. He resembled a portrait of the Lord Rhys, his distant renowned ancestor, that I had seen in Wales. He bowed towards me, no doubt assuming I was a parishioner, and proceeded from the room.

"Wait, David, come meet your Aunt Carys," said Thomas.

"Excuse me, madam. I am most happy to meet Gwyn's mother," he said with an eager grin, flashing white, even teeth.

"David, of course, I have heard much about you from Gwyn and your father. I'm so happy we could meet here in Philadelphia. How long will you stay?"

"That is unsure at this point. I am making inquiries about purchasing a business here."

"Oh, I see. Well, I hope you will come to see us at our cabin soon. Your father promises to come, to our delight. I must get back to that cabin now, as they will be needing me and I have stayed in town much too long."

David bowed again. "What a pleasure to finally meet you, Aunt Carys!"

I nodded at Thomas as I walked out the door. Outside, the sun was beating down and I had a dusty, ruminative walk to the cabin. At least the humid heat of the summer was lifting, signaling fall's approach.

Several days later, we met at the cabin with Ardath. Gwyn had told us to proceed as we wished. She liked the plans to buy property, but she was busy with other matters. Ardath, having looked at property with Smythe sometime back, thought we might have enough silver for several plots.

She was sitting up in bed, looking quite well and beautiful, red curls tumbling down onto her white bed jacket. I sighed as her Uncle Thomas came into the bedroom to join us, for my worries about her niggled at my mind.

"Don't sigh, Mother," she said. She read me well.

"Ah, Uncle, how good it is to see you, finally," she said to him.

He answered with a lovely smile. "It brightens my day

just to see you looking well." He removed his tri-corn hat and smoothed his graying hair with his palm.

"Please sit, Thomas," I said, gesturing to a straight chair. He and I brought our chairs nearer, so that we formed a triangle with the bed.

"What have you brought us, Uncle?" Ardath was not one for small talk. She jumped right to her purpose.

Thomas smiled with affection. "I believe I have made good progress for us. My parishioners, the Bains, have returned to England, asking their agent to rent their house for the coming year while they attend to their business there. It is a lovely house on 4th Street. Of course, it stood vacant during the yellow fever, but the agent has tended it well. I believe it would be a good residence for you and Major James, when he returns, or if he brings his sister, she could use it. I could show it to your mother if you wish, since you must not go about."

"I trust you to know what is needed, Uncle," Ardath said. "Let us lease it. Now, about the land that we might buy, have you looked into the plots previously belonging to Mr. Graham?"

"Yes," he said, spreading out a map of Philadelphia streets and plots on her bedding. I stood to look over his shoulder. He pointed to some rectangles on the map. "These are your current plots here, and here. Mr. Graham's land comprises these three here. He has no heirs, nor any will, so the land can be sold by the Land Office, with the funds returning to the proprietors. They will sell them at close to the original price just to be rid of the problem, because they have so many issues to deal with following the fever. There have been improvements made of course, so you would be getting a very good deal. You have plenty to buy these. There are no squatters yet, so it would be good to move quickly."

"Uncle, what good news!" said Ardath. "Would it not be best to have the two plots that join these properties to ours?" She pointed to the blank spaces between them. "But perhaps there is not enough money for them all?"

"I would like to purchase those, but in your name, and Gwyn's," said Thomas.

Ardath's flushed face reflected her astonishment. "That is so generous, Uncle, but…."

I said, "But Thomas, you have your own son and heir. Wouldn't you rather spend the funds on something for him, or leave the funds to him?"

He turned to me. "My dear Carys, David is making his way most splendidly all by himself. Neither would this purchase drain me of all my resources. This is something God wants me to do; I've seen it clearly while in prayer."

"Thank you, Jacob," I said to myself as I sat in silence, overcome with his generosity. Never had I expected anything of substance from Jacob's family, nor had I thought that his brother would become an important part of our dear inner circle. I saw that he was becoming that, and I looked at him with grateful eyes.

Chapter 26

James
December, 1753

To Elizabeth's evident distress, the journey across the Atlantic was as stormy and unpleasant as could be. Autumn and early winter are not settled times for a crossing. The ship rocked and creaked as it jerked along, as if atop a wild animal. The ocean was always dark gray, the sky not much lighter.

It was a matter of endurance for both of us. The smells and confinement below decks were noxious, driving us to venture above decks. The air was better on deck, but we were likely to be caught in cold sprays of salt water that drenched us as soon as we ventured there. We stayed mainly in the small open area below, attempting to play whist or some other game to distract us. Luckily we did not often suffer seasickness.

Elizabeth had many questions about Philadelphia and the wilderness as well. I tried to prepare her, but there was no way to convey the scope and difference that the New World presented to one as sheltered as she had been.

Finally, some two weeks into December, we docked in Philadelphia, having been aboard ten grueling weeks.

"Listen to me, Sam! I'm never leaving dry land again. I'm bound to be a resident of this New World forever," declared my sister, as the cold wind whipped her hair from her bonnet and slapped it across her face.

I had to smile at her. "I know exactly how you feel," I said. All I wanted was home, and Ardath in a warm bed beside me. I hoped we might have a child by now, or even better, that I might be there for the babe's birth.

We arranged for our goods to be carted to the cabin. I hailed a carriage to take us there in all haste.

As we settled into cold leather seats, wrapping our cloaks around us, I said, "Remember, we do not live in luxury here. It is a small cabin. It will look primitive to you."

"Yes, Sam, you've told me many times. At the very worst, we will soon have more suitable lodgings. Your friend Smythe will know of something, if he hasn't engaged one already." She sounded sure, yet her gloved hands twisted a lacy handkerchief.

"You look worried."

"I only want to be accepted by your wife's family. It's so important to me, you know."

"I know, but I'm sure you will be, with no doubt," I said.

She sat back into the seat, but I could see she wasn't confident.

When we arrived at the cabin, I swung her down onto the path. Paying the driver, I took our hand baggage up the walkway to the house. How happy I was to be home!

When we walked inside, the homely smells of cornbread and buttermilk greeted us. Elizabeth looked around her in confusion and sniffed the air; I could tell it didn't smell like home to her. Mrs. Rhys was the first to receive us, skirts rustling as she hurried forward. "James, you are here!" she said, grinning widely and coming into my open arms.

"Mother, how good to see you. This is my sister Elizabeth."

"Oh, please come in. It's a nasty wind today," she said.

When we crowded inside, she held out her arms to Elizabeth, who tentatively opened her own.

Next, Mrs. Perry came in wiping her hands on her apron.

She greeted us with a big smile as well. "So Major, you've come back."

Before I could answer her, here came Dougie, running in with complete glee, jumping up and down. Pointing to me, he clearly said "Horse!", so I dropped to the floor to let him climb on my back for a ride. Before he was ready to stop, I dumped him off and tickled him into good humor.

Elizabeth was standing, still somewhat stunned, until Carys took her back to the hearth room for a drink of warm cider. I followed them but refused a cup.

"Ardath?" I said.

"She has been confined to bed these many weeks. She will be so overjoyed to see you," said Carys.

"Confined to bed?" I asked. Alarm struck my chest.

"Just being careful about the pregnancy," Carys said. "It's fine to go up."

I ran up the stairs, finding Ardath wrapped in covers, glowing pink-cheeked in a yellow bed jacket.

"It took you long enough!" she joked, laughing and holding out her arms. She moved away from the edge, so that I could sit with her in bed. My eyes consumed her greedily. She leaned into me, but her great stomach pressed between us.

"Umm, you smell like the ocean," she said. "Yes, I'm big all right. I've been imprisoned here without you, with no one but the babies to keep me company."

"I'm so glad I've made it in time for the birth. But—babies?

"Only two," she said, green eyes gleaming at me.

"My God! What a lucky man I am." I felt like I was drunk

with whiskey. "I worried, you know."

"I've had the best of care," Ardath answered.

I took off my frockcoat. "Yes," I said, burrowing into the warm covers closer to her. Soon we were kissing, long and slow, saying so many things that had no words.

We paused, panting.

"I have some things I must get off my chest," Ardath said.

"Such a lovely, full, firm, beautiful chest."

"Settle down, please, this is serious. I have to confess to you. In the fall, I became obsessed with finding Ahmed and the other thieves and getting back the stolen coin. We were barely getting by without funds, and confined here by the epidemic of yellow fever. Foolishly, I set off in a wagon with Omar, going north to track them. We did succeed in finding the two villains and brought back the silver. Ahmed had hidden the gold, and had insisted they return all the money to us. For that, they sold him into slavery in North Carolina. The thieves are in jail and we have been searching for Ahmed." She paused; she looked troubled.

"And you were confined to bed after going on that journey?"

"Yes, thank God for Mother's stern commandment. I might well have lost the babies from the jostling journey on hard and rutted roads, fighting the thieves, and the return trip when I felt the pain, and knew I had injured my body."

I was gazing at her, wondering how best to respond. Her lovely eyes were downcast with something like shame. "But you didn't lose them."

"But I was so foolish, and I might have." Wide, stricken eyes climbed up to mine. "Can you forgive me?"

"There is nothing you could do for which I would not forgive you!" I said. We were so close now that I could put my arm around her shoulders, which relaxed in relief. Her head nestled into me. Once again I was struck by my good fortune in finding such a woman. Yes, she could be foolhardy in her bravery, but I couldn't help but admire it. That might be my madness, but so it was.

"How close is your delivery?" I asked, after a time in which we contented ourselves with simply being together.

"Any time now." She smiled up at me.

"Well, let me know if I should run for your mother," I said.

She laughed. "I thought I heard more voices below. Is your sister with you? Are you an earl? If I should bow, I may not be able right now." She patted her huge stomach.

"Yes, Elizabeth is with me; no, I am not an earl, though I am now next in line when Father dies."

"How is that?" she asked. So she hadn't gotten my letter from England. I explained the results of my trip to her.

"Ah," she said. "So it is likely that you will be earl." She pulled back from me, examining my face.

"Please let's not talk about that now," I said. "I am sorry to have left you with so little financial help, because now I do have substantial means through gifts from my father. Those will be ours whether I become earl or not."

"Well, you deserve it. You have worked hard to be a good son, joining the army as he wished, searching for your brothers, and helping to put the estate in order."

"About the army. I have resigned my commission. There is too much happening for me to be a good officer. My father doesn't know about it yet."

"Does Elizabeth?"

"Oh yes, we have no secrets."

"That's important. I will be glad to hear more of that commission story at a later time. We have arranged a furnished house for Elizabeth, closer to the center of town. The servants have kept it up while the owners are gone. My mother and uncle have also helped us spend our silver on property the proprietors or other owners have sold us."

"You are a woman of business." I grinned at her.

"I might have said a woman of leisure, though it's a forced leisure."

"That will be over soon! My father hopes you will have a son, so he can be assured of the family line."

"And you?" She quirked her full lips.

"I shall be happy if all are well."

"Oh, really?"

"Well, I think we know how to make more…." I couldn't stop thinking of matters of the bed, with her voluptuous body in my arms. She sighed, but pulled away.

"As for Gregory, well, I don't know what letters reached you, but he has been very ill with the yellow fever. Gwyn has nursed him through it, but he hasn't been able to inquire about properties as he did in the past. Mother and Uncle Thomas approached the Land Office. Some properties were available because men had died of the fever with no interested heirs, as happened in the case of Mr. Graham. We were able to get his stables and horses for a good price. Furthermore, we bought the land between his and ours, so it is all contiguous. We have our own little Duchy here."

"That's a good investment. I feel sure that as the city grows, it will all be quite valuable."

"I hoped you would think so," Ardath said. "We could build

our own house out here."

"Yes, we could. However, if it would suit you, I would like for us to live closer to the social center of town near Elizabeth until she finds a suitable husband. Since she is a widow, she could respectably live alone, but I know she isn't prepared to do so."

"Oh," said Ardath. I could see she hadn't thought of that.

"Would you like to think about it for now?" I asked.

"Well, yes. But I can't consider leaving here until I am sure the babies are well, anyway."

"Perhaps I could stay with Elizabeth for a day or so—"

"Oh, no you will not!" Ardath said, pushing me off the bed.

I landed with a thump upon the floor. "Now they will truly wonder what we are doing up here," I said. She was bent over, giggling.

"Well, maybe Gwyn could—"

She sat up farther in bed. "Gwyn, well, that's another story," she said.

"Is she still with Gregory?" I asked.

She cleared her throat. "No, she's back here with us, as they decided that he was well enough to be cared for by servants. It would not be favorable for her reputation if she lived with him unmarried."

"That is true, but do you think they will get married?"

"I couldn't say," she said, while casting her gaze toward the roof.

"Hmm. Ardath, tell me what is going on!" I sat forward in the chair I had occupied since she threw me out of bed.

She sighed. "Oh, Gwyn is so wishy-washy. Honestly! Our cousin David from North Carolina came here, asking her to marry him."

"But I thought she wanted to be here, not North Carolina."

"Oh, well, he planned to start a business in Philadelphia, but he heard that his son was sick and went home by the fastest ship. Anyway, she had turned him down."

"I see. And does Smythe know of all this?"

"No, and please do not let it slip."

"Don't worry; I wouldn't cause any harm to either of them, but what a situation for them all."

"Well, the only good that might come of this is that David agreed to search for Ahmed, who is in the Albemarle region."

"But how will he get Ahmed from the plantation owner? A blacksmith is a very valuable commodity."

"We have sent along papers proving that Ahmed is a free man, or if necessary, David will buy him back."

"Well, I leave here for just a little while and all hell breaks loose."

"Just a little while, eh?" Her white foot kicked out at me from under the bed covers, but I caught it and pulled her off her pillow. I gave her foot an amorous kiss before she tucked it back in. Like the rest of her, even her feet smelled good, lavender scented.

"Oh, I don't know if I can wait," she cried.

"Well, if it wouldn't harm the child…."

"No, you must get your sister settled first. Please hurry on to do that. Gwyn should go too. Come back tomorrow morning. I'll keep the bed warm." She sent me a lascivious smile and arched her copper brows.

"I'll see to it," I said, pecking her on the cheek.

I ran down the stairs, finding that Gwyn had joined the others in the hearth room. Her eyes lit up to see me. "Brother, welcome home," she said.

"Dear Sister, so good to see you again!" I said, struck with her maturing beauty.

"We have been discussing Elizabeth's new home," said Gwyn. "I was there just yesterday to see that all is in readiness. It's a quite fine house; I think you'll find it to your liking."

"Thank you. Such good news! I'm going to see if I can intercept the luggage and have it taken there. Elizabeth, I will return as soon as may be, to get you settled."

"I will go to the house while you get the luggage. The fires should be lit in readiness for your arrival," said Gwyn.

"Gwyn, could you stay there with Elizabeth tonight?" I asked.

"Certainly," she said. She gave me the address and I rushed off to tend to the practical matters.

Chapter 27

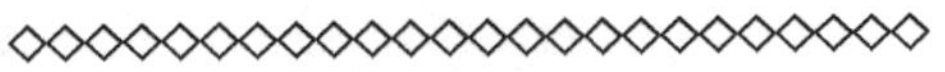

Gwyn

I was very happy to see James home at the cabin and to meet his sister also, but, of necessity, I went rapidly to the 4th Street house we had let. Elizabeth's new house was not far from Gregory's and I knew it well. I entered the gracious, well-appointed foyer. The wide oak floors were a pleasing honey color and set off a lovely Turkey rug of rich reds and blues. The foyer had lamps lit, but the rest of the house was in a gloom that echoed the gray skies outside. We were in for wet weather, whether rain or snow, I couldn't say yet.

The servants of the owners, the Bain family, were honest and experienced. Mr. Hinch, the butler, appeared at the end of the hallway. He was a rather spindly man with large feet and hands, who had come from England with the family and exuded proper English dignity.

"Oh, Mistress Rhys, let me take your cloak," he said.

"Thank you, Mr. Hinch, but I believe I will wear it for a while. It's quite chill out now."

"Of course. Let me light the fire in the library. What else may I do for you today?" he said.

"I am so happy you are here, because your new mistress has just arrived. We need the house to be warm and glowing for her. I will be spending the night here as well. The two front bedrooms should be prepared and a supper ready. Please don't worry the cook about anything elaborate, just something warm, perhaps soup, would be appreciated."

"Of course. I will tend to it right away," he said. He turned to the library door, which, when opened, revealed a maid dressed in black, with a crisp white apron and white mob hat. "Isabel, please make up the two front bedrooms and light all the lamps and fires. Mistress Gwyn and Mistress Elizabeth will stay tonight; ask Cook to make a light supper."

"Yes sir," the maid replied, her homely face a study in concentration.

"Major James should arrive presently with luggage," I said to Hinch. He nodded and left me to warm by the fire.

I thought back over a very active fall season. Not too long after I had resolved to tell David that I would not marry him, I had an opportunity to talk with him alone when we met in the street. I explained that I was set to become betrothed to Gregory Smythe, and that I thought we should relate simply as cousins and friends, regardless of our strong feelings for each other. He was disappointed, of course, but eventually took it like a man, which made me regard him even more highly.

He related that he had not found an opportunity in Philadelphia that pleased him. When word came that little Solomon was sick, he rushed off to return home, with my love and best wishes to take with him. It was an extreme relief to me to have that matter settled.

I awoke from my reverie when James knocked at the door. Hinch hurried to open it. A stiff wind blew freezing air and snow into the hall. The luggage on the front stoop was mountainous, with a drayman bringing still more from his conveyance. The driver and Hinch struggled to get it all in the door, even with James helping.

"Good heavens!" I said. I had never seen anything like it.

James gave me a lopsided grin. "You should have seen what she left behind," he said.

I pulled him towards the library, to stand before the fire, which crackled away there. "Come in; get warm," I said.

"Whew! I had thought to go by Colonel Ellis's today, but I believe it can wait," said James, edging his boots closer to the fire.

Like magic, warm toddies spiced with clove and cinnamon appeared on a tray held by the maid. "More English than England," he commented, on the service, and perhaps the house as well.

"Not the usual here in the colonies, but I hope Elizabeth will feel at home."

"Elizabeth will be happy as long as she doesn't have to get back on a ship," he said. "Yet, I can't help but feel she will have much to adjust to."

"Hmm, I expect so. I understand that you are looking for a husband for Elizabeth. Do you think she wants to stay here? Do you want to stay here, in the colonies?"

"Dear Gwyn, we have much to catch up on. So many things in our lives are unsettled. I may not have a choice in these." He then told me of the status of the earldom. I cringed inwardly at the idea of Ardath as a Countess. I didn't think she'd mind telling other people what to do, but she was too much a person of action to go to the endless teas, visits, and parties I envisioned as part of a Countess's duties. I thought James was a little too sanguine about the possibilities.

"You seem optimistic about Ardath's role as Countess,"

I said. I took a big breath and leaned forward to look at him closely. "What do you really think it would be like?"

He groaned and put his head into his hands. "Oh, Sister, I am greatly concerned! I think she would hate it. It is a frankly insipid position for someone of her vigor."

"Ah, I was thinking the same. I know how much she wanted to go farther into the wilderness at one point, and you also, I believe."

"I cannot even imagine our future. It may be best to suspend any plans until we see how the birth goes."

"I'm sorry if I have brought up difficulties of the future. You are right that we must see what happens in the near future."

"It is quite all right. What does your mother think about the possibility of a fortunate outcome for the birth?"

"It would be best to ask her that, though no one can know everything ahead of time."

"Not even you?" he asked with a smile.

"Oh dear! I should never have intimated that I could know what might happen, ever. But, James, a thought struck me just now. Ardath is a very accomplished businesswoman. Why not let her take over the running of some aspect of the estate? That would relieve the burden on you and give her something productive to do."

"I like that idea. One thing about being an earl is that you can do eccentric things and get away with them if you do not mind the ensuing gossip. Hmmm."

He looked thoughtful for a moment, then laughed. "Good. Thank you, Sister, for this brilliant idea. There is one thing I do know in all this, that you will make Elizabeth welcome to Philadelphia and even more welcome to your wonderful family."

We heard a knock on the door, which Hinch hurried to answer. "Ah, here is Omar with Elizabeth and our hand luggage,." James said.

We rose to greet them. I was struck again by Elizabeth's English rose beauty, heightened by her windblown cheeks.

"Don't worry, we shall be quite fine, James," I told him. "I know you are eager to return to your wife," I teased.

He and Omar went back into the cold, while Hinch delivered the bags to Elizabeth's room.

Elizabeth smiled at me. Another sister, certainly a very different one from Ardath. "Do hurry to the fire, Elizabeth," I said.

Again, warm drinks appeared and we both sat down with a sigh. Cheeses, dried fruit, and fresh bread came shortly thereafter. We sat to enjoy them.

"What a day this has been for you!" I said.

"Thank you, Gwyn. It has indeed. Your mother welcomed me so sweetly, though, making me feel quite at home. Such a cozy home and full of good smells and good cheer."

"I'm glad!"

"And little Dougie was so charming. He and my brother seem to have an excellent relationship. How old is Dougie?"

"He must be close to three years old now. My mother said he was born in March. His birth was certainly memorable, as that was the night my mother was abducted from Wales. We thought her dead for many months. Thereafter we started our voyage to the New World with our father. It was on that ship that we met your brother."

"Ah, he has told me the story of that harrowing voyage. What courage it must have taken to endure those trials." Her eyes shone with something, perhaps admiration.

"Of course, there just wasn't a choice, but we did survive." I had never thought of us as courageous; we did what we had to do. Now I noticed Elizabeth gazing at her pretty hands, as lovely and pink as the rest of her.

"Are you tired? Though it's early, you might prefer to go to your rest soon."

"No, please," she said. "I need to tell you something, though I wish to keep it secret between us. Sam tells me that you are to be trusted."

"Of course," I said. I rose to close the door, leaving us secure in the library. Something was weighing on her; her lips were pressed and tucked into her mouth as if keeping a secret back.

"It's just that, well, seeing Dougie, today. My son would have been about his age. I imagined that he would have looked like Dougie too. But I never really got to see him." An unmistakable sob escaped her lips. I sat in perfect silence, respecting her need to tell her story. She mistook it for judgment on my part.

"You'll think me a weak and weepy person, as well as a scandalous one."

"Oh, no. I'm so sorry that you lost your husband and your son too," I said.

"Well, that is what we are telling people," she said.

"Don't tell me more if you think it best, but whatever you say, I will not share with anyone else."

Suddenly, I knew what she might tell me. A creeping tingle ran up my spine. Lights flashed blue and green in my brain, so that I took in a harsh breath. Could it be? If so, whatever divine providence there might be had played a mighty trick on us all. I struggled to keep a calm expression on my face. "Do you want to tell me about your son's birth?" I asked.

Her eyes ran all over my face, and she made her decision.

"Yes, I must, and I believe you."

I groaned inwardly. "Thank you for your trust."

"You see, there was no husband." She flushed from neck to brow. "I had become involved with a village boy and was with child. My mother was horrified and hid me away. When it came time for me to give birth, she brought a midwife from another area and forced her to deliver me. Then she drugged me, but I heard her tell the ruffians who had brought the midwife to kill her and the baby."

"Ah, how dreadful!" I said.

"With such shame, I could never be married, you see, but if we tell the story of a marriage to a sickly man and of losing him and a child, then no one would expect a virgin. I hate lying. I hate it, but I want to marry a respectable person and I want children."

"I understand. Do you remember what the midwife looked like?" I asked, holding my breath while my heart beat quickened.

"My mother tried to keep a veil over my face, and I could only vaguely see the midwife. She was kind and insisted that I should be allowed to breathe freely, without the veil. But the light was dim and I was distracted by sweat and tears in my eyes and the birth pains."

I had to still my quiver. I looked at her and took her hand gently. "You have had courage too, it seems."

"It's just, you know, Dougie's age and your mother being a midwife, well, it set these memories off in me. I want a child so badly."

"I understand, and I don't doubt that you will have children. You are beautiful; you are the daughter of an earl; you obviously are a gentle person. You will find someone to love, I feel certain."

"Oh, I have burdened you with this. I am sorry!" She looked horrified.

"No, you needed to tell your story. I hope it will give you peace."

"Gwyn, you are so kind. I believe I will go to bed now, if you can show me the way."

"Of course. I have some things to tend to, but I will be just next door to you tonight."

"I am glad of that, dear Gwyn," she said.

After I had walked her to her room and rung for the maid, I returned to the library. I sat thinking a long time, shaking my head in disbelief. I wouldn't break her confidence, but I wondered who next would realize that Elizabeth was Dougie's mother.

Chapter 28

James

After settling Elizabeth in her new household, I could no longer delay reporting to Colonel Ellis. I found myself at his doorstep, twisting my hat in my hands while the wind whistled past my ears.

His usual maid opened the door. When I asked for the colonel, she said, "Yes sir, Major. He will see you immediately. Please wait in the drawing room." She fetched him a little too quickly for my taste. I could have used more time to compose myself as I looked around the heavily decorated room at the wall hangings and brass candlesticks. He strode in, dressed in full uniform, his florid face reflecting the red of his coat.

"Major James, how good to see you again. We have struggled along without you through a damnable epidemic and all sorts of disturbances. I hope you found things more settled in England."

"Good to see you as well, Colonel. I'm afraid my story is a long one."

"Please, please, sit down by the fire and tell it all to me. Frances will bring us tea, or would you prefer something stronger?"

"I will take whiskey if you have it. Thank you, sir."

He nodded at his maid, who left us. "James, you have no idea how much I missed you. The Germans are pouring in and don't want to follow English ways, or even learn our language; the squatters are everywhere; and the French encourage the Indians, even those who used to be friendly, to turn against us. My pleas for more troops fall on deaf ears in England. Franklin tries to raise militia, but the colonials don't want to support a fight for King and country."

The maid entered with our whiskeys. "Ah, good," he said, as she left.

His chair was opposite me as we warmed by the fire. I could clearly see his shrewd, pale eyes piercing mine. I would have to get to the meat of it soon or he would guess I had an unfavorable report.

"Sir, I found my father in poor health, and my brothers missing, as I told you before I left."

"That is hard news. I had hoped your brothers would be found before you reached England."

I took a deep breath. "My eldest brother Stephen died in a shipwreck off the coast of France and, though the next in line, Richard, survived, he cannot remember who he is and lives as a simpleton in a small coastal French village. It took quite some time to find them and to restore some order to the estate at Ensleigh. Also, my widowed sister Elizabeth needs my protection, and I have brought her to Philadelphia with me."

"You have many troubles of your own, I see." His face had relaxed into an almost kind expression.

"Yes sir, I have had to make difficult decisions. At present, when my father dies, I will inherit the title and all its responsibilities. Further, I love my wife deeply and she is soon to be brought to childbed."

"Perhaps you wonder how you will manage all this and remain in the King's service," he said, rather grimly, I thought.

I looked straight at him. "Sir, I hate to tell you this, but my only solution was to resign my commission while in London. I do not feel I could serve my country well and still carry out my other responsibilities."

Ellis sighed. His mouth twisted. I couldn't tell if he felt sympathy or disappointment in my decision, or perhaps both. He took a large draught of his whiskey. "I can well see how you arrived at that decision. I tell you truly, though, that I am appalled that you are leaving. It is a terrible time to lose such a man as you."

We both gazed into our whiskey, and the silence grew.

Finally I said, "I understand. Thank you. Perhaps there are things I can do as a private citizen, such as help train militia. I know Franklin has done it before, but even he says that he is no soldier."

"That would be a good help to us." He paused. "I don't want to lose touch with you. Who else can beat me so thoroughly at chess?" He actually smiled, but it was a weak effort.

"Well, Franklin might, I suspect," I said.

"He is too busy to bother with games. He's been elected to the Assembly." He scratched his moustache. "Well, the town has returned to something like a normal state following the epidemic. Is your sister ready to be out in society? My wife has been back in town for some time. She might arrange a party for Elizabeth."

"We just arrived today and it was a rough trip, but I'm sure she will be recovered in a few days. She has completed her mourning period. We would be most grateful to have her introduced into Philadelphia's society."

We sat in a more comfortable silence together. All in all, I was pleased that Colonel Ellis had been so gracious to me. Perhaps I had expected the same unfair response I would have received from my father, if he knew of my resignation, despite the extenuating circumstances.

Chapter 29

The Birth

Ardath:

James did return from getting Elizabeth settled, as he had promised. I had been so excited about having him in my arms that I'm sure I couldn't have slept anyway. But when he appeared, flicking the snow off his tousled, wet hair, I felt such a surge in my breasts and my loins that I pulled him onto the bed in haste.

"For heaven's sake, woman, have some decency," he said, with a wide grin.

"No, I want your body on me!" I said.

"Agreed! But let me dry off a bit." He found a cloth on my clothes rack and proceeded to slowly disrobe and dry himself on all parts, including the one which stood more and more upright, until I thought I'd have to jump out of bed after him. His grin didn't fade either. Cruel man! He was teasing me.

Finally, he nudged me over in the bed and claimed the warm spot before lowering his cool mouth to mine and kissing me practically unconscious. When his searching lips found my breasts and sucked gently, I thought I might explode.

"How I have missed you and wanted you!" he exclaimed.

Suddenly he jerked away our bedcovers, pulled my hips to

his and was in me to my root. Moving, insistent and full, until I was gripped by a power beyond myself. We groaned together, came together, such beautiful pain.

When I rose to full consciousness, I became aware of his now hot body held above me by stiff, strong arms and of the warm wetness of the sheets below me. We sighed as he let his firm body down beside mine, covering us up with the quilt. He laid his head on my shoulder. Warm bliss swirled around us.

After a pause, he murmured, "Does the bed seem especially wet to you?"

My reply was stopped by a hard, gripping pain and an involuntary growl. "James, get Mother. My labor has started."

I felt him leap from the bed. He dashed on his clothes, hurrying from the room.

Carys:

I hadn't really gone to sleep yet, though both Dougie beside me and Mrs. Perry in the other bed snored gently. I could hear Ardath and James across the hall even with both doors closed. They had lost no time in finding each other's body. I was nodding off, though still clothed, and happy for them, when I heard the unmistakable groan of oncoming labor. Before James even reached my door, I was on my feet, fully clothed, and out in the hall.

James was startled to see me, but pulled me across the hall in haste. "She's, she's, I don't know. She says she is laboring. I hope I didn't hurt her. I don't know what to do." His eyes were wild.

I took a moment to face him and look him in the eye. "James, all is well. You didn't hurt her. It is just her time. Please go to the hearth and stir up the fire. You will need to boil water and bring it up when you can. Remember, I am a midwife. I do this all the time."

He visibly relaxed, turning to run down the stairs.

Ardath's eyes were wide, glinting with the reflection of the candle that burned beside the bed.

"Mother," she said, a cry of relief. Though she had helped me at times with births in Wales, nothing prepares a woman for her own first childbirth. She was between pains, so we were able to place the pad beneath her. The pad and clean cloths had been in readiness in her room for some weeks now.

"The bed is so wet. Have my waters broken?" she asked.

"Yes, so if you will turn on your side for a moment, I will pull the wet sheets out." This we did with no little trouble. Ardath was a large-boned woman and very heavy with child. I helped her lift up her hip, just as another wave of pain hit. We breathed through it together. I could see that she was frightened by her body taking over control.

When that wave had passed, I reminded her, "Your body knows what to do. Do not try to fight what is happening. Remember the pain has its purpose, to help you be delivered."

She pressed her lips together, taking a deep breath through her nose.

"I need to check the position of the baby." She nodded. I felt the abdomen. "The baby is in a good position, with the head pointing downwards," I said.

She bobbed her head, swept with another spasm. The contractions were rather close together. But I was able to get my ear trumpet on her stomach as she relaxed.

"I hear a good heartbeat," I reported.

She tried to smile. "It happens too fast; I'm afraid," she said.

"I know, but you are doing well, my brave girl," I said.

I heard the front door open and then a brief conversation at the hearth. Soon Gwyn was with us.

"You just knew?" I asked. She shrugged her shoulders, as if it were a mystery to her also.

Ardath lay with her eyes closed. "I'm here too," said Gwyn, "just as we were in the wilderness."

For the first time, Ardath shed a tear. "Dear Gwyn," she whispered. Despite Ardath's sometimes brusque manner with her sister, I saw how much Gwyn meant to her.

Her eyes opened, fixed on Gwyn's face. "I am afraid I have hurt the baby by going after the thieves, Gwyn. I was so careless, again!"

"I know, but that is past and gone. We are here with you, now. You are not alone. Use our strength too," said Gwyn, in that soothing way that made her a good healer.

She listened to the baby's heartbeat also, nodding approval.

Ardath drifted off to sleep. Gwyn asked me quietly. "Why do we not hear the second heart?"

"The first baby could be in the way. Or there may be only one alive now. I haven't heard the second for the last week or so. I haven't told Ardath."

"Oh, Mother. She will see that as a judgment on her carelessness."

"Yes, but hopefully the joy of the first, if it is healthy, may help somewhat."

The labor had slowed. James appeared with hot water. Mrs. Perry had taken Dougie down to eat his breakfast and play in the front room. She brought us warm porridge, bacon, and tea. James retired to my bed, as he was very weary, and fell asleep there.

"Is this usual?" Gwyn asked me about the slowing.

"No, but it is a blessing. The baby hasn't moved down, and the parents can use a rest."

She sighed.

"Is Elizabeth established at the Bain House?" I asked, settling back in the rocking chair.

"Oh, yes," she said in a distracted manner. She paced around the room for a moment.

"What's wrong?" I asked.

"Hmm, oh nothing, just thinking about Elizabeth. She really wants a husband and children. I hope she finds someone here, but I don't know who would be of her social class."

We were interrupted by a new groan from Ardath, who pushed herself up, face in a grimace. Labor continued apace. Gwyn brought in snow, with which we cooled cloths to place on Ardath's reddened face. James appeared at the doorway, hair awry, looking like a man who was in his cups, or otherwise beyond the reach of reason. Gwyn led him away gently, murmuring softly. That was good, because I had to focus all my energy on Ardath, who fought the pains with wild thrashing, no matter how I coached her to accept them and see them as progress. She was tiring herself out. I checked the baby's position, which was still good.

"Ardath, stop thrashing!" I spoke in a loud voice, hoping to get her attention.

"No, Goddamn! It hurts! I'll thrash if I want to!" she said, glaring at me. Well, Ardath had never been one to face things meekly. Her labor proceeded normally, by which I mean it took many hours more than either of us could believe.

In time, Gwyn was back to help me deliver a healthy, if rather small, red-faced boy. I rubbed his hot body with clean cloths and sucked out his nose and mouth. His squalls resembled his mother's. After we cut the cord, Gwyn swaddled him and handed him to Ardath.

"Put him to your breast, Ardath. It will help you both," I said.

This she did, tears streaming down her face. "My baby!" she whispered, looking down as he latched onto one breast, while the other one released a creamy trickle as well.

I was very thankful that she was distracted because something was terribly wrong. Though the afterbirth came quickly and completely, she did not stop bleeding. Ardath groaned with more pains rapidly compressing her stomach. In a slippery red flood, the tiny bluish body of a baby girl rushed out. She was inert, unresponsive, and had little warmth. Turning from Ardath, I faced Gwyn, who, without a sound, hurried to wrap the doll-like body and turned herself away.

Meanwhile, Ardath fainted with the boy at her breast. I scooped him up, swaddled him and lay him in the prepared cradle with a sugar tit. Ardath's face whitened; the blood still gushed. I packed the vagina with cloth and pressed hard on her abdomen.

Gwyn:

The small, pale body lay in my arms. I chafed at her with cloths, suctioned her nose and mouth, but no call came forth. I put my mouth on hers and blew breath gently into nose and mouth with no response. I wanted to cry for her, but I couldn't take the time. Like animals I had nursed as a child, I would do anything to bring life to this little creature that love had created. Ear to her chest, I listened. No heart beat beneath that pallid skin, which began to cool as I touched her. In desperation, I pushed on her breastbone several times with my fingertips and blew in her mouth some more. I would not let her die. I kept this up until I heard a tiny gasp from her. Round blue eyes looked into mine and she began to breathe. With this, I saw the miracle through my own bleary eyes, of her skin slowly turning pinkish in color. I pushed away my bodice and her cloth and held her to my bare breast to warm. I leaned forward enough to cut and clamp the cord, then back to the warmth she went. And oh, she did warm! She breathed. She was alive!

I turned to mother, who was bent over my unconscious sister. I saw the gobs of red cloth in the bed. Ardath had bled prodigiously. Blood still ran from her body, where Mother was affixing a pad to catch it.

"Gwyn, keep pressure on her abdomen; It has been a struggle to stem the bleeding." I stepped next to Ardath and pressed down. It seemed to help.

"Mother?" I asked turning my head toward her. "Will she live?"

She drew in a great breath. Her chin quivered.

"Mother?" I asked more sharply.

"She lives." She looked at me. "For now," she said.

"Oh, oh, Mother. This babe is alive for now also. Will you look at her?"

"The babe lives? That is a miracle I did not expect."

Mother came close to me, while I unwrapped the cloths

away from my breast. "I did not hear a cry," she said, as she examined the small head covered with fine black hair. "There she is, a nice pink baby. I thought her gone. You have accomplished a miracle, thank the Goddess Brigid!"

"I thought her almost beyond hope, but I blew into her mouth and pumped on her chest, much as those actions scared me."

"And you got her warm. Good work."

"Yes. What about Ardath?"

She watched me closely. "I don't know if she will survive. We must prepare for the worst. And we need help."

"I can get Mrs. Perry and Ibrahim could maybe come. What do we say to James?"

She looked grim. "Help me clean up this bed. We should bring him in, while Mrs. Perry prepares some broth and warms some goat's milk. We must tell him that Ardath has lost a lot of blood."

We proceeded to clear away the bloody cloths. The whole room looked better and smelled less raw as a result. I still had the baby girl wrapped up in the sling. I kept her on my chest with a small blanket around her, only my bodice between us.

Down the stairs I went, not knowing what time it was, or who I might find about. I dumped the big bundle of bloody sheets and cloths under the storage bins in the storeroom.

Mrs. Perry was at the hearth. I whispered to her what had happened.

"You'll be needing strong broth, which I have already prepared. Do you need goat's milk?"

"Yes, let's bring Trude into the animal room. Is Omar here?"

"Yes, working with the barn animals."

"Could you please ask him to go for Ibrahim?"

"Of course, dear Gwyn. What else?"

"Occupy Dougie."

"Of course. I'll go for Omar first."

James was in the front room. He sat in the large armchair with Dougie on his lap as they rested by the fire. He looked up, fear and hope in his eyes.

"Congratulations, James. You have a little boy and a girl. You can go up to see your son and Ardath. Here is your daughter. I'm keeping her warm next to me." I showed him the sleeping baby.

"She's so small." He sounded completely undone, just looking at her.

"Yes. That happens with twins sometimes," I said.

"And Ardath? How is she?" he asked in an anxious voice.

"She is sleeping. She lost a lot of blood."

"Oh. Can I see them now?" His face was so weary; I felt for him.

"Yes. I'll sit with Dougie while you go up," I said. James gestured for me to take his seat, lifting Dougie to rest next to me.

"We have new babies?" asked Dougie in a sleepy voice. I showed him the little girl.

"Yes, we do, but they won't be ready to play with you for a long while. They sleep a lot at first."

"Tiyed."

"Yes, tired and growing too."

Yes, we were all tired and the house was at its limits for space too. Thank goodness for Mrs. P, who fed us all at every chance, since there wasn't much sleeping, except for Ardath. Even through her weakness, she insisted on feeding their son. She showed little interest in her daughter, who luckily took to the warm goat's milk. The children didn't have names yet, but I privately called her Lilly. I felt in some way that she was mine and I tried to be there for as many of the bottle feedings as I could. When I wasn't there, Mrs. P or Mother wore the baby on her breast to keep her warm. Most of the next several nights, I spent with Elizabeth. James was often at the Bain house with us at night. Though he wanted to stay with Ardath, she was too weak to converse, or really, do more than feed their son. There was not enough space at the cabin. We did set up a space where their son could safely nestle with her in bed. She had only to pull him over when he wanted to nurse. When I was at the cabin, I made Mother go to bed. During the day, James played with Dougie and helped in any way he could about the cabin. He was exhausted with constant work and worry.

Ibrahim came by each day to check on everyone, especially Ardath. He and Mother wouldn't pronounce her out of the woods until at least a fortnight had passed without infection. They wouldn't speculate on how long her great weakness would last either.

At the Bain house, James took frequent deep breaths. He confessed to me and Elizabeth that he didn't believe he could survive without Ardath. I tried to keep my focus on the baby. Although I had many more people in my life now, I didn't know

how I could exist in a world without Ardath either.
So much had changed so suddenly.

Chapter 30

Gwyn and Ardath

Gwyn:

Having Lilly on my chest was like cuddling a kitten. She slept most of the time and was silent. Even if wet or hungry, she didn't cry, only made a small "meep" sound. She looked up at me while eating, eyes intent and round, cheeks stretched thin over bones. I wondered at her survival and whether she could ever be hearty. Yet she had a lovely spirit.

Ardath lived through those first days and even began to regain some of her color. I almost felt sorry for her, since Mother and Mrs. P plied her continually with beef broth and liver, rich ale and custards. James had gone out in the awful weather to kill a deer. When he returned, Mrs. P made venison pasties and, of course, more broth from the rich organ meats. All of us appreciated the fresh meat, but it was most essential to help Ardath regain her vitality.

"It'll be a slow process, you can bet on that," said Mrs. P, who had helped other women after hard childbirths.

Mother and Ibrahim agreed. They tried to help us keep our expectations low, especially about Lilly. I had to remind myself that I wasn't Lilly's mother. If I saw her in that way, I would be in trouble of many sorts.

I grew somewhat melancholy from the worry and the work. "Mrs. P, I know you are stretched thin with working so hard, but I need to get out of the cabin for a while. Could you keep Lil, uh, the baby, while I go to see Gregory?"

Mrs. P, who never seemed to get tired, said, "Of course, my dear one. Getting out will do you good." She patted my cheek. "Let me have this little girl for a turn."

We took the sling from my shoulder and placed it on Mrs. P's ample breast. "What a dear little babe!" she said. I almost cried with relief. Mrs. P seemed in her element, while the rest of us stayed worried.

I washed my face and tried to make myself more presentable, but I knew Gregory would not judge me for some speckles of goat milk on my shoulder. I pulled on my warmest boots, which were oiled leather lined with rabbit fur. The snow was high in the streets near our cabin. I took up my walking stick, thus feeling secure in my footing. The sky showed a clear blue; the air was crisp. Light snow blew from the trees, sparkling in the air. My breath frosted before me. It was an invigorating walk of six blocks to Gregory's.

It was a delight to enter Gregory's home. Mary greeted me at the back door. Mary and Robert had taken our ideas for improvement and made them real. The parlor, well-warmed from the blazing, popping, fire, gleamed with polished wood tables and brass candlesticks. Long curtains, a bright teal with cream stripes, puddled to the floor. Best of all, Gregory sat straight in his desk chair, working with some papers. He immediately rose at my entrance.

"My dear Gwyn, what a pleasure!" His warm arms surrounded me. He drew back to look me over. "Ah, you have been working very hard," he said.

"I had hoped to hide that from you," I said, smiling despite myself.

"Never worry; I have occult powers," he said. "Now sit you down and let us fuss over you. Mary, please bring us some tea and those lovely cakes." Mary nodded. She closed the door discreetly.

"I love to see you looking so vigorous," I said.

He nodded. "I'm following a program to build up my strength. James recommended it. Tell me," he said. "I want to know what's on your heart."

"Oh, Gregory, please just hold me."

This he did, so that we cuddled together in his large padded chair near the fire. His heart beat strongly next to mine. I felt at home, relaxed, comforted.

Next, the words tumbled out. "We have been so worried. Ardath lost so much blood, I don't know how she has survived. The baby boy is small but seems all right. The girl arrived blue and without breath or heartbeat. She is tiny; I've never heard her cry, but we try to keep her warm and dry and fed with goat milk. I don't know why Ardath won't feed her. In general, James suffers greatly. We are all upset except Mrs. Perry, who seems to take all in her stride."

"I am glad you came here. It must be most distressing to be submerged in all this. You are not responsible for making everything all right, you know," he assured me.

"How can I be a doctor if I worry so much?"

"First, it is your own family you are helping, which makes it very much harder. You are sensitive; that trait will make you a fine physician. Second, the process of becoming a doctor, I believe, will help you develop some equanimity in the face of disease and uncertainty. You won't be alone, with training from Ibrahim and your mother and their advice to rely upon. And you will come home to my love each day. I swear that will never fail you."

I sighed. I was in the right place. Mary brought in the tea and left us.

"Of course I do realize that some things are beyond me no matter how hard I try to help or heal them."

"Hmm. Whom are you most worried about?"

That took some thought. "Honestly, it is the girl. I call her Lilly. She was practically dead at birth. What harm might have come to her when she was not breathing?"

"I assume that your actions saved her?"

"Yes, but it is not possible to prevent a bad outcome. I don't wish that I had not tried to save her, but I feel responsible."

"Is that all you feel about her?"

"No, no, I love her. Deeply… Ah, there it is. Somehow I didn't quite know how deeply."

"One day you shall love our child like that," he said.

I was staring at the fire and hoping for that day, when I felt Gregory pouring the tea. The Willinghams' flowered cup rattled as he put it into my hand. Even the fragrance of the tea made me feel better. I looked at him with gratitude and love, as a lock of his blonde hair fell over his forehead.

"How is James doing?"

"Oh, well, he is overwhelmed, I think. He could probably use a friend at this point." I smiled as he nodded.

"And Elizabeth?"

"Elizabeth could use a good husband," I said.

"Well, I do have a few men in mind," he said.

"Aha! Do tell me," I said, feeling perkier.

"In time, in time." He smiled as I nudged him.

"Elizabeth is quite beautiful, with an English rose complexion and large blue eyes. James has told me that he has a sapphire necklace and earrings for her. He has planned for Mrs. P to make her a blue gown the color of her eyes."

"I can't believe I haven't seen her yet…And will James be earl, do you think?" said Smythe.

"Oh, yes, I think so, and now he has a son for his heir. He usually sleeps at the Bain house, where Elizabeth and I are staying. Won't you come over tonight to talk with him? Come for supper."

"Of course. A good idea," he said.

"I need to get back to the cabin." We kissed longingly. With all the goings-on we had postponed our wedding, but Gregory had become healthier each week and that was what really mattered.

When I arrived back at the cabin, Ardath was awake and nursing her son. The room was warm and homey. It smelled of new baby and mother's milk.

I spoke to her quietly. "Ardath, do you not wish to nurse your daughter?"

She frowned at me. "No," she said.

"But she needs you, even if she can be sustained on goat's milk."

"Gwyn, don't be tiresome," she said, but a tear slipped down her cheek.

"Well, you feel something for her," I said.

"I know something; I killed her. There, does that satisfy you and your vexatious urge to hound me about it?"

I subsided into silence. I didn't try to convince her otherwise. Ardath would not easily change her mind. She had turned away her wet face.

I left her room, returning to the hearth where Mother held Lilly. When Mother looked up, we spoke in hushed tones.

"Ardath won't nurse this baby because she is convinced that she killed her."

"Why in the world would she think that?" Mother asked.

"I don't know, but I fear the guilt prejudices her against her baby."

"Oh, that is not good." Mother's brow wrinkled. "I will have to think about a solution."

"We all will have to come together on this. I will tell James, poor man," I said.

"I felt that she is too fragile to say anything to her now, or at least that I should not."

"I agree and this isn't to fall on you, my dear one. I'm just grateful that she admitted it to you," Mother said.

"She does look better to me, though."

"I think so too. Let's hope we are right," Mother said. "Gwyn, could you tell James? We could meet here tomorrow and talk to Ardath as a group of concerned family."

"Yes, I'll ask James to be here, about ten or so."

In the evening, James, Gregory, and I met in the parlor at the Bain house. James looked tired, and I'm sure I did also. James had been with Ardath most of the day. While others helped her, he had become the caretaker of Dougie, not an easy thing nowadays.

Gregory spoke first. "I can't help but comment that I haven't seen you and Gwyn look so weary since the worst days of our Atlantic voyage, James."

"Oh, I'm sure that is true," James replied. He uncrossed his legs and slumped down in his chair, legs out before him.

"Let me help where I can. I could send Mary or Robert, or both, to the cabin to relieve those on the front lines. Carys and Mrs. P would be welcome to rest at my house without a worry that they might miss a cry."

"Oh, Gregory, that is very kind," I said. He shrugged his shoulders.

"Thank you," said James. He turned to me.

"Gwyn, can you tell us how you think Ardath is? For one thing, I worry that she doesn't see or ask about our daughter."

"Just today I found why that is true. She feels guilty that she 'killed' her, I suppose by risking that journey after the thieves." Both James and Gregory knew that I had revived Lilly after she was born.

"My God!" James said. "No wonder then. Is there any truth to that?"

"We all worried that she might have had some damage to her own body, but there is no reason to expect that it caused problems for the babies. Twins are difficult in any circumstances. Frequently one twin is bigger than the other, for example." I did not admit that there could be problems in the delivery related to the jostling in the wagon. That was not a known fact and I would not have expressed it anyway.

"Mother wants us to meet at the cabin at ten tomorrow to talk with her."

"That sounds good. I had planned to do what I could for

Ardath in the morning."

I nodded. "I will be there. We must reassure her. Have you any thoughts on names for the babies?"

He smiled. "Have you? I know you are very close to the baby girl."

I rubbed my nose in embarrassment. "I call her Lilly," I said.

His eyes lit up. Gregory was smiling his secret proud-of-you smile.

"I really like that name," James said. "I'll suggest it."

I realized that we were talking as if Ardath and both babies would live. That was a cautious conclusion at this point.

"Oh, I need to tell you," I said. "I have word from David that he has found Ahmed at a plantation near the coast. The weather hasn't been conducive to travel there, but he plans to go as soon as possible. Apparently, Ahmed is well treated as a valuable worker. David will probably have to pay for him."

"It is a relief to know he is treated well," Gregory said.

"Yes, that's good!" said James. "I know you all want to get him back, no matter the price."

After a pause, he turned to his friend. "So, Gregory, Gwyn tells me that you have some suitors in mind for my sister."

"Well, it's been hard to find the idle, rich noble here in Philadelphia, with so much going on, but there are some young men I am impressed with, mainly merchants and businessmen, if such could be considered."

"Of course. Elizabeth wants a new experience, more someone of a noble character, rather than noble blood. We both insist she should find a love match. There is more to life than elevated status."

"Hurrah to that!" said Gregory.

"Hurrah to what?" Elizabeth said as she entered the parlor.

"Hurrah to love," I said, smiling at her. I introduced her to Gregory, who bowed.

"Well, of course," she said, rosebud mouth pursed. "Dinner is served. Cook has outdone herself tonight."

It was lovely to simply sit down to elegant food that I hadn't worked to make myself. Mr. Hinch first set out a hearty vegetable soup, followed by mince pies, then rabbit fricasseed. Somehow, I must ask Hinch how, each dish was accompanied with fresh greens, which should not be available in January. Perhaps he knew someone with a hothouse. Dessert was a cherry and rhubarb pie with cream. Even eating a little of each left me sated.

"I hope you'll not be expecting such fare on our table, Mr. Smythe, after we are wed," I teased him.

"Why certainly! I shall chain you to the stove at the start of each day. You will be the warmest person in the house, at least," he said with a grin.

After she had listened to my thoughts about Ardath and the babies, Elizabeth asked me to tell her more about my training to be a doctor.

"Well, a very pertinent question," I said. "After the babies, no one has time to teach me, nor do I have time to learn, except what the babies teach me. Since I was the younger of us sisters, I've never had babies figure in my life. They are very dear."

"Yes," she said, looking down at the table.

I realized I had trod on a sad subject for Elizabeth, and changed my direction. "Really, the best thing to learn right now is which herbs will be best used in winter to work with agues and catarrhs. Well, not exactly table conversation, is it? Tell me what has happened with Mrs. Ellis, wife of the colonel?"

Elizabeth brightened. "She is a delightful lady, so full of

warmth and ideas. She has taken me under her wing, advising me of the prominent families here, and which have eligible young men." Here Elizabeth blushed. "She plans a morning gathering of ladies. Ladies are the first group in which to gain allies for my entrance into society. It is to the good that some work in charity for the less fortunate in the town, especially widows and orphans."

"They have much work to do here, I believe," said Gregory, "especially after the fever passed through like an avenging wind."

James nodded, though I could see his mind was elsewhere. "I like your plans, Elizabeth, and you must keep us informed of every step."

He rose. She smiled up at him. "Always my protector," she said.

"Smythe, what say I walk you home tonight?" said James.

"That would be welcome," Gregory said.

Thus the party ended. I admit to falling into bed at the first chance.

Ardath:

I was dozing on my bed with Ed asleep beside me, when I heard many footsteps coming up the stairs. James appeared first and I was surprised to see the baby in his arms. Surely they must know that I didn't want her in my presence.

"James, how could you? I don't want her here. Take her away!"

Before I had finished speaking, Mother and Gwyn entered the room, and even Mrs. Perry. They had all gathered against me!

"Don't start in on me. I know I am an unnatural mother." I

felt a panic rise up in me. I twisted away from James, glaring at him and at the others also.

"Ardath, you know how I love you, but you must accept this child as our own. She is very much alive," James said.

"No," I sobbed. They were here to shame me. "If I had not gone on that reckless wagon trip—"

"Ardath," Mother said, "we all love you and no one blames you for those difficult births. We admire your courage and your fight for life, your own and the babies'. You have killed no one, but you have suffered greatly. Now don't spurn your little girl for that."

Gwyn then approached, while I sat rigid in my bed, my former sanctuary. She lifted the girl from James's arms, letting the blanket fall away from her. The tiny face looked out and seemed to search the room.

"Speak to her, Ardath. She misses the voice she heard all those months inside of you."

I wondered if she could truly know my voice, so I reluctantly looked at her and murmured. "Are you my little girl? Do you even want me as a mother?"

From under the blanket the tiny star shaped hand reached out to me. Gwyn put her to my breast and I heard the babe sigh with contentment. Bleary little blue eyes blinked, staring up at me with complete devotion. I sobbed out my shame and sorrow. She really was alive and she didn't blame me, it seemed.

Without looking up, I sensed everyone but James leaving the room. "She's ours and she really needs you, almost as much as I do," he said.

I smiled through my tears and placed the babe on my nipple. She had a surprisingly strong suck and my milk came down for her. We were going to be close; I was determined.

Chapter 31

Carys
Early 1754

Of course, I knew as soon as I had seen and heard her, that Elizabeth was Dougie's true mother. Everything about that terrible night of his birth was burned into my memory. I thought that Gwyn probably knew also, just from the way she looked from Dougie to Elizabeth and back, in the weeks following their arrival.

I couldn't share this with anyone, however, as we must all commit to the story of her widowhood and a lost child. It pained me not to be truthful, but I couldn't decide if it would be worse for her to know. How would it affect Dougie if he came to know? She would know Dougie as his aunt and in any case, she would be in his life. Still it left me with a moral dilemma. I was uneasy, but decided to wait for a better time to tell her.

Since Ardath's labor began the night James arrived, I had no time to deliberate. The subsequent weeks had been focused on bringing Ardath and the babies safely through. Bless the Goddess, all had survived. Their son, whom they had named Ed, bloomed particularly well. Little Lilly was still quite pale and petite, but very curious about her surroundings. Ardath had gained weight and color after her alarming delivery. Her irascible nature had mostly receded, to be replaced by a sweeter devotion to her family than I would have thought possible. I believed that she favored Ed somewhat, but with all of us persuading her, she had overcome the idea that she had "killed" Lilly. And, I had even become used to the notion that I was a grandmother.

In March, James received a letter from his father, who was very pleased about a male heir for the estate. James only raised his eyebrows about it, but I believe that took a great pressure off him.

Elizabeth had been surrounded by suitors throughout the winter and early spring. Mrs. Ellis took it upon herself to play the matchmaker, something I would not have been able to do, but which she enjoyed immensely, perhaps because Elizabeth was the daughter of an earl. Elizabeth radiated health and youth. She glowed in her dark blue mantua with golden traceries, made by Mrs. P and worn with the sapphire and diamond necklace and earrings that James had surprised her with. In accordance with the less extreme colonial fashions, her panniers were modest in size. It was a good thing that she inhabited the large Bain house, mingling with others of the upper class she moved among. I didn't really want to be part of this society. I would much rather be useful. In any case, I had not the time to do it. I did go to the "family" party that Mrs. Ellis put on for us. It included a young man named John Stewart, with whom I was very impressed. The third son of a duke, he was making his way very successfully in the New World with his intelligence and hard work. He and Elizabeth seemed attracted to each other.

As I thought about these things, Gwyn came to the back door.

"Mother," she said, hugging me with wool sleeves cooled by the fresh wind. "I think it's about time we stopped dreaming by the fire." Here we both laughed, since there had been little time for dreaming!

"What should we do instead?" I replied.

"We should plan my wedding!" Gwyn said. "All Gregory wants is for us to be married, in any way I wish. I would like to have a service at the church, so that Uncle Thomas could conduct it."

"I think that's a splendid idea! I'm sure he would be very pleased."

"I always loved Uncle, but his wife Priscilla made it hard for us to be close."

"I understand and I think he does too."

"Good. I'll ask him today. Now, as to a guest list, obviously our 'family' here, Elizabeth, and I think the Colonel and his wife, as she is very close with Elizabeth. Is there anyone else? Do you think there will be objections to the Africans coming into the church, or maybe they will feel strange since they are Muslims?"

"On the last, I hope not, as Muslims regard Jesus as a prophet. I will ask Omar, if you want?"

"Yes, please. I will ask Thomas about the other. I don't know about the Franklins, as Ardath was the main person he knew. I'll ask her what she thinks. We definitely don't want a lot of people, so Gregory thinks he won't ask any clients, although I wonder if that is politic."

"Hmm, maybe inquire of him again?" I said. I paused, watching her enjoy the discussion. "I'm happy to see you excited."

A wide grin flashed across her face. "Really, like Gregory, I just want to be married."

"That's good because marriage lasts a lot longer than the

wedding," I said. "Are there other things you wish to know about the physical act?"

"Not really, having heard you and Ardath speaking about the women you have helped, but I do worry some about the broken ribs I had after Aunt Priscilla kicked me. Could that have caused problems for my womb?"

"I will speak with Ibrahim about that, since he treated you, but I would not expect it to be a problem."

"It's just that after Ardath's ordeal...."

"I know, but that was an unusual situation," I said. I hope! I thought.

Gwyn kissed me and ran off again, to talk with her uncle and Elizabeth, who loved to speak about such matters. She and Gwyn had become good friends. I smiled; Gwyn hadn't even taken off her cloak.

I had other things on my mind as well. I was just wondering when we might hear more about Ahmed when Thomas appeared at the back of the house.

"Dear Carys, I was hoping you would be here."

"Come in, come in, Thomas. May I offer you some tea or ale?"

"No, thank you. I have had a letter from David. I didn't even open it, as I wanted to share it with you."

"Oh, thank you." I found I was wringing my hands in anticipation. We sat side by side at the scrubbed hearth table.

The letter cracked open at the red wax seal, which fell in pieces on the wood. Thomas put on his wire eyeglasses. "Ah, let's see. David has made his way to the plantation of a Mr. Merrill, not far from Wilmington, where he did indeed find Ahmed employed as a blacksmith. Hmm, Merrill didn't want to give him up, even when he saw the legal papers. David returned with a magistrate's decree releasing Ahmed, but to smooth the waters, David did pay him back what the thieves had sold him for."

"That seems fair, as that money was part of the silver Ardath recovered," I said. "We will give you the funds to pay David."

"Thank you. It seems that Ahmed is very grateful to you all for searching him out. He's eager to return to his family here. David has put him on the packet boat 'Emma Lee' to come back to Philadelphia, hmm, any day now. Wonderful news!"

"Yes, it is. Omar is working here today. Let's get the news to him." I rose to fetch my cloak, but Thomas forestalled me with his arm.

"Please let me bring him in. No need for you to go out," he said.

I laid out some biscuits for them and they were back almost before I put the plate down.

"Mrs. Rhys, Mr. Reese says dere is good news," said Omar.

I wanted to hug Omar, knowing how worried he had been, but I just said, "Sit down a moment." Thomas and I took turns telling him the news.

"Oh, oh, I must go to Isa. De building work is done in de barn and de animals are fed and happy. How can I ever t'ank you kind folks enough. Bless you," he said, taking my hands in his calloused ones to give them a quick kiss.

"Of course, go," I said. "We are all so happy for you."

Thomas and I looked at each other, content. "Thomas, stay for supper, please."

"I will, and gladly," he said. We had become as comfortable with each other as brother and sister by blood would be.

Chapter 32

Ardath

Mother appeared in my bedroom door after supper.

"Ardath, David has found Ahmed in North Carolina and put him on a boat to return here," she said.

"Finally! Well, I never thought much of David, but he's coming through for us now, isn't he?" I said.

"Just because Gwyn isn't marrying him doesn't mean he's a worthless person."

She cleared her throat. "Of course, but you never saw David in the state we found him in, in North Carolina. He was a drunken, useless fool."

"Perhaps true, but he was mourning his wife at that time. You can surely spare him a little compassion in those circumstances?"

"Hmph!" she said, turning to her side. "Anyway, I can't wait to see what Ahmed will say about the gold he stole from us. I'd dearly love to see that again! But I never heard from the constable where we left those other thieves. Since the silver had been recaptured, I suspect he threw the thieves out without a trial. It's been months now. They have probably gone right back to where Ahmed hid the gold, dug it up, and now they're somewhere in New York City enjoying our money."

"Well, let's hope that didn't happen, Ardath." Mother's

mouth was tightly drawn. She judged me to be too harsh. Men! I thought. She ought to know they were not to be trusted for the most part.

Several days later, Mother and I were sitting by the hearth fire while the babies slept upstairs. I had been able to make my way down the stairs for the first time. Omar came to the cabin door with Ahmed in tow. Omar's face split into a great grin.

"Mrs. Rhys, Mrs. Ardat', here is my son Ahmed returned to us t'rough your kindness."

"Ahmed, I am so pleased that you are back home. Are you well?" Mother asked, standing to look him over as best she could. He towered over her and his father. He didn't appear to be injured, or starved.

"Yes, ma'am, I'm well. De didn't whip me 'cause den I couldn't work and my work made dem money."

"Oh, I'm glad of that then. Won't you come in for some tea?" Mother asked, looking from him to his father. She was being so sweet I almost screamed. Instead I kept a wooden smile on my face.

Omar answered, "We are going to tell all de family he's here."

"Of course. I'm honored you came here first to let us know," she said.

Omar's face contorted; I thought he might cry. "So grateful, ma'am!" He turned away quickly.

Mother sensed their embarrassment, grew crisp, and shooed them to the door. "Go then and spread the news. Remember, this was not just something I did, you know. Everyone helped."

They fled through the door so we couldn't see their faces.

"Mother, you should have asked about the gold." I sighed. "I am going back upstairs." If I could have, I would have stomped.

Ed had waked and was crying for the breast. I welcomed his hard suck as I was full to bursting. Mother had followed me up the stairs. When she entered, Ed pulled off the nipple with a loud pop. His red lips oozed milk. Nursing the babies made me content.

"It was good to see Omar and Ahmed so happy! You could have been more welcoming, since Ahmed has been through hard times to get here," Mother said.

I felt some shame then. "But I honestly strained just to keep quiet while they were here," I said.

"Well, the gold is not as important as having Ahmed back," she said. She shook her head with disapproval.

"Oh, I am sorry," I said. "You know I am obsessed. I'm trying to be better, but…."

"You are married to a man who will likely be an earl. You will never want for any material needs," she said.

"I know, but though we have all been sharing our skills and resources, and coin, I was the one who got that gold. That was my contribution."

"Hmm. That's not your main contribution. Everyone knows that you were the bravest and smartest person on that ship, as well as very hardworking, then and since," she said.

I sighed. So much had happened to me, but that was true of us all. My confinement and the giving of all my strength to the babies made me feel unappreciated and exhausted. James did seem to love me still, though I wasn't my normal self.

"I know you must feel depleted, with the babies, but you

are doing the most important job in the world," Mother said.

I felt like rolling my eyes at that, but it was true that no one else could be their mother.

Later that day, when all had been told of Ahmed's arrival, he came back to the cabin. I was at the hearth with Mother again.

"Mrs. Rhys, Mrs. Ardath, I have sinned against your family," he said, twisting his hat in both hands as he stood in the hearth room. "You have every right to give me to de constable for jail." His handsome face reflected his misery.

"No, Ahmed. We will not do that," said Mother. "We feel that everyone should have a second chance. But you must stay away from the drink or laudanum if you wish to continue to be welcomed by us." I was glad to hear that condition expressed.

"Yes, ma'am, I have learned my lesson about dose poisons. Den, I ask you if Omar and I can take de wagon and get de gold back to you."

Just then Omar appeared through the back door. "Is it all right with you, ma'am, and you, Mrs. Ardat', if we take de horses and wagon? Not a very long journey, I t'ink."

"Are you sure that you don't want to wait until the weather improves?"

"No ma'am. We want to do it now," Omar said.

"Of course take the wagon. Let me pack some food," said Mother.

"No, t'ank you. Isa has done it. We will go now and be back in a few days if all goes well," said Omar. His large dark eyes brimmed with hope. I wished I felt as sanguine as he did.

As the main manager of our collective money, I didn't

know if we could always trust Ahmed, but I did know we could trust Omar. I needed to check with Smythe about whether we paid him enough for all the work he did. I smiled at them more sincerely this time. They certainly realized how important that gold was.

"Mother, we should ask Smythe to buy us a large iron strongbox to put this gold in. If they find it. I think it will be gone when they get there. Anyway, I'm not relying on digging a hole in the dirt again for our valuables!"

"I agree; that seems wise," Mother said.

When I wasn't feeding the babies, I paced the floor in agitation. If they didn't find the gold, I thought nothing could keep me from hopelessness. I didn't eat or sleep for several days. Mother hounded me to take care of myself, and I tried to at least nibble bread and drink ale.

In a few days, Omar and Ahmed returned with a heavy, muddy, and moldy leather bag. As they entered the hearth room, I saw that they were smiling, though tired and dirty. I grasped the slimy bag and did the honors, rolling out the shining, untarnished coins on our hearth table. Everyone gasped at the marvelous sight. I felt a warm glow of happiness that burst out as a huge smile on my face.

The first thing I did was to give Mother and each of the Africans a gold coin for their own. Omar and Ahmed were effusive in their thanks. Mother just beamed at me.

"Ahmed, could we employ you to help with the house and animals until you can obtain blacksmithing work, since Omar needs to return to his carpentry full time?" I asked.

He accepted humbly. "I will start tomorrow," he said.

"Why do you think the thieves didn't come back and find the gold?" I asked.

Ahmed smiled. "I told dem the wrong place to look," he said. We all smiled again at that. Ahmed was a sharp-witted man.

"We must leave now to clean ourselves and change our muddy clothes," said Omar.

"Of course, and thank you again," I said.

"The prosperity of this family grows with each day," said Mother. "I don't mind the security it brings. It is certainly better than the life we ever could have had in Wales."

"So much better than anything I could have imagined there," I agreed. I felt a great relief. We would do all right with the resources we now had.

Chapter 33

Gwyn
Late March

"Elizabeth, what would you think of a periwinkle blue for my wedding gown?" I asked. She had just come into my room at the Bain house after I got back from Mother's.

"Oh, perfect for you. You can wear my sapphires. Do you have some material?"

"Oh, dear, not really. I was just dreaming of the best, I guess. I never knew I could be so scatter-brained as I'm finding myself lately."

She hugged me, so loving. "Any bride deserves some completely frivolous thoughts. I hope to be having some myself soon."

"Aha! Is it John Stewart? He would be a fortunate fellow."

"Gwyn, he's very handsome, but also very accomplished and practical. He has already started a company for the manufacture of iron for the colonies and a trading company between Philadelphia and the Caribbean Islands, rather than England. He thinks our future here is to produce and trade for our essentials, without so much reliance on our distant home country."

"Hmm, I can see why you admire that. There's so much to explore and new ideas to try here," I said. I thought of my own desire to be a doctor. Some things might not be realized, but possibilities still abounded.

"So, when might you know?"

"If he doesn't ask soon, I might ask him." Her mouth twisted in a withheld grin.

"Why Elizabeth, I didn't realize you had been so influenced by Ardath."

She finally laughed. "I could never be anything like Ardath. I am awed by her fearlessness."

"Hmm," I said. "When will you see him next?"

"Mrs. Ellis is planning a soiree on Wednesday. I think that will be the night."

"Very exciting!" I said. Out of courtesy, Mrs. Ellis and others invited Gregory and me along with Elizabeth to their many gatherings. I had seen so much social life since Elizabeth came that I soon ran out of gowns to wear. Fortunately, we were of a similar size and she generously loaned me many of hers. Mrs. Perry practiced her skills with other gowns she made for me, saying that I would need them as a prominent solicitor's wife. She wouldn't take any money for them, but I bought the material from Ardath's and my funds. She had a way of designing gowns so that they were reasonably comfortable. I helped to advertise her business by mentioning her skills to anyone who complimented my dress. Soon she was going to need her own shop and an assistant.

All of this helped me be ready to assume my role as a wife in polite society, an aspect of marriage I hadn't really thought about. Being with Gregory in society made it an easier task than I thought possible; he was never at a loss for words. His assured manner and natural humor were contagious.

I was a happy woman, yes woman. No longer did I feel the doubts that used to assail me about my youth and competence.

As well, Gregory and I had made changes to the house. His office remained much as it had been, but, with Omar in charge, we separated out part of the parlor with a new wall to enclose a space for me, for my study now, and then for when I should be ready to practice medicine on my own.

Throughout the house, we had torn out the aging window hangings, had the dusty windows scrubbed, and placed new colorful draperies. The floors had a new coat of varnish. The furniture was cleaned and oiled. Walls were repainted in the softer colors we both preferred. It was a gracious house and now it felt more like our own.

The one problem with all this activity was that I was spending very little time on my studies. Everyone else was busy too, so Mother and Ibrahim had little time to teach me. It looked like I would have to get married to calm things down. Elizabeth had better marry soon also.

"I don't know him well, but I know John Stewart has proposed and I hope she will marry him," Gregory said to me in a quieter moment. We were enjoying tea in our new parlor.

"I do also," I said, "but I am a little worried that he is entering the iron business."

"So you know about the King's law forbidding finished iron products made in the colonies?" he asked.

"Yes, that's on my mind, but I didn't say anything to her about it. I hope he's not some form of outlaw. I don't know why, but he makes me a little uneasy."

"I know that forges are operating in most colonies that have access to the iron in the western mountains. Apparently, the ore mined here is better than anything English finishers can buy in Europe. So they can get it cheaper from here, but I haven't heard that any of the governors are prosecuting that law. After all, nobody tries to export the finished product.

"It's more worrisome to me that we may have battles coming with the French and their Indians soon. The French have built forts in the Ohio Valley. The Virginia Militia is active, I've been told. Militia Major George Washington has been negotiating for the French to leave the Ohio Valley. Prominent Virginians want to develop that land. I think you met Washington on your travels, did you not?"

"Yes, near Winchester. He's young, but seemed a steady gentleman."

"If the French and allied Indians decide to take a stand, there will be trouble."

"How do you know all this?"

"General rumor, but more precisely, from James and Ellis. James keeps up with it. Though no longer in the army, he will do what he can to help."

"Do you think he will be recalled to England when his father dies?"

"Sooner or later. I know he hopes it will be later," Greg said. "He told me that he has received news from France that his brother seems at peace, but is no closer to knowing who he is, so Richard is no candidate."

"What will happen if we are at war with France? Will James even be able to be in touch with the people there?" I asked.

"That is a question no one can answer. Are you worried for James?"

"Partly, but also for Ardath. She can't take those small babies on a ship."

"Come here, worrywart. Let's not talk of things we can't know, but discuss those we can. For example, how would you feel if I did this?"

He kissed my neck, which he knew tickled me. How nice it would be to be married to this lovely man, being with him every day, and fully the mistress of this house!

Chapter 34

James and Ardath
March, 1754

James:

I would have cheerfully faced any number of dangerous battles to avoid what we had all been through with the children's birth. In many men's opinions, males didn't have the tender feelings of "the weaker sex." Hah! In my opinion, we had the feelings, but didn't know what to do with them. Fortunately, I had friends, both male and female, who could tolerate and understand.

Smythe stood out amongst the men I knew in this respect, perhaps because he was reared as the only boy, with several sisters in his family. While he possessed modest physical abilities, his sensitivity and knowledge of people were exceptional. He listened to me and actually heard what I can only call my soul.

I had thought my whole little family was going to die. Even now that they have survived, the thought still leaves me devastated. I see that many things must be done to keep them healthy and at ease. We must have a house and servants here in Philadelphia. No more making do with pallets on the floor!

I came into the cabin to the smell of baking apples. Mrs. P was at work, caring for Dougie, cooking, and sewing all at the same time.

"Hello, Mrs. Perry, how do you do today?" She looked up from her sewing with a bright eye.

"Splendid, my lord," she said, standing and bowing.

I grimaced. "None of that 'my lord' business! You know better!" Then I grinned at her. Dougie had heard me. Running in, he tackled my knees in a wild embrace.

"Ouch, man, don't hurt me please!" I said, making a big face for him. "Is Ard awake?"

"Yeth, yeth, come on," he said, tugging at me to follow. We both clambered up the stairs to her room.

Ardath, of course, had a baby at her breast. She seemed the picture of contentment. "My darling, how is it today?" I asked her.

Dougie climbed on the bed, giving Ardath a sloppy kiss. She grimaced briefly and held him at arm's length. He had been rather naughty since the babies were born, and I ended up trying to manage his wild behavior on many a day. Between that and my worries, I was more exhausted than I had ever been. I did everything necessary so that Carys, Mrs. Perry, and sometimes Gwyn, could take care of the babies and Ardath.

"I am well." She turned to Dougie. "Mr. Dougie, can you go help Mrs. P?" she said. He nodded and thudded down the stairs again.

I took his place on the bed. "You are so very beautiful," I said.

"Oh surely that's a lie," she said, pulling at a strand of uncombed hair. "Look at someone who is pretty." She moved aside her nursing cloth, showing me a tiny but happy Lilly.

"I can't believe my good fortune!" I said through the lump in my throat.

"Hmm, yes," she said. We sat in silent appreciation for a

moment.

"What's happening with Elizabeth?" she asked.

"I think she has actually chosen a good and prosperous man, John Stewart, who has asked me for her hand. She has said yes. He travels in his business and most likely the wedding would have to be soon, before he goes to the West Indies."

"Well, that is satisfying! But it's so strange, you being out in society for Elizabeth's sake, and I'm just here with the babies," said Ardath.

"That's true. I'm sorry not to be with you more. She felt some urgency to see what her prospects were. She really wants children as soon as possible."

"When she marries, will they continue in the Bain house?"

"No, he has a large house already." I cleared my throat. "Speaking of houses, I'd like to find a suitable place near Smythe's for us to lease or buy. I know you are bursting at the seams here. We need to establish our own household, as much as this feels like home to us both."

"Oh," she said, "I had thought we would build out here." Her forehead creased, wild tuffs of red hair floating about it.

"I know, but I believe you should save that property as an investment for the future. Also, I would like to be more in the center of things and I don't want to have the house building as a distraction from settling ourselves as a family."

"Hmm. You have thought about this. Have you looked at some houses?" She searched my eyes.

"No, I wanted to talk with you first. I know you wanted to wait until the babies were proven healthy, but I think that will be soon if not now. And spring is coming, with weather that will let us move about more easily. I don't want us to be confined to a small space then."

"What about your promise to Colonel Ellis, to help train militia?"

"Another reason I'd like to be settled soon."

"Mother and Mrs. Perry are taking good care of us here."

"I know. It feels like home, but you are a married woman now and a man has needs." I grinned to show her I was partly joking.

"Hmmpf. All right then, let's look at furnished houses to lease and make it as simple as we can, agreed?"

"Agreed!"

"James, Mrs. Perry needs a shop, too, while you are looking. Please ask Smythe to help, as he knows the town best," she said.

"That I will. Let me hold Lilly."

"Good. It is about the time Ed will be getting hungry too."

As soon as she gave me Lilly, Ed began to move about and finally cry. She stretched her back and picked him up. Ardath's life was absorbed by these two. I almost felt guilty adding the idea of a change of place to her mind. I really would have to make it as easy as possible for us all, but with our own house, we could hire servants to help us.

A little warmth to the breeze, a few daffodils, a mild blue sky hinted at spring. I had found a house very close to Smythe's to lease, furnished adequately and with a small garden. He helped me find a housekeeper, cook, nanny, and a houseman. The preparations went at a fast pace. The nursery and main bedroom were separated upstairs, and I insisted on the nanny living in, so we could get some sleep. During the day, we could keep the babies in a small room off the drawing room.

On the day we moved in, Ardath and I walked together to our house. I lifted her over the threshold, setting her down on a comfortable sofa in the parlor. She wore her green linen gown. Mrs. Perry had let it out over the bodice.

"Ardath, please close your eyes," I said. I was excited to finally place around her neck the emerald teardrop necklace the goldsmith had created for her. Holding a mirror before her, I said, "Now open them."

As I had hoped, she gasped to see the pendant. It nestled most becomingly between her breasts.

"Oh, James!" she exclaimed, eyes glinting, my passionate, wonderful woman. We had a moment to kiss before Mother and Mrs. Perry arrived with the babies. We didn't have time for more, though I knew we both longed for it. Mrs. Rhys and Ibrahim had made it clear that there was to be no congress between us until Ardath was more healed, and no more children for a long while, if ever.

Ardath:

James and I were nestled in our new bed in the leased house. I held Ed and he held Lilly. The open window gave us a cool breeze. I couldn't remember ever feeling so content.

Our new "man," Charles, knocked hesitantly on the bedchamber door. He was a retired British soldier who stood with an erect carriage. He had lost one half of his left ear in battle and probably had many other wounds we didn't see, but he was able-bodied and unfailingly loyal. It was comforting to have another man in the house for protection and heavy work.

"Charles here, sir, with a message." Handing Lilly into my

other arm, James rose, with that feline grace I so admired, to answer it.

"Thank you, Charles."

"Yes sir."

"Oh dear," I said, when I saw the large red seal of the Ensleigh Estate.

"Hmm, perhaps I should save this for later," James said, settling beside me again.

"Oh, no! What have I told you about not treating me like an invalid?"

He grinned, feeling caught in the act, I presume.

"Very well. You are correct as usual."

Both of us were tense as he broke the seal, the parchment crackling in his hands. He relaxed, seeing that it was a report on the animals and repairs at the estate. James had been keeping me abreast of the "business" of both the main and other estates. He wanted my help in making decisions about everything from expenses to the shearing of sheep, both of which the agent there, Mr. Appleton, tended.

"Ah, that's good; the shearing has gone well. We should do well in the wool market this year," he mused. "The wool from our sheep is the best in the Cotswolds. It is our true wealth."

"Hmmm. We hear very little from your father in these letters," I noted.

"True, but as far as I know, he has never been inclined to write. Of course, when I was just the third son, I wasn't worth writing to…."

"That is really sad. He doesn't, or didn't, know what an accomplished man you are."

"At least we are not exposed to my mother, who really seems to hate me," James said.

"That's just unbelievable to me, a mother who doesn't show love to her son. How horrible for you, that you haven't known a mother's love!"

"That's one reason I cherish being around your family. Your love for each other is so easy and natural. It makes for a joyous household. I want us to have that kind of family, even if we have to live in England. But, our children will be of a noble class, under expectations of being 'correct' Englishmen. I don't want them to have the same warp as I did, warped, in the sense of twisted like a thread out of shape. I have come to hate the very idea of a life in England, but duty would call me there if my father died now. With Richard so disabled, there is no one else to take it on," James said.

"Oh, James, that is horrifying to me," I said. We sat in silence for a while, until we heard crying from the nursery.

"Well, I think someone needs a mother's love," I said, relieved to interrupt our rather gloomy conversation.

Chapter 35

Gwyn

"Gwyn, you should be married first. You and Gregory have waited a long time," said Elizabeth.

"Thank you, but remember, you and John will want time to 'settle in' before he takes ship." She blushed at all that thought included. "You must go first," I insisted.

"Gwyn, I have never had a friend like you. In so many ways, my life has become very different since I arrived, unsure and afraid I might not be welcomed, especially by your family. I can't believe John and I found each other so quickly and how completely I trust and admire him. In England it's all about leisure, entertaining ourselves, and status. Here everyone seems so energetic and purposeful. He may not be an earl's son, but he is of noble descent and of noble character, and on his way to considerable wealth. His manners are impeccable also."

"Yes, that's true. He's very handsome too, with the dark hair and eyes and manly figure. And, I was very happy when we first arrived here, to find how enthusiastic most new settlers are. Perhaps it comes from the many opportunities to be seized," I said.

I admit to some curiosity about whether Elizabeth would ever tell John about Dougie, but I didn't see how she could at this point. First, there was the story we had all adhered too, about her being a widow who had lost a child. Most importantly, she didn't know that Dougie was her child. All this was far from the best. I came out of my reverie with a slight start when she addressed me again.

"What will I do when John is gone on travels for his business?" she wondered. "My life thus far has been about obtaining a suitable marriage."

"You will manage a household, and probably become a respected hostess for parties," I said. "Perhaps you will host artists and intellectuals, or raise funds for orphan children."

She looked thoughtful. "Hmm, I'm going to ask Mrs. Ellis about it. She seems fulfilled in her life, although she doesn't do anything as purposeful as you will do."

"Yes, good. And don't forget you'll have your own children soon!" Elizabeth again blushed at that, so I changed the subject. "Which gown do you think to wear?"

"I am decided on the creamy pink one, the one that has a rosy tone to it. I have pearls that will look well with it. Did you find material in a periwinkle shade?"

"Yes, fairly close to it. Mrs. Perry is at work on it already."

Thus we spent our leisure in happy preparation. Ardath would have scorned us for wasting time on this, but she wasn't there. She had a surfeit of her own things to occupy her.

Elizabeth and John were married in April at Christ Church in a "society affair" reported by the Gazette, with all the prominent citizens attending. She was beautiful and transcendently happy, but not more so than her tall, elegant bridegroom with his wavy dark hair and shining eyes. I stood up with her and James presented her to be married.

At the reception at the Bain house, I whispered to Gregory, who proudly held me by the arm, "Oh, dear, we will never match this."

"Hmmm, always my desire to have a society wedding," he said, quirking his mouth to tell me he was joking. "It is not so much the wedding I look forward to, anyway," he said, waggling his eyebrows in a lascivious manner.

"Oh, don't. It's not nice to laugh out loud at a wedding," I said, pressing my lips together.

I noticed that Mother had approached John, who was standing near us at the time.

"Mr. Stewart, I am pleased to see you again and on such a happy occasion. I'm Carys Rhys, mother of Gwyn."

"Of course, Mrs. Rhys, I am very pleased you are with us," he said with a small bow.

"I understand that you will soon be leaving for the Indies, and wonder if you have met a friend of mine named Captain Alex Whitsun. He lives in Jamaica and has built a merchant vessel to transport goods from there to our Eastern seaboard. It seems your interests might dovetail nicely," Mother said.

"Indeed, I have heard of him. Do you know what goods he might trade?"

"I knew him in Jamaica until last summer. He has access to cinchona, also called Jesuits' bark, a highly valued herbal treatment for malaria. We would like to buy some for our apothecary shop. It should be even more important in the colonies south of here."

"Ah, that is just the sort of thing for which I am searching, as well as fruits, and also salves made with tropical plants," he said.

"I am impressed with those made from the aloe plant, which Captain Whitsun could also get for you. It's very good for burns," Mother said.

"How fortunate that you spoke with me. Is he near Kingston?"

"Yes."

"Then I shall go to him first."

"Excellent. I will write to him, letting him know to expect you," Mother said.

"Thank you, and may I tell you how much I value our friendship with Gwyn?"

"I'm very glad to hear it," Mother said. "Have a good and safe journey."

Their conversation seemed pleasant and agreeable, but something about John was cold and overly polite. He moved away from Mother as soon as he could, as if she were beneath him.

We followed Mother away to the "groaning board" on the dining room buffet, where every sort of treat was laid out in sumptuous splendor. The centerpiece was an entire crackly roasted pig with an apple in its mouth and greenery surrounding it on a huge platter. Of course there were the usual treats of pickled onions, green gooseberry tarts, apple tarts, jumble cookies in their traditional "S" shape, tansey, syllabub, and the enormous, dense, spiced wedding cake, with dried fruit and nuts crowded into it. They even had managed to get hothouse strawberries. All of it glowed richly in the mellow candlelight, and the smells enticed us.

I felt a lurch in my heart when their carriage took them away to John's house. Elizabeth seemed forever changed in her new position as a married woman, though I knew we would continue to be friends. And I would soon be in the same position.

My wedding was to be in May, as the flowers were blooming across the city. We tried to make it a small affair, but the number of guests far exceeded that plan. Uncle Thomas officiated with delight. Ardath stood up with me and Mother presented me to be married. I wore the exquisite dress, really a mantua, that Mrs. Perry had elaborated for me out of what I had planned as a simple dress of periwinkle silk. The outer mantua was embroidered with small silver stars and crescent moons. James had surprised me with earrings of sapphire and diamonds as a wedding present and Elizabeth loaned me her sapphire necklace. I felt like a queen.

I loved walking down the church aisle with my mother, thanking God that she was there to do so. I had no anxiety because I faced my bridegroom with so much love and surety in my heart. He, in turn, beamed with love for me.

We received guests at our newly furnished house amid much celebration of friends I had grown to cherish. While the party went on, Gregory steered me to my "surgery." He made me close my eyes, and when I opened them, I found that it was now furnished with every herb and medical instrument one could think of, including a huge magnifying glass on a stand, which even Ibrahim didn't have. It would help me see into and clean wounds. I touched it with awe.

"Oh Gregory, what a surprise! All of this is truly the best gift you could give me!"

"Ibrahim and your mother helped me with it," Gregory said.

"Oh, it's perfect. If I can't help people here, it will be my own fault," I said.

"I want only for you to be happy," he said. We fell against each other, kissing, and might never have returned to the party if there had not been a discreet knock at the door.

"Gwyn, folks are asking for you and Gregory," said Ardath's voice.

So we went back to the friends socializing in our parlor, well-wishers all. To keep from going into a dream state, I concentrated on Gregory's hands, as I had in the church. When he reached out to slip the ring on my finger, I appreciated the long slender fingers, the cleanly cut nails, the surety with which he clasped my hand in his, so competent, so warm, so welcoming. His were the hands of an artist, made for writing poetry or painting, sensitive, loving.

Now he held the wine glass with elegance as they toasted to our marriage. I must have held one too, but I wasn't aware. The warmth of the crowd around us made my head swim. Or perhaps it was the ruby red of the French wine that swirled in our glasses. I, however, longed for silence and the ease of being alone with my husband.

Finally they all left except my mother, who dressed me for bed in a white, lacy gown, hugged me tightly, bent my head down, and kissed my forehead.

She left through the open bedroom door, nodding to Gregory, who stood just outside. Besides his long white shirt, he wore a large woolly nightcap designed to start our night with a laugh, and we did.

"Oh my!" he said, "You are so lovely, my Gwyn. I think I must be in heaven."

"I don't think a woolly hat would be the proper attire there,"

I said. He slung the hat across the room, the better to slide, seated, onto the bed beside me.

"I want to see all of you; please stand up." he asked.

"You must do the same," I said.

We stood before each other. His hands gently pulled the nightgown over my head. I did the same to him. His eyes glowed at me; he cupped my chin and kissed me until my knees threatened to fail me. Those fine fingers traced my face, slid down my neck, and settled on my collarbone. All the while, he whispered soft words, like love and beauty.

I held him around his waist, aware of the powerful chest he had developed since he was well again, lightly sprinkled with soft blond curls. Though he was slender, he was well proportioned, like a marble Greek statue.

Next, he was cupping my breasts with both hands, kissing and tugging at them with an open mouth and such a tongue! My private parts gushed with moisture; I was melting.

I had seen men all over of course, but I had never seen a cock stand up like this one did. We threw ourselves onto the bed. He kissed me all down my body and mouthed and tongued me instead of entering. Now my back arched and I was away in a different world, where we were no longer in two bodies and minds but in a primordial sphere where we merged and floated together, throbbing.

He whispered to me, "This might hurt," as he entered me. It did, sharply for a moment. Then he slowly drew his cock in and out until I was frenzied. Suddenly I felt an explosion, whether his or mine, I couldn't say. We lay back panting.

"Was it what you expected?" he asked. His hands smoothed my wild hair away from my face. They smelled of me, the me that I was just beginning to know.

"Oh, I didn't know what to expect," I said, still gasping for breath. "I am completely astonished!"

Chapter 36

James
Late May

I enjoyed my stroll down the Philadelphia streets on a day in May. The scents of the locust and chestnuts in bloom, the pleasant clatter of life in the city, the sounds of birds rejoicing in their freedom from winter's siege, all surrounded me.

Before I left our house, I had looked out of the window of my office on the second floor down to Ardath and our babies lolling on a white quilt in the bright green grass of our back garden. Ardath, with her gleaming head thrown back to catch the sun on her face, the babies giggling next to her. I was a very fortunate man!

Now I was on my way to take our "fortune" in gold coins and jewels to Smythe's office for safekeeping in our new iron strongbox ordered from John, Elizabeth's husband. The box weighed more than two men could lift, not easy to steal, and I felt better to have our wealth secured thus.

Smythe greeted me at his office door. "Oh, I'm surprised you didn't bring your man Charles with you," he said, when he spotted the full leather satchel hidden beneath my coat.

"Well, I should have, I suppose, with many thieves about, but was lulled by the beauty of the day."

"Indeed, what a day! I'm absorbing the news. I suppose you

have heard about George Washington's attack on the French at Jumonville's camp."

"Yes, the Virginia Militia is proceeding to defend our Pennsylvania borders. Meanwhile Franklin has had no success in procuring funds from the Assembly to train our own militia. I agree with him and Colonel Ellis that those members who held out against a militia were woefully short-sighted. Inevitably, the conflict over the Ohio valley will affect us in Pennsylvania directly, as there are already settlers pushing at the frontier in this colony. At least the Assembly might contribute some funds to the Virginia effort."

"The Virginians have a large stake in what happens in the Ohio country, having formed a speculative company to sell land there. Whether war will come between the British and French is now a moot question in my mind," said Smythe.

"I agree, and the French have only a tiny foothold in the lands they claim, a population of mostly fur traders and forest runners. I believe the French can't win in the end, although they do have professional soldiers," I said.

"The Indians will lose; that's for certain. To put it bluntly, we are taking their land," said Smythe.

"True. In the south, I observed the admirable culture of the Cherokee. Perhaps there's a way to live with such natives so that each culture benefits, but I'm not optimistic. I would consider joining Washington in the fight, but I don't feel I can leave until the children are older."

"We shouldn't repeat our sentiments about the Indians in public. People would think us distinctly strange."

"Oh, I know!" I said, shaking my head.

"Weighty matters, but I'll put away these valuables. Will you take some ale?"

"With relish," I said.

As we sat to enjoy our drinks, to my surprise, Charles appeared in Smythe's doorway.

"My lord, a letter from England," he said. "It looks official so I thought to bring it straightaway."

"Thank you, Charles, but I am not a lord, remember?"

In response, he bowed and left us. He backed away as if I were a king, which both amused and irritated me. Smythe also had a thoughtful smile on his face.

"Well?" said Smythe. "Looks like the Ensleigh seal."

"I should wait for Ardath, I suppose, but it's probably just Appleton reporting on the spring shearing. She was in the back garden enjoying the fine day when I left."

"Ah," said Smythe. "But go ahead if you wish. I can give you some privacy."

"Oh, no need. I no longer feel such trepidation as once I had about these letters."

I cracked the seal with impatience to hear how the spring had gone on the estates. It began:

To: The Earl of Redfern:

My Lord, it grieves me to inform you that your father, the late earl, has died on April 2nd, 1754. His was a peaceful death, passing in his sleep, and he had been alert and cheerful to his last waking hour. He has been interred in the family plot and is mourned by all. The Countess returned from Wales to attend the ceremony and resides at Ensleigh.

Your father's fervent dying wish was that you return to England with your family to fully take on your proper role and title as soon as may be possible.

Your most obedient servant, P. Appleton

I sat, stunned, rereading to be sure, though there could be no doubt what this letter said. I felt as if a great wall of stones had collapsed on my head. I wasn't trained or prepared to be the earl! This was it, the circumstance I had dreaded and yet to which I thought myself inured.

Smythe gave me a sympathetic pat on the shoulder. "I see by your expression that it has happened," he said.

"Yes…. Of course my father's dying wish was that I come to England soon with my family. Smythe, how can I do that? Take those little children there when they can't even walk yet?"

"Perhaps you needn't hurry to be there," he said. "Your father would appreciate your dutiful impulse, I'm sure, but he isn't there to see them or you. They are certainly safer here."

My friend's brow was creased with concern. Here was another thing I would have to leave, the friendships I had made here that were precious to me. The present and future I wanted to make on this new continent. No, I was about to be pulled into the past, the life my father wanted for me. And there was need there too, a responsibility for those who lived and worked on our great estates. Father had not been able to see directly to the conditions of our tenants in the past years. Although Appleton was a conscientious warden of the several estates, he hadn't time to travel to them nor the authority to make changes. My mother was probably creating havoc in every way she could. I became aware that I was pacing with tension.

"I have to go, Smythe, but I can't take the family." I paused to see his reaction.

"That is certainly reasonable. Everyone here is settled and there are more of us to see to needs of the others. Elizabeth has her own house in hand and John is returning soon; you have settled your family. All is well with The Reverend Rhys and Carys, Ibrahim and Omar's family, and not least, Gwyn and me. As of today, your wealth is secured here and everyone is sufficiently housed and well engaged in work."

"Once again, you reassure me, friend. It is certainly not the worst of times to leave. It will be strange to enter our old house at Ensleigh with so many gone."

"Will you miss your father greatly?"

"Hmm, I will miss him, yes. At least he was always there, an integral part of the estate, no matter what other feelings I had about him." I paused. "Well, there will be more time to accustom myself to all of it. I must take ship as soon as possible."

"We will be here waiting for your return," said Smythe.

"Yes, I will surely return," I said, feeling brighter at that thought. "Just in case I do not, through unforeseen accident, we must make my will."

"Whenever you are ready."

"I must get the news to Ardath."

"May I tell Gwyn when she returns from Ibrahim's?"

"Oh, yes of course."

As I hurried back to my house, my mind filled with a thousand questions, I hardly noticed the beauty of the day. Deaf to the sounds of the city, the bird calls, or anything else, I tried to figure out the words to tell Ardath.

She was still in the back garden, just gathering the children up to take them inside with the nanny.

With one look at my face, she asked the nanny to take the children. "I'll get the things inside later," she said to Margaret.

When they were gone, she turned to me.

"What has happened, James? Were you robbed?"

"Oh no, all is well ensconced in the strongbox," I said, pulling her into my arms, my face buried in her flying hair. She smelled like clean children and sunshine.

"But…."

"I got a letter from Ensleigh. My father died there in April," I said on a sigh.

"Oh, no!" She pulled me tighter into her arms as if she could prevent my going.

We stayed there, locked together, for a long while. Finally, I drew a deep breath. "I'll have to go and see to the estates, but I will come back as soon as I can."

"I want to go with you," she said pulling away from my arms, but fixing her eyes on mine.

"I know, and I wish I could have you there, but in good conscience, I must leave you with the children."

Her lips thinned into a straight line. "I don't think I can stand it! Not again."

"I know, I know."

"The children are weaned; they don't need me so much. The weather should be good for the crossing. I can help you at the estate; you know I can. You've made me learn everything about it, after all."

"That was in case I should have to stay there permanently, but now my thought would be to go long enough to set things in order and then return here. Or do you think we should go together and live there, give up our lives here?"

Warring moods tumbled over her face. "I fear you will get caught there," she said.

"You can trust me."

"I do trust you, but I don't trust the ways of the world, the things we can't control."

I had no answer to that. Life contained enough dangers. It was always possible for me to meet with some accident and not return. But if we dwelt on those things we would be unable to risk any adventure, or even necessity.

"Well," she said in a cold voice, "of course I cannot leave the babies. I believe I'll walk and try to sort my thoughts. But I fear that you will desert your family here, to go to those who don't appreciate or need you as we do."

"Some time alone will help me too. I don't want this any more than you," I said to her back.

I could think of no way to change my fate. I could only hope that Ardath would understand in time, that I had a duty which compelled me to England. It was partly a matter of honor, a vital thread in my fabric.

Chapter 37

Carys
Spring to Summer, 1754

After Ardath and the babies had recovered, I had been busy this spring of 1754 with midwife duties. Some of my mothers were eager not to have a child as frequently as nature allowed. There was no way to shield them completely, though some herbal oils and patches to be put in the vagina discouraged pregnancy.

Also, I explored the resources of Philadelphia for condom materials. By befriending a local butcher, I was able to obtain lamb's intestines. I had to tell him I was using them to make mounds of sausage, though whether he believed me I didn't know. Perhaps he thought that the strange Welsh people had sausage at every meal.

Some churchmen and other "learned" men thought condoms were evil and encouraged licentious behavior, so it was best for me to be private about it. I know that our family must be seen as unconventional at the very least, perhaps heretical, and the subject of much gossip. My late husband Jacob and I were only a generation removed from nobility, and I could still remember the many restrictions placed on that class, especially its women. We were actually more part of a working class now, and I frankly embraced the greater allowed freedoms. However, I suspected that only James and Elizabeth's status as children of an earl kept us from being total outcasts amongst the local gentry.

At any rate, making condoms was a smelly, nasty process using sulfur and lye on the intestines. Hardly a thing for the indoors or the winter months!

"Mother, what on earth are you doing?" asked Ardath, when she found me at the back porch on the first decent day. I waved her away from the sulfur fumes. I had on my sealskin gloves and a hat with a heavy linen veil all around it.

"Well, we have talked before about all the things you used to prevent a child and still you had the twins, so it might be foolish to depend on those methods alone."

"You are saying I shouldn't be with child again soon."

"Ardath, don't sound so surprised! You know how Ibrahim and I feel about that."

Her lips quirked. "Well, so what are you cooking up that smells so foul?"

"I am experimenting with lye and sulfur to process the lamb skin, to make condoms. It must be soft and without leaks." She examined the folds of intestine that lay on a board beside me.

"Does James know what you are doing?" she asked with a grimace.

"No, I am relying on you to tell him," I said, hiding a smile.

"Disgusting! I'll have no part of it." She stomped off to the barn to check on the horses.

I thought that, with condoms, if I could make them work, it would be the men that would protest. I had not found any for sale in Philadelphia, but perhaps that was only because I hadn't been to the brothels here. Being seen to enter a brothel would seal our reputation in the town. Furthermore, I wouldn't rely on any that could be bought. The need was too close to home. Ardath shouldn't have any more children, at this point. Gwyn might need them if she wanted to wait for children until her training was more complete. They should be using only the best and cleanest and I was determined to make those. However, the process was horrible enough to be one I would not undertake frequently.

Mrs. Perry witnessed the process of making the lambskin condoms. Being ultimately a very polite person with me, she didn't wrinkle her nose noticeably, but set to work making linen sheaths put together with extremely fine stitches, which she then treated with lavender oil to soften and make them waterproof. I was relieved that there was a reusable and more pleasantly made condom.

When we had made some that I knew wouldn't leak and were comfortable, I gave them to Gwyn and Ardath. I also gave one to one of my patients, a woman who already had six children whom she could hardly feed. She thanked me with tears in her eyes. As a healer, I couldn't deny that these were important products. I would find myself giving out more, I felt sure. They could prevent poverty and death for many a woman.

As for the claims that the condoms led to licentious behavior, I believed that licentious behavior was its own reward and having a condom wouldn't encourage it, no matter what a clergyman might say.

The sun shone brightly on a June day to rejoice in. Elizabeth came to me at the cabin with the hope that she might be with child. She had bloomed since her marriage, cheeks pinker than ever, a ready smile on her lips, filling out her clothes more fully.

"I haven't had my courses since John left," she said as we sat at the hearth table with the back door open to watch Dougie running about the yard.

"Ah, and you are hopeful?" I asked.

"Oh, yes! I want a child so much."

"Well then, come out and lie on the hammock. There's no one around. Hmm, how many months have you missed your courses?"

"Only three, but it feels like the first time."

"The first time you were with child?"

"Yes, you know we decided on the story that I was a widow and had lost a child, but if you are to be my midwife, I must tell you the truth and rely on your silence."

"You may indeed rely on that."

"I trust you. I had a babe born at the full term and he was healthy, but he was taken from me as my mother didn't want the scandal of a child out of wedlock."

"I see."

"The midwife took him away, but my mother wanted him killed. I always hoped he somehow survived, but I don't know." She looked at me with tear-filled eyes.

"That is a very hard thing to sort out." I had finished my examination. "I am delighted to say that you are with child now, Elizabeth."

Now the tears streamed down her cheeks. "I just knew. I'm so happy. John will be pleased. I really want to please him any way I can. But," she paused, "I wish I knew about the first. He was made with love, you know."

I helped her out of the hammock. Dougie had quit playing around in the yard and came over to us. He was a beautiful boy of more than three now and speaking very well.

"How are you, Mistress Elizabeth? Why are you crying?" He held his head on the side and looked at her with kindness as well as curiosity.

"Why, Dougie, I have just heard good news. These are happy tears."

"That's good," he said. "Mother, may I go to the stream?"

"Yes."

"I must ask you," said Elizabeth as he ran away, "to tell the story again of how you found Dougie."

I took a deep breath. "I think you may know the tale as well as I do," I said, raising my eyebrows. "You must suspect that Dougie is your little boy. I struggled about telling you, as I knew the importance of your story about losing a baby and I feared it would be harder to maintain the story, or perhaps even distressing to you, if you knew."

Peering through the fingers with which she had covered her face, she stared at me in wonderment. She jumped up from her seat, shaking her arms as if to bring back circulation. "Oh God! What a relief! You somehow saved him. He is so beautiful and happy. He even looks like Sammy when he was a child. How I have wondered what happened to him! My mother admitted that she had told the men who brought you to kill him and you as well."

"I persuaded the men to sell us into slavery instead of killing us. A woman on the slave ship had just lost her baby and was able to nurse him."

"This is the story of a marvel, a marvel you created, out of your many adventures." She paused, biting at her lip. "But I can't let on that he is my child. That would ruin me, and John as well. John is most polite and well-spoken, but just on the cusp of being a gentleman, so he would permit no disgrace to mar his name. I believe he would put me away if he knew I had a child out of wedlock. Nevertheless, this is a miracle."

"Dougie is the miracle in all this," I said. "You are welcome to spend all the time you want with him. You are his relation by marriage, after all, and no one need know any different."

At this, Elizabeth straightened her spine, a look of determination on her face. "Dougie is very fond of Sammy too, isn't he? Perhaps he will be happy to play with Ed and Lilly, and my little one, as an older cousin. How I hope that Sam will not have to stay in England for too long and that he will not take Ardath and his children away. I will never return to England. The bad memories are too painful there. Anyway, Sam will rejoice when I tell him this news about Dougie."

I sighed. While it was a relief to me that Elizabeth knew, and was happy that Dougie should stay with me, I felt there was danger in telling anyone, even her brother, about Dougie's beginnings.

"You are making a new life here, as all of us are. I'm very pleased that you are with child, as you had wished. I would advise you, however, to tell no one else, about Dougie, even James, or 'Sammy' as you call him. Every person who knows increases the chances of John finding out. It seems he might reject you over it."

"I found out fairly soon that he is a harder man than he first appears, and unfortunately lacks a certain good humor, especially when it comes to following social conventions. Most of my appeal to him must have been that I am 'a lady of high birth.'"

"Umm," I said in sympathy.

"Oh, Carys. It's terrible to say, but I'm glad John will have to travel frequently. My children and the society of your family and mine will be the center of my heart and my life. Meanwhile, I cannot thank you enough for bringing me this joy, for saving my son, for having the strength to claim him as your own."

"It is my constant pleasure!"

She hugged me and went off to speak with Dougie. I could see her looking deeply into his eyes and could only imagine her feelings as she did. She took his hand as they walked about the yard, with her leaning over him while he chattered away. Though it was sad that John and James couldn't know, the future was bright for both Elizabeth and Dougie.

How different Dougie's story and mine might have been, were it not for some strange circumstances and my determination that he should live.

Chapter 38

James
Early Summer, 1754

The skies thundered. The wind gusted in my face, driving a pitiless rain, as I walked on board the ship to England. I pulled my cloak tighter and my slouch hat lower and thought how the weather reflected my mood. Leaving my family here made me lonely in a way I never would have thought possible. The children didn't know how long it would be, of course, as they gripped my hands with their pudgy fingers. Ardath put on a stoic face for our goodbyes at home. I didn't press her to see me off, as we had not the warmest of relationships since we had argued about me leaving them. I actually dreaded hearing from her by post, as I thought either her silence or her complaints might continue.

Even in this weather, Gwyn and Smythe had come to the docks, and waved at me as I looked back at them. I managed a smile and a hearty salute, then gestured for them to go home. I went below to get settled. The smells of dead fish, rotting timbers of nearby ships, and fumes from the tannery downstream were enough to overcome my nose. Nevertheless, I opened my porthole for some "fresh air."

I had brought the minimum of baggage. The clothes I would need in England I could find at Ensleigh. I no longer needed a uniform. My life had changed utterly since I sailed from England less than a year ago.

My dear sister Gwyn had loaned me the book cherished by her family, "The Adventures of Robinson Crusoe." Instead of dwelling on my ruminations of the future, I opened it carefully to the first page and began to read as the clatter on deck signaled that we were leaving port. It was written as if it really happened, but I didn't think it real. Somewhat ironic that I read it on board, as the narrator was shipwrecked!

I knew from my experience last year that the voyage to England was generally swifter than its return, and indeed we had smooth sailing. The winds and the very water seemed to speed us along. With the help of sunny days and Mr. Defoe, we pulled into London in less than eight weeks.

Once again, I traveled by swift horse to Ensleigh. It was high summer and I used the long days to ride as long as possible. As I rode the Ensleigh drive, everything seemed the same, green fields, flowers, birdsong, horses and cows in the near meadows, sheep on the surrounding low hills. Someone had kept the place in good condition and though I might have felt forlorn about my oldest brother's and father's deaths and the disability of my brother in France, I was happy to see my British home.

Well-known servants greeted me warmly at the door. Everyone bowed and called me "My Lord." I wasn't happy about that, but I realized it was important to their traditions. After the rest left, I approached Mrs. Bailey, the current housekeeper. She had been with us since I was a child. When my mother slapped me and my father ignored me, she would take me to the kitchen and give me a biscuit. If the rains or snows came down, I could stay there in the warmth as long as I wanted, or I could retreat to the river and woods on a clear day. Her kind snub-nosed face was now wrinkled, but the smile was the same.

"You'll find your room aired out and ready for you, sir," she said. "You must let me know of any need you have. We are sorry for your losses and we welcome you home."

"Thank you, Mrs. Bailey, and you must let me know of any needs amongst the staff."

"Yes, sir. I will give you a full report when you have had time to rest from your journey. I have arranged a bath in your old room now if you wish. The Countess occupies the earl's rooms. At your decision, those rooms will need to be decorated to suit your wishes."

"The bath will be perfect. I'll go get ready for it. I'll not poke the hornet's nest with my mother. She is welcome to her old rooms.'"

"Sir, I must warn you," she said quietly, "Your mother is out riding and I don't believe she understands that you will be taking over as earl. She has been trying to command Mr. Appleton in his duties. He has been struggling to keep the estate in order regardless of her interference."

"Thank you for your warnings, Mrs. Bailey. I will attend to her in time."

I slung my saddlebags over my shoulder, but she said, "Oh, no, sir, Jim will take those for you." A thin but eager boy took the bags, bowed again, and ran upstairs. It was going to be difficult to do anything for myself here. The windows were open in my old room and the curtains pulled back. Mrs. Bailey knew I loved fresh air. A deep copper tub stood ready for its hot water. Several maids brought in two buckets each, making several trips. Steam began to rise from the tub.

"Thank you, that is plenty," I told them. I locked the door, stripped off my travel-stained clothes, and stepped into the tub. The water felt wonderful, but I would have been as happy to immerse myself in the tub in the Philadelphia kitchen with only Ardath as my attendant. I didn't let myself follow up that unbidden thought; it was too painful.

I ate in the small dining room, which was still too large for one person. I had peered into the formal dining room, which was filled with ghosts. I shut the door on that. Happily, my mother had taken her supper in her room, so I was able to enjoy my food and wine in peace.

I was at breakfast the following morning when Mother entered the small dining room.

She stopped abruptly at the door. "Whatever are you doing here? I thought I told you not to come back. Wait until Stephen returns. I'll have him cast you out as you deserve. You have never done anything of worth for this family and you won't be allowed to use Ensleigh for your leisure. Well, at least you have not brought your ill-bred wife and her brats with you. Or that slut that calls herself my daughter."

Despite my resolutions to the contrary, my gorge rose. I tried to find the most important aspect of her attack to answer. "Mother, you know that Stephen will not be returning to Ensleigh. You must know that he died in France."

"Don't spread that horrible rumor about. Don't you dare contradict me. Now that your father has died, Stephen is the heir we trained to become earl," she said. "I have been taking care of the estates until he can arrive, with no help from any man."

"I understand," I said, for I could see no way to persuade her of her delusion. "I shall go about my business with the least contact possible, but you must allow Appleton to make decisions about the estates. He has the best knowledge of any of us about their current status."

"Appleton is no noble; he should not take on a noble's task."

"But the day-to-day business of the estates shouldn't be done by a noble person such as you. It is beneath you. You should just enjoy the fruits of the lower classes' labor."

She looked askance at me, but had no reply to that idea, at least not yet. I would ask Appleton to make use of the concept for now.

"I believe I shall take my meals in my rooms until you make your leave," she said, with a sour expression that did not improve her appearance. She left the room as haughty as ever.

"That seems a good solution," I said, heaving a sigh of relief. I knew this was not the last of her foul manners, but it might help for now.

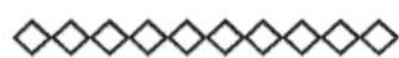

After a good breakfast, I met with Appleton in his office above the stables. I would gladly have given him a room in the business wing of the house, but he had said he liked smelling the horses. I suspect it was because my mother didn't often appear in that part of the stables.

When I entered, he stood and bowed. I waved him down and shook his hand. "Thank you for taking on all the responsibility of the estates all these months. Everything looks good here, but I'm eager to hear all you have to tell me."

"Yes, sir. The shearing went well. We lost very few lambs this spring. The weather has been good, thank heaven. The profits and expenditures for the year are shown on this sheet." He laid a page before me. I gasped before I could stop myself. The estates of the earldom were worth so stupendous an amount that I couldn't fathom it.

There was a long pause while I felt my face blanch. "This is the profit for one year? Is this what it has been in years past? Where is the money that we have made before?"

"Your family has major accounts in several reputable London banks. This year was better than some, but there has been a substantial net profit each year."

"What in the world did my father do with these funds besides save them?"

"In the last few years, he hasn't ordered any changes, so funds have grown."

"But surely there are expenses that have not been addressed. I see very little spent on repairs to the cottages, for example."

"I believe that you will find some things in disrepair. I suggested to your father that we should have a builder look at the cottages on all estates, but he didn't seem to have the strength to address it. The countess has forbidden me to undertake repairs, and in truth, I have not had time to address them anyway."

"I see. Has anyone assessed the state of the main house, the roof, and so forth? What about the fields?"

"No, nothing has been done. The staff hasn't seen any evidence of leaks, but I haven't had time to have the house inspected. I apologize for that."

"No, don't apologize. You have had a tremendous burden here, more than I should have expected you to carry."

"It is my duty and honor to serve you," he said.

"Well, the first thing we do is increase your wages," I said. "Then I need your help to make a list of the things that need tending on the estates. By the way, what is the status of the Glenmorgan property?"

"Your father had asked me to close the Welsh house after your mother returned to Ensleigh. There is a local man who watches it for us, keeps vandals out, tends the lawn."

"All right. I will need to visit all the estates before I can set priorities, but we'll start here."

"Yes sir, it is wonderful to have you in charge," he said.

"Well, my mother may try to push me out, but we are clear to work right now," I said.

The next day Appleton and I rode to the largest of the crofts. It wasn't far from the main grounds. It had the richest, flattest land, where vegetables for the house and fodder for the winter sheep were grown. Mr. Cook had very prosperous fields, currently being prepared for harvest. We drew up our horses before the stone house, where stood a man of sturdy build with a red, round face, which he wiped with a cloth before bowing to me.

"My Lord," he said.

"Your crops grow well, Mr. Cook," I said, looking around us.

"All the better for your profits, sir," he commented.

I thought this a rather strange reply, which seemed to contain some hostility. "I am new to the management of the estate and would appreciate your thoughts on how to make things better for the tenants," I said.

"'Tis hard work to make these farms successful. With the rents so high, I can't hire enough workers to keep things as you see them. This is too big a piece of land to work mostly by myself. I'm thinking of moving to my daughter's house and giving this up."

Appleton had told me that Cook was a good tenant and he didn't seem to me old enough to retire. "I'm very sorry to hear that. Had you spoken to my father about this problem?"

"I did, but nothing changed." His reddish lips tightened.

"Well, I'm here now and I see your point. Appleton, let's see what we can do to correct this. I will speak with you personally very soon, Mr. Cook. I want you to consider staying," I said. His expression didn't reflect hope, though.

We nodded to each other and rode on. Every tenant, many of whom looked undernourished, had some sort of problem to deal with, a roof that was almost falling in from disrepair, many who were struggling with the cost of rent, one that wanted to retire and ask his son to take over, which needed my permission. Their small yards were overgrown instead of neatly weeded and used for their own produce, which told me of a lack of time and hope. I could see that these folk were overworked and hardly getting ahead, while the estate raked in the great profits I had seen in Appleton's ledgers. Father had perhaps an excuse in his own illness, but more should be going back to the people who worked here.

I rode to neighboring estates to investigate their tenants' wages and conditions. The squires were very cordial to me and welcomed me to their community. I tried to get to know them and not ask too many questions. I observed that most estates had somewhat better conditions than Ensleigh. I had to be cautious that I didn't make drastic changes at my estate, as my neighbors could well resent me for it. However, even small changes in rent and efforts to help would reduce some misery. Over the following weeks, I lowered rents considerably. I gave my families chickens to raise and sent garden crews to prepare small vegetable plots for them. Each family received a nanny goat or a milk cow, as they chose. I repaired leaky roofs and walls and asked about their health, providing medicine as needed.

I visited them personally. At one cottage, I found three children lying on pallets on the floor, all crowded up together, all with the pinched faces of hunger and disease, eyes too big for their faces. At my direction, Appleton was quick to call in the doctor for them and Mrs. Bailey had soup, bread and cheese delivered that same day.

Mother found out about some of the changes. She confronted me in the great hall one day. "You again, making changes Stephen will reverse, when he gets word of them. You would coddle these villains, use our funds for them, when they do so little to earn them."

"Mother, I am acting as earl, in accordance with Father's wishes in his will. We cannot let our estates, including our tenants, fall into ruin because of money." I knew it was probably useless to use reason with her.

Her eyes sharpened, her disheveled head shook on her stalk-like neck. "Stephen will tend to you, you imposter. He will stop your foolish ways."

I merely raised my eyebrows as she swept away.

I became less resentful about being earl when I saw that my presence made a difference. After correcting things at Ensleigh, I made trips to our closer estates and then to Glenmorgan in Wales. Tenants and staff had remained loyal and hardworking even when conditions were far from ideal. Perhaps they had no better place to go. I lowered their rents as well and ordered repairs, and had their own gardens fixed as I had at Ensleigh. When I returned, having arranged necessary changes to all the estates, I again examined our funds.

Even with the improvements for staff and tenants, the estates were wealthy beyond compare. I sent letters to our lawyer in London, asking him to take substantial notes from various bank accounts that I could exchange for small bars of gold and a good deal of coin that I planned to take back to Philadelphia with me. I asked for secrecy about this, not being sure that English authorities wanted resources to leave the mother country. I still believed that the future lay in our colonies. Investments in the colonies were investments in the future. Either gold or coin should be accepted by anyone in the cities there as fair exchange.

Chapter 39

James/Sammy
Summer 1754

By the time I had reviewed the conditions of all the estates, I began to receive some mail from Philadelphia. There was Ardath's looping handwriting on one, which I tore open first. I feared that she might continue in her anger about me leaving the family in the colonies.

"My Dearest Love," it began. How I treasured that phrase a hundred times more than any of the "My Lords" to which I had become accustomed. She had written it only days after I left, but reported all the children's progress and antics. Lilly had rolled over so many times that she had flopped into a wall; Ed was getting teeth and liked to chew away on a cool spoon. It was hot in Philadelphia and she had taken to wearing only one cotton petticoat beneath her gown and going barefoot at home. I had to smile, but I ached too, wondering how soon I could get back to them. I appreciated her friendlier tone to me and hoped it was the beginning of an understanding about my responsibilities in England.

Elizabeth wrote next, with her suspicions that she might be with child. As I had prepared to leave Philadelphia, when I told her of our father's death, she took it well enough. Of course, her mourning period had to commence right away. However, aside from wearing the requisite black clothes for our father, she was generally happy. She was practicing motherhood on Dougie, as Ardath had done, and hoping for a boy like him, to satisfy John. She was concerned that her husband might not be as tolerant as he had first seemed and had high expectations for her. It was clear we must never let him know that Elizabeth had had a child out of wedlock.

John was still gone, of course. She found herself spending more time at the cabin with Carys and Mrs. P, for whom she was doing some sewing. Though she had been overcome with the strangeness of their life at first, she now relished her affectionate relationship with them. They included her in the simple chores, and the down-to-earth conversation. She even enjoyed the homely smells of cabin life. She was learning how to made corn pone, a kind of Indian bread that was popular with the colonists. I shook my head, but all things were new in the New World. Mother could never know this, as she would be horrified how her daughter had come down in the world.

Smythe wrote that his law practice was busy, and Gwyn spent more and more time delivering babies with her mother and learning how to tend injuries and illnesses with Ibrahim.

The next letter I saw was not from the New World, however. Father Guillaume's script made me eager to hear of my brother. I translated from the French.

TO: Samuel Booth James, Esquire, The Lord Jesus' greeting:

I pray that you are well and finding your way with matters of the estate.

Mrs. Poschette and I are happy to tell you that

your brother's health has improved. He is speaking more clearly about his life before the shipwreck. He even asked to see his brother's grave.

He still enjoys his work in the gardens, but seems more restless as well as more alert. I told him that you are in England and he says he would like to see you. We have not told him about the death of your father. It may set him back to know of this and we wonder if you should be the one to tell him, especially if you can come here to see him.

Please let us know your thoughts on this. In the meantime, we shall continue to give him our earnest support. He seems like a good man and often joins us in our worship.

With deepest respect, Father Guillaume

I was astounded that such a change had come about in Richard. His French friends had surely made it possible. As soon as an estate agent could be hired to oversee the changes that Appleton and I had started, I would go to France, this time not to wander the coast, but to hurry directly to their little village by ship. I wrote this to Guillaume and sat with a glass of wine to look out over the peaceful deer park. The sun set in a burst of reds and oranges, finally settling on purple slashes that faded slowly from the sky.

Would I be able to help Richard regain himself and perhaps even have a fitting relationship as two brothers might? What would he make of our mother's increasing signs of madness?

I had made myself an office in the library where I could muse on the events of the estate and imagine the life of my family in Philadelphia. The servants watched the door and I locked it from the inside, so that Mother could not disturb me. My desk overlooked green fields and the river beyond, through windows that jutted out over the garden hedge, letting in light all the long days. The chair was comfortable, as was the room. "Lord of the Manor" I said to myself in amusement. Though I could cherish the quiet contemplation, it was a lonely place to be. It still smelled faintly of the cherry tobacco Father had smoked in his pipe. It was strange to be in what had always been his private place.

What if I could persuade Richard to come back, regardless of how limited he might be? Elizabeth would never return; I was sure of that. I could visualize myself and Richard here. Mother could not live forever. When I tried to imagine my youthful family in residence, it was difficult. Mother had not allowed any boisterous play when we were children, so we never played in the house. Did the place have to be as stodgy as I remembered? Perhaps I simply lacked the imagination to picture it otherwise.

Appleton had found a well-suited candidate for estate manager, a Mr. Staton. We hired him on a trial basis. I conferred with him for several days, then left it to Appleton. I went to London. I didn't know what to do with the club membership my father had kept there. I stayed the night and was treated with the greatest deference and with the assumption that I would take up his membership. Leaving the question open, I hired a ship to take me to France.

Fortunately, we had no storms so the trip was almost pleasant, taking only two days.

From the ship, I was rowed in a small boat onto the beach. It was a wet landing but I cared not at all. Boots splashing down, I went directly to the church, feeling its familiar warmth, which seemed to glow like a light from the Almighty.

Father Guillaume was puttering around near the altar. When he raised his head, he viewed me with great joy and hobbled down to embrace me. This man felt some godly connection with me, I'm not sure why, though I felt the same towards him.

"Guillaume, how splendid to see you," I uttered from a grateful throat.

"And you my brother!" he said. "Come, come, let us sit and talk, or do you want some refreshment? I have some wine cooled."

"Perhaps we can go outside, so that I may remove my wet boots," I said.

He laughed in that natural way he had. "Outside it is. Wine?"

"Wine would be welcome too."

We sought the bench in the shade of the church and I upended each boot while we watched the water and sand gurgle from it. "Sorry," I said.

"All that matters is that you are safely here. Thank you for sending your miniature so that I could remind our Joseph of his brother."

"I hoped it might help."

"And it did. I told him that you would try to come here, and he was glad, though I think he worried how you would view him after a childhood of brotherly rejection."

I smiled. "True, but that was childhood for the most part. After that, my brothers ignored me."

"Ah… but let us have some wine and you can tell me more."

I waited while he ducked inside his little stone house and returned shortly with some light green wine. "Thank you, Father." I sipped the wine and found it light and refreshing. "So, I am eager to hear how Richard is doing."

"Well, he has told me of his youth on the estate, haylofts to tussle in, horses to ride, great woods to roam in, hunting with Stephen and your father. He says they left you out of activities, teased, called you names, and attacked you, and generally thought it was fine to blame you for their own mischief."

"Yes, that's all true. I had to be solitary in those days and didn't have friends until I joined the army."

"Your father's idea?"

"Yes, but it was a good one. I flourished there, and if not for the army, I would not have gone to the New World."

"As you have told me, if Richard recovers, you are to yield the earldom to him."

"Yes." I shifted on the bench. This seemed like an examination to me. "Do you think he might recover that much?" I asked, feeling my eyebrows rise.

"How will you feel if he does?" he asked. He looked at me carefully. It was an examination.

"Honestly, I would be very happy with it, and not only for his sake. I could do a good job of running the estates, but it's not the life I want."

His gaze was thoughtful. "Hmm," was all that he said, but his kindly face was wreathed with gentle smiles. "Well, let us go to Mrs. Poschette's house for a visit, then. First, I will get a cloth to finish drying your boots."

We walked slowly up the hill. I was tired and Guillaume was always restricted by his old injuries. As before, Mrs. Poschette's house and grounds were covered in flowers. Ardath would know their names, but for me they were merely an array of every bright color.

It was as if he waited for us. Richard stood in the arched stone doorway, his hand on his forehead to shade his eyes. To my surprise he grinned broadly and hurried to us.

"Dear brother, you have come!" he said.

I know my chin dropped. The tall and assured man before me was not at all what I had expected. He was in fact, a miracle of health and cheer. I found myself enveloped in strong arms which gripped me, seemingly with great affection.

"Richard," I said, overcome with the possibility that one of my first family had returned to me.

"Please come in. Mrs. Poschette will want to see you," he said.

As before, we entered the cool house, and Mrs. Poschette greeted us with a twinkle in her eye. "So you see how well your Richard is!" she said.

I turned to Guillaume, who now had the same twinkle in his eye.

"We wanted to surprise you," said Mrs. Poschette.

"You did, and how grateful I am for your healing care of my brother," I said.

"It is God's miracle," said Guillaume.

We sat and had champagne, Mrs. Poschette's favorite drink. I was hardly able to make polite conversation and kept staring at Richard.

"You will want to walk and talk together, I am sure," she said. "Then return to us and we shall have a feast in honor of your reunion."

"Come, I will show you some of the gardens," Richard said. He walked through the French doors onto the terrace where just last year he had slouched and stared at the ground without knowing me, or himself.

So, please, Sammy, tell me how things are at home. How are Father, Mother, and Elizabeth?"

I had thought he wouldn't be ready to understand and had not prepared myself to speak about our father's death, so I started with the better news.

"I suppose Guillaume has told you that I fell in love on the way to the American colonies and married my wonderful Ardath. She bore twins at Christmas and is at home there in Philadelphia. Well, Elizabeth thought to start a new life also, and went back there with me last fall. She has married and is hoping for a child this coming Christmas."

"She married a colonial?" he asked.

"Yes, a merchant with ships and an iron manufacturing enterprise."

He sighed deeply. "And you have children, all on a major's salary?"

"Father has been generous in his help to me."

I wondered if the look of amazement would ever leave his face. We had come to a bower and sat to catch a breeze on its benches. The heady smell of the sea reached us there.

"I have truly missed much in the time I was insensible," he said, his expression somber.

"Yes," I said. I leaned forward with my elbows on my knees, dreading the next news I had to deliver.

"I know that we were in a storm which wrecked our ship and that Stephen died. I have been to his grave, but I still can't believe he's dead."

"I have trouble believing that too," I said, putting my hand on his knee. Looking up at his troubled face, I hoped maybe I could evade the next news for a while.

"So, I am next in line to inherit when Father dies," he said slowly.

"How does that seem to you?" I asked.

"Wrong, terribly wrong," he said with a wrinkled brow.

"Well, that's not something you have to deal with now," I said.

"Sammy, I want to apologize for the way we treated you when we were younger. We were horrible to you."

"I believe I am almost recovered," I said with a real smile.

"But Mother and Father too! No one treated you well."

"Thank you for thinking of me, but since then I have known real love and friendship, and that's made all the difference."

"I want to be a good brother to you." Tears ran down his face.

"And I to you." I looked at him with compassion. I saw that he had learned from the care he was given here.

"No, you have always been a good brother. I will only try to be worthy of your kindness," he said.

"It is hard that we have been parted, but now we can know each other in a different way," I said.

"I have one more thing that I fear, but desire too," he said.

"Then we shall try to make that real."

"Sammy, I want to go home, but I don't think I can without your help."

"What is it that you fear?"

"Hmm, I have been in a sort of cocoon here. The world outside is harder than I am prepared for."

"What would be hard about going home?"

He laughed, a strangled noise. "I think Mother and Father will have no use for me. Stephen was a bulwark for me, but now he is gone. Perhaps they will resent my survival."

I stared at him. All these years, I had thought he and Stephen were equally beloved and valued. "Are there other considerations about going home?"

"That Father will not think me worthy of being the heir, that I am weak."

"Oh, Richard, you must not worry about that. I, for one, am very grateful that you live. You were always the leavening in our household; do you remember? You were the only one who made us laugh. Father has not been the kindest, it is true. I believe we all have suffered from that. Mother, well, I believe her mind was never quite right."

"Neither of them has written to me in all the time I have been here, Sammy." He looked at me with the most forlorn expression yet. I had, then, to get past my dread.

"Richard, do you trust that I care about you and want to make your situation better? When you are ready, I will surely take you home."

"Yes, I trust you. And Guillaume has told me of your efforts on my behalf." He paused. "What about Mother?"

"Mother was in Wales most of the time; she isn't capable of understanding what is happening at the estate, or even with you and Stephen."

"Oh, well that might explain why she never wrote, though I don't think she really liked me much."

"I'm afraid she is incapable of truly loving, or even liking, anyone."

"Ah, perhaps that's true. Does it seem unfeeling that I don't care much for her?"

"No, I feel the same."

"What about Elizabeth?"

"She has just been married and seems happy in the New World."

"Oh. So Father is alone on that great estate."

"I think he was suited to being alone. He was ill and had Appleton running the estates for the most part."

"Then I must ready myself to get there and assure him that my wits have returned to me."

I needed to tell him. It couldn't wait any longer, or I would be lying.

"One of the reasons I am here is that Father died in April." A stunned silence. I watched him closely, wondering if this would dissolve his new poise.

"No, no, that can't be correct," he said. He must have been flooded with overwhelming feelings. He put his head in his hands. "No, I can't accept it!"

And there it was, what we all had feared. He finally lifted his head, but his hands shook mightily.

"I'm so very sorry to be bringing you this news," I said in a low voice. I ventured to put my hand on his, but he drew away as if burned.

"It isn't true! You have come just to torment me," he said, his mouth a jagged gash in a pale face, his body pulled away from mine. A patch of red burned on each cheek.

I waited with him, a sigh of pity escaping me. We sat this way for what seemed like hours. Nothing but a low moan came from Richard as he stared at the ground. The sun was tending toward the west when Father Guillaume limped up to us, but stopped when he saw the scene. I shook my head and he knelt in the grass to pray.

"I can't," Richard said finally. At least this made some sense.

"You don't have to do anything you can't manage," I said, "but you are shocked right now. It's too much all at once, but we will take things slowly from here. You are not alone; I am here with you."

He looked at me with a bleary eye.

"Would you like some wine?" I asked. He gave a definite nod.

Guillaume arose from his prayer. "I will fetch it," he said. I was grateful to stay with Richard; I felt I shouldn't leave him.

"I'm sorry for shouting at you," Richard said quietly.

"It's all right. Don't feel badly on my account."

"All the death; all the death," he said. "There are only the three of us children left. I am bound to my duty, but I cannot do it."

"Please don't concern yourself about that. I am acting as the earl. Appleton helps me. You must take time to consider whether you want to go home now or stay longer in France. That is all you will need to decide for the foreseeable future."

His shaking had subsided to a tremor. He took an exhausted breath. Guillaume arrived with a dark red wine that should give us all some temporary strength. He bent toward Richard to serve him.

"Remember, God is with you, Richard. God will give you everything that you need. Just receive it in His Grace."

"Thank you, Father," Richard said, his eyes red from emotion.

Though not a religious person, I myself prayed for my brother. I knew what it was to be faced with more than I thought I could bear.

Chapter 40

James/Sammy
Summer 1754

After I had told Richard about our father's death, Mrs. Poschette invited me to spend the night with them, which I did. In fact, I stayed in Richard's room in case he should have another attack of distress about his ability to face both the past and the future.

To my great surprise, he slept fairly quietly and I was the sleepless one. I had dared to hope that Richard might eventually be able to manage the responsibilities of the earldom, if I eased him into it. The legal process ahead of us wasn't simple either. He had to be deemed competent in order to be earl. I was no longer so hopeful. However, I realized that I could take him home. In fact, I really should get him out of France in case the situation in the colonies caused war to break out between Britain and France.

Despite a quiet night, Richard straggled into the dining room. His clothes were rumpled. His hair stood out from his head; his chin bristled with a prickly growth; his face was pale, eyes downcast. He greeted me with a wan smile and sat to eat what Mrs. Poschette laid before him with a desultory air.

Mrs. Poschette gave a sympathetic "tsk" and left the room to us.

"Richard, did you sleep well?" I asked.

"Yes, did you?" he asked, not raising his head.

"No, not well," I said. "I so regretted having to tell you the news I brought."

"Can't be helped," he said. He pulled his chair closer to the table with a harsh scrape.

Silence stretched between us. He was definitely worse. I cleared my throat.

"Look Richard, I am your brother and I love you, but you must soon make some decisions. You know that you can stay here. Mrs. Poschette has offered you a home as long as you wish it. Or… I can't change what has happened to our brother and our father, but I can make it as easy as possible for you at Ensleigh. You need not take on anything you cannot do there. Do you still wish to go home?"

"I must go home, Sammy. I can't stay here forever," he said, finally looking up. He seemed as tired as an old man. I stood and put my hand on his shoulder.

"Are you sure? Do you think you can handle Mother?"

"Yes, somehow," he said. "I'm going to the garden now."

Mrs. Poschette came into the room as I sat absorbing this exchange.

"You had a most difficult day yesterday," she said.

"I think I shall give him time by himself for a while," I said. "I'll go visit Stephen's grave."

"A fine idea. I hope you will approve of the stone we have erected as you requested," she said.

Walking down the hill to the churchyard, I wondered at my responsibility for this family, including those already deceased. I shrugged my shoulders. Nothing in this life was sure. Presently, remarkably, I was the head of the family.

As I had expected, Stephen's stone was of high quality. Perhaps we should put a plaque in the family graveyard for him and not attempt to move his remains back to England. Elizabeth hadn't been close to him and wouldn't mind. I'd ask Richard what he thought about it, whenever I found him in a reasonable state of mind.

I couldn't put it off. I must return to Mrs. Poschette's house and talk with Richard further. I tried not to grit my teeth; so much of my future depended on the ungovernable state of my brother's mind.

I found Richard happily pulling weeds in a border bed of summer flowers that would soon be gone over to fall's whims.

He looked up when he heard my approach. "These weeds have needed tending for several days now," he said.

"I can see you love gardening," I said.

"I find it soothes my mind greatly."

"Ah, yes, I can believe that," I said, squatting to join him. We contentedly pulled white roots from the rich and savory black soil for a long while. I left it to him to begin any conversation.

"I've been very happy here," he said.

"I'm glad of that."

"What would you think if I asked to stay?" he said. For the first time, he looked at me directly.

"Is that what you want to do?"

"My duty lies elsewhere."

"I asked what you want?"

"I am pulled in two directions," he said. "I want to do my duty, but I don't want the responsibility of running the estates and especially of going to the House of Lords. I thought Stephen was perfectly suited to all of it and I would, at the most, be some sort of assistant to him."

"I have commented to Ardath that an earl can be as eccentric as he wishes, if he doesn't mind the gossip. You could be working in your Ensleigh gardens, if you wish."

He actually smiled at me.

"But the running of it!" His face fell again.

"We can set it up so that the estate managers really make most decisions and you just live in luxury and work in the garden. Also, the House of Lords, well, it would depend on your interest in politics as to how often you would attend Parliament. I don't think they can throw you out."

His smile spread wider. "And is that how you have managed things so far?"

I raised my eyebrows. "Well, of course," I teased, "there is the providing for an heir…"

"Oh my, I had not even considered that."

"Does that seem a great chore?"

He actually blushed. The blows Richard had endured rendered him not only less secure, but seemingly younger than his actual age.

"Should I ask if there was someone you admired in England?"

"Not in the neighborhood of Ensleigh. But there is always the London season. Is our aunt still alive? I could perhaps stay with her," he said.

"Yes, she is, and she would welcome you, I'm sure. Also, there is our house in Barkley Square."

"I'd rather not be alone in that big house, and I can't see taking Mother there."

"Then you wouldn't have to do it," I said. "You will gradually see that you are in charge of your own fate."

We still squatted above the flowerbed, but he slowly rose.

We retired to a nearby bench in the shade of a large oak. He seemed deep in thought, head bent, arms resting loose on his thighs while he stared at the grass beneath us. I could hear the bees buzzing among the flowers and smell the flowery fragrance on the breath of warm air.

"I am a man," he said, "but I have been feeling like a child, thinking like a child too. I must turn away from childish things."

"You have always had a child-like spirit and humor. I hope you won't lose that, but I believe you will be able to assume the qualities you need as a man also."

"You are the younger brother, but you will need to teach me."

"Of course, I'm very willing to do that."

"But, Sam, even if I become earl, I don't want that to mean that you have no share in the proceeds of the estates. One single man or his family does not need that much, if it is as wealthy as I imagine it to be."

"Please believe me, it is!" I said.

"And," he paused, "don't you resent the idea that because I am alive, you would no longer be the heir?"

"I don't, truly, Richard. I love the unexplored richness of the New World. My wife and I want to go further into it, to travel into places of vast promise and unexpected beauty. Perhaps one day, you will visit us and see more for yourself."

"Oh, my travels have not been fortuitous so far. I shall be happy just to see our part of England."

"Then are you ready? We could go to England before the weather gets rough."

"I'm ready," he said. His shoulders straightened as we strode towards the house.

Father Guillaume and Mrs. Poschette exclaimed how much

they would miss their Richard, but were very pleased he felt like going home. We would leave on a passenger ship within a few days, headed to London and thence to Ensleigh.

Chapter 41

Ardath
September

As I raised my head from tending my children, to look around me, I noticed Philadelphia changing. The skirmishes on the frontiers caused by the French and their allied Indians meant the city was experiencing refugees. Some of the Germans from farther west of Philadelphia were trickling into town, their wagons filled with dusty-faced children and tired mothers. We saw more of our friendly Indians coming into town as well. I didn't know where they all would go. The churches might feed them, and they might camp in the squares, I supposed.

Well, I had certainly been engrossed in my children for these many months, but having seen the new refugees, I felt it necessary to ride out to our western properties. Those properties would be some of the first land that people fleeing the fighting would come to, and squatters had rights if they improved unoccupied lands, even those already owned. With Gwyn's permission, I had steadily added to these plots, spending some of the gold we had returned to us, so that now we had considerable holdings.

I'll admit I also wanted to be thoroughly alone for a while, such a luxury being limited for a mother and householder. I told no one of my plans, except Margaret, the nanny, knew I was going out and might spend the night at my mother's house. I wore my divided skirt and packed the brace of pistols James had left, just in case. I knew I should have asked Charles to go with me, even though I really thought I would be safe. Well, if I ran into trouble, I could always retreat. I was tired of being looked after and looked over. I wanted some of my freedom back.

At Mother's house, I sneaked into the stable for tack and, in the field, whistled for my favorite mare, the chestnut. She lifted her lovely head, running eagerly toward me, like a dog for its master.

James and I, having not parted with best of feelings, still wrote frequently to each other in a cordial manner. I had come to see that his past was steeped in a sense of obligation that boded ill for fulfilling his own desires. That meant I was also to be thwarted in my desires. It seemed terribly unfair that he should put his family above our own. Would we be caught by tradition to live the past instead of the future we wanted? I knew I would never be happy as "the earl's wife." I needed space to think about that possibility.

I rode quite a long time through lands we owned. It was a beautiful September day, cool, with a crisp blue sky above. The thuds of my mount's feet were muffled by the pine needles and leaves beneath us. Her warm body felt good on my legs, the more so because a sudden cloud cut out the sun and a cold wind sprang up.

Rough sounds ahead of me focused my mind. There should be no one in this area. I made sure that I could easily reach a pistol. I heard several men's voices in the clearing ahead. I checked the pace of my mare, leaving her tiptoeing slowly on the woodland carpet. I meant only to see what was happening.

Then I should go for help.

I came to the edge of the trees to see three large men in coarse brown clothes chopping a tree. Preparing a shelter that was laid out in a square in the middle of the clearing. If they put up a shelter, they could claim the land as squatters. My anger was a ball of molten lead in my chest. After all we had been through to make this our land! I couldn't allow that to happen.

My mare took one step too far and a branch snapped under her hoof. The men startled as they saw me. One leaned down to pick up his rifle casually.

"You are on my land," I said. My mare danced around in agitation.

"Nein, Nein!" one cried in German, following with a quick stream of words while they all pounded on their chests. They seemed to believe it was their land now.

"No, not your land," I said as I shook my head at them. Any German words I had learned from the Moravians fled my mind. I was angry and not thinking straight. Still shaking my head and jabbing my finger, I dismounted and approached them making shooing motions. Foolish!

At this, their faces turned to stone. They silently surrounded me. I kept my eyes on the one with the rifle in hand. He leveled it at my chest and growled. I hadn't time to draw my pistol, but I dodged to the side, so that his bullet only grazed my arm. I charged him, trying to get under the rifle, throwing myself at his chest so that he went off balance and fell. I drew out my pistol but I hadn't reckoned with how close the other two were. I felt myself pushed roughly into the wet grass. My pistol was wrenched from my hand. Now two of them were armed. The third held me down. The others stared at me over their guns, eyes flickering with contempt and hate. I knew they were thinking, "No mere woman can stop us!"

They made quick conversation. The one who held me face-down rocked on my bottom as if he wanted to rape me. I heard his harsh breathing. He apparently argued that he should have his way with me. The others disagreed. They urged him away. As soon as I could, I scrambled for my pistol. I pushed to my feet.

The man with the rifle turned and this time got off a wounding shot as they ran. I felt no pain although I was thrown back by the bullet. I could see nothing but grayish fog surrounding me, racing at me from all sides. Then all was black.

I awoke but wasn't in my bed. Cool night winds blew; I seemed to be on grass. I was cold, but my chest was a boiling hollow of pain. I heard the sound of a horse munching near me. I tried to call to her. She had stayed with me as I lay there. How many hours? I hadn't told anyone where I was going.

I awoke again later. The moon had risen. I wasn't at home. Where was James? I wanted him to come and warm me up. Where....

Something was licking at my face. A broad smearing tongue. A warm nose blew on my neck, nudging me. Where was James?

Light cracked through my eyelid. Why were the candles lit? I wanted to sleep. I coughed and tried to breathe. I was under water. If I breathed I would strangle, but I had to breathe. I tried to pull myself up. I couldn't manage it. Sharp, cutting pain!

The earth itself was thumping at me. It should be quiet. The babies might wake up and then what? I couldn't breathe.

Mumbled sounds around me. The villains were back to kill me. I struck out with my arms. I kicked with my feet. My chest exploded. Blackness.

Chapter 42

James/Sammy

So often it happens that our future is determined by the circumstances of others rather than by our own choices. After seeing Richard undone by the news about our father and the possibility of his becoming earl, and after our talk in Mrs. Poschette's garden, I was left with a downcast heart. I saw how he lacked stability. It shall be as it shall be, my future and that of my American family. I knew not what I could do about it. At least I was taking him home, and that felt right.

Over the next several days, I made arrangements with a nearby captain whom Guillaume knew, to pick us up on the beach with his small boat, which the crew then rowed to their ship. Richard had cleaned himself up and wore some of my clothes, which Mrs. Poschette's maid had altered for him. We both looked at least respectable.

It was a clear and sunny day for the trip, with the sails caught by a steady wind blowing us from France toward England. I blessed the weather, but when I took a walk around the deck, I returned to find Richard gripping his seat with white knuckles and a face stamped with dread. I sat close to him, putting a warm hand on his cold one.

"It's a day for clear sailing," I said.

"It started like this before. It started like this, last time. Then we were in the freezing water."

"Well, the Captain says good weather is expected all the way across," I said. "I am here this time. I have sailed a lot and I will protect you. Did you hear me?"

His eyes flitted around. He peered over the side, eyeing the water almost with longing.

"Richard, look at me, please."

He did so.

"I am here. You are safe," I repeated several times.

"Will you take me home?"

"Yes, we are going home. You are safe. Do you want a drink? I have your favorite whiskey here."

"Yes, but I have to watch the sea. That's where those waves started."

"You can watch the sea while you drink."

I had prepared for his fear with a tincture of laudanum, which I put in his whiskey. I was disappointed that I must resort to that, but I feared he might relive his former voyage by throwing himself overboard.

"This whiskey is bitter," he commented, but drank it down regardless. Soon he became sleepy and leaned against me until night fell and I helped him to his bunk below decks. A full moon rose and the captain decided he could take the ship onwards. I thanked God that we could make this trip faster as a result. Still, another day did not improve Richard's state, so I was forced to feed him another whiskey and laudanum dose. We arrived at a London wharf as it was wearing off. Richard made his way off the ship still leaning on me.

I had a carriage take us to our aunt's house, hoping she could take us in. Fortunately, she was home and happy to greet us, serving an English breakfast which I needed after the lighter French fare.

"Aunt Charlotte, I need to take care of some business here in London. I don't want to leave Richard alone. Would you stay with him here while I am gone? You can see that the voyage here has been hard on him."

"Ummm, I shall, certainly. Tell me, Sam, do you think going to Ensleigh will somehow cure him?"

"Oh, no, of course not, but he wanted to go home and I wanted him out of France."

"Well, that was surely a good idea…. Certainly, I'll be here with him."

"Thank you." I bowed and left her getting out cards to play a game with Richard.

I went to our family solicitors to find out what it would take to have Richard declared competent through the courts. There would be an extensive examination. It was easier to be declared incompetent than to prove competence. Perhaps Father and I had been too hasty to set out the will in such a way that now might prove difficult. I hoped there might be a way around it, though I didn't say that to these important bewigged gentlemen.

Next, I went to a bank to withdraw funds from our accounts to take to the New World. I put these into silver coin. I also purchased small gold bars from the goldsmith. He was a friendly fellow with wire-rimmed glasses perched on his nose and wearing a heavy leather apron needed for his work.

"So, sir, as we have done business before, I recall that you have a home in Philadelphia. Will you be returning there soon?"

"I don't know yet," I replied, uneasy with his curiosity. I rubbed my chin.

"Well, I don't mean to pry, but you know the Crown doesn't like great wealth to leave England heading for the colonies." He studied the gold filings on his counter, stirring them around with a finger.

"Ah, and do they ask you if you have sold gold that might be headed there?"

"They keep a close watch on us all, sir. They prefer to have goods made here which are easier to tax before they leave the country. They do allow me to send some gold to my brother, who is a goldsmith in Philadelphia. I can say that this load is intended for him."

"And I can use your brother for my business there, I assume," wondering if that was his reason for being friendly.

"Yes, that would be good. He knows how to advise you on the customs and taxes there. I would also warn you that officials check on the amount of silver coins leaving the country, though they might not be so scrupulous with an earl."

"I know all this, of course, but I want to invest in the New World."

"Gold is a safe commodity, but getting it there and using it is difficult. Now Spanish dollars are in wide use there, and solid gold might be exchanged for Spanish dollars. Or solid gold could be put away to be used in later years, should the laws change."

"Well, that's something, I suppose. However, about this gold, I am requiring a large amount for gilding the chapel of our estate in Wales. You can refer them to me if questions are asked."

"Certainly, no one will question an earl for needing it on his estates. Hmmm. Most people have no sympathy for the colonists, but my brother writes to me of the difficulty in dealing with funds there. In the far past, some colonies have resorted to using 'shillings' made of wood, or even Indian wampum. Now it's mostly different kinds of paper money, I believe."

Oh, my God, I thought, what next? A tax on the air the colonists must breathe? I thanked the man for his advice, also leaving him a reward for his help.

He nodded as one man of business to another.

I normally supported a decision of the Crown as a faithful countryman, but I could see that the government view of the colonies was becoming, perhaps had always been, as merely a source of riches to be plundered for the mother country. I resolved to put the gold and most coin under a false bottom in my trunks, whenever I was free to return there. I was interested in getting some resources to the New World without so much taken out by the Old World.

When I returned to my aunt's house, she met me in the parlor. Richard drowsed in a chair by the fire. She gestured for us to slip into the library across the hall.

"Sammy," she said, taking my hand as we sat on a sofa. "I know you love and hope for the best with Richard, but he is in no state to assume the earldom."

"Well, of course not yet, but I— "

"But nothing! He is, practically speaking, an idiot."

"But he is worse from being on the ship!"

"I'm sure that is true, but he has no stability at his core. You can put him in a good suit of clothes and he would look competent at times, but this kind of instability will not resolve by being in a familiar place, even given all the love and care in the world."

I sat, feeling the alarm rise from my gut into my chest. "Surely I could...."

"No! Stop fooling yourself! I would be willing to bet that you saw your solicitors today about how to get him declared competent. Well, did you not?"

"But in the future…."

"Oh, Sammy!" she tsked and fell silent, more worrisome than any stream of words.

My face burned. I was scalded by her surety. I would not feel this way unless deep inside I believed that she spoke the truth.

Aunt Charlotte sighed. Her hand patted mine. "I am sorry to be so blunt," she said. "It's just that Caroline's brother, your Uncle Howard, showed some of the same problems after he was in the war."

I looked at her eyes, encased in well-earned wrinkles. Truth shone there, but caring also.

"Well, we got along all right today," she said. "I could come with you to Ensleigh to give him some security that he is not alone."

"Oh, Aunt, you would do that? What about our mother? She still thinks Stephen is coming home."

"Oh, Caroline! I'm not surprised that she is going the way of her brother Howard. I can deal with Caroline! And I could use some time in the country and make the neighbors feel we have not abandoned the place completely. There are one or two people there that are not completely tedious."

"But he won't be alone. I will be there," I said.

"No, you will not; you will be teaching me anything I need to know about the estates sand introducing me to the managers with instructions that they are to listen to me. I used to run my husband's estates and I have rather missed it! You will go to the colonies to be with your wife and children. I can stay at least long enough to be sure things are running smoothly."

I no longer felt like a volcano set to spew. "I sit in amazement," I said.

"Oh, I know," she said, smiling with all teeth showing. "By the way, your wife sounds like a woman I'd like to know."

"She is a woman quite like you," I said.

"Oh, that is good. You will do well, then."

Chapter 43

Gwyn
September-October

I left my bed early in the morning. All night I had suffered from a growing alarm that something was wrong. Gregory had already gone out on business. I dashed on my clothes and ran to the cabin to check on things there. All was quiet. Dougie hoed weeds in his own little garden that we had helped him plant. Mother had awakened after a long night of midwifing. Mrs. Perry stirred a steaming pot of porridge over the fire. She urged me to eat some, and it smelled rich and good, but I must hurry to Ardath's house next to find out what was wrong.

Thank God, Charles, James's houseman, came to the cabin just then, to report that Ardath hadn't been home after leaving the house yesterday. At the time, he had been working in the basement and hadn't seen her go. His torn ear blazed red in the low light. He had been running hard. Ardath had told Margaret, the nanny, that she might spend the night at the cabin. They had thought they would see her this morning. They were greatly worried about her.

After we told him Ardath was not there, Charles shook his head, teeth gritted, and ran out again to continue looking for her. "I'll get the constable to start a search," he said.

Mother was calm, but worried of course. "Where do you

think she might be?"

I had been thinking hard as I hurried to the cabin. "Have you checked the barn? If they aren't finding her in the town, maybe she took a ride. I know she worries about our land to the west of here. She could be checking it, though she should be back."

Mrs. Perry watched Dougie while we went to the barn. Ardath's chestnut mare was missing. I searched the ground for hoof prints. The trail lead west as I had thought it might. Mother and I looked at each other.

"I'm going to the house to get Robert. If she's fallen, we'll need a man's strength to carry her."

"I'll hitch the dun mare up to the wagon. Robert can take Rascal."

Need gave me wings and I was soon back with Robert. Mother had Rascal saddled. She and I took the wagon.

Following the trace of a trail, we went as fast as the narrow track would let us. Ardath had ridden a long way, to the westernmost property, and the trail was grassy and hard to see prints. Robert was well ahead. He shouted to us. We almost missed the turn into a clearing.

There we beheld the awful sight of Ardath, still, lying on her side in a puddle of her blood, which had soaked into her hair, maroon in the rust.

"Oh, my God, Mother! It's Ardath!" I cried.

Robert was already off Rascal. Mother and I were close behind.

"Is she alive?" I asked. Mother kneeled at her side.

"She is breathing," Mother answered. She had brought along her medicine bag, from which she pulled cloths. "Check her neck," she told me.

As I touched her, she struck out at me with feet and hands. She groaned horribly and passed out again.

I felt each bone with care. If anything was broken in her neck, we must not move her. "It's not broken," I said. "I think she had dismounted before she fell. Where is the blood coming from?"

A deep sigh from Mother. "She's been shot. Help me press on the wound."

Robert had walked around us farther into the field. I looked up for a moment and saw that he had the other mare, Ardath's, in hand. He was taking off the saddle and hitching her to the wagon.

After cleaning away some of the blood, we could see from where it ran slowly from the wound. "Her lungs?" I asked.

"Either that or lower. Let's straighten her out. Robert, please help."

"Yes ma'am, I'll pull her legs straighter," he said.

Ardath had curled around the wound. We turned her gently onto her back. The hole was large and frightening. Rays of dark blood spread across her shirt. Her skin glowed a glossy white.

"It doesn't seem to have hit a major vessel, but it's not good," said Mother.

"I didn't see an opening on her back," I said.

Mother's mouth was grim. "The bullet didn't go through. We need Ibrahim."

"Should we take her straight to him?"

"That's more time in the wagon, but I don't want to take her to the cabin."

"We can't take her home either, but we could take her to my house," I said.

I rode in the wagon, kneeling beside her, attempting to keep her body steady. Meanwhile, I pressed on her wound. It felt like a very long trip. With a grunt, Robert carried her into my medical office and laid her on the cot.

"I'll go get Ibrahim," he said.

In the meantime, we cut off her clothing with the very sharp scissors I had on hand. She breathed, but not easily. "I think it has nicked her lung," I said.

"Or it could just be the shock her body has had, I hope," Mother said.

Robert appeared in the doorway, panting. "Ibrahim is coming."

Again, it seemed like a very long time before Ibrahim arrived, though I knew he had run, because I saw him, his long robe flying behind as he came down the street towards us. He got to work right away, approving all we had done so far.

Mother couldn't wait. "Is it in her lung?" she asked.

His large brown eyes looked into hers. "I don't think so. I don't think she would be alive if so. It may be in the muscle right below the lung. Has she lost much blood?"

"It certainly appeared so," I answered. "It had soaked into the ground around her. She was cold."

"Fetch Robert. We must put her on the table."

The two men lifted her up from the cot to the table. I jerked the curtains open and brought our brightest lamp to hold over her. In the globe of yellow light from it, Ibrahim washed his hands thoroughly and doused them in alcohol before parting the edges of the wound. I wet the pincer in the alcohol and handed it to him. He had to probe for the bullet. I admired his sure and almost supernatural skill as he swiftly found and pulled it out.

I heard him murmur a prayer to thank Allah. "It is whole, not fragmented!" he cried. "Obviously, no major vessel bleeds, but I will try to find the source of blood."

He spent some minutes probing the area. He shook his head. "I can't find it. The bullet must have crushed many smaller vessels. We must rinse this out with salt water, then I will use herbs. Do you have yarrow powder here, Gwyn?"

"Yes," I said reaching onto my shelf for the jar.

"Excellent!" he said.

Mary came in with the warm salt water. She had boiled it as I asked her, then cooled it. We poured it into Ardath's wound slowly, washing out the old blood, which I collected in a basin.

I applied powdered yarrow to the wound. "Spider webs as well?" I asked.

"Yes, and then I will stitch. I know you both are good at that, but this is your child and your sister, after all. I'll stitch loosely for now so we can monitor the blood flow and leave the wound mostly open to the air. It is a blessing that she remains unaware at this moment." After deftly wielding needle and thread, he placed a loose linen patch over the stitches.

We smiled in relief and gratitude. My cheeks felt stiff from hours of apprehension.

"However, you know that the wound can still putrefy, leading to an infection that can cause death. You must watch her carefully. Come to get me if the wound begins to smell, even a little. But, forgive me, I don't need to tell either of you these things. Gwyn, can she stay here? I would not like to see her moved far."

"Of course, she can stay here, on the cot."

The men moved her the few short steps to the cot. She lay there pale and remote. This felt like the aftermath of the children's birth all over again.

"Who has done this?" Mother asked. Her hands clutched her skirts.

"Ma'am, I believe it might have been squatters," said Robert. "I saw that someone had started putting up a shed in that clearing, and there was a little trail leading into the woods, where they ran away."

"Oh, Ardath, why didn't you come for help?" Mother said.

"Maybe they saw her before she could get away," I said. "There are some desperate people out there now."

We both shook our heads. Even what we considered the city was no longer safe.

Robert went to tell Charles. Mother went back to the cabin. Thank God, Greg came home soon thereafter. He offered to sit with Ardath so I could check on her children. Mary brought him food and tea into my office.

Margaret, the nanny, had remained outwardly calm for the babies. When she knew Ardath was alive, however, her tense body relaxed. Nevertheless, both babies turned to me as soon as I entered the yard. Ed crawled to me and held up his hands to be picked up. I did, but then sat on the blanket with him and Lilly, who hadn't crawled yet. She gazed at my eyes with an intent question.

"Ed and Lilly," I said. "Your mother is all right. She is resting at my house for now. She will come home when she is able."

I saw Lilly's face light up. Ed smiled and showed me how well he could pick up the ball beside him.

Ed was developing rapidly in his physical abilities, but Lilly was behind in those respects. She spoke through those large blue eyes, and it was a language I knew. Many times, I saw those eyes looking into the distance as if she were receiving a message from the universe. I suspected that she had "the sight" as I did. I hoped that the sights she saw were comforting. I still felt that deep connection with Lilly that I'd had since her birth. I pulled her into my arms. She nestled her warm sweet body into mine and sighed. Then Ed settled on my other side.

It was strangely comforting to sit and hold the children for a while, their little bodies pressed against me, heavy, yet yielding.

I had not become pregnant in all these months since my marriage to Greg. In some ways, it made no sense to try, as I was training hard every day to become a healer, but we would welcome a child when the time came.

I wondered how long it would be until Ardath had the pleasure of her children again. With a stab to my heart, I realized that she might not recover. I shook my head as I sat in that garden, trying to dislodge that thought. Her little babies without a mother was an idea too horrible to consider. Still, my mind would not let go of that tortured feeling.

Ardath didn't waken for several more days. I kept giving her small sips of water, by the spoonful, which she did swallow, thank God. Mother came frequently to sit with her. We talked to her as if she could hear us, telling her all that was going on with her babies, the weather, anything we were learning or doing, letting her know each time how much we loved her and wanted her to return to us.

When she awoke, I happened to be with her, trying to get her to swallow.

"No," she croaked.

I was so startled I almost dropped the spoon I was holding to her mouth.

"Ardath, can you hear me?" I asked.

"Yes. Stop talking!"

I was never so happy to hear her grumpy voice.

"How do you feel?" I asked.

"I feel terrible. I want to get up."

"I'm sorry, you can't get up yet. You'll pull out your stitches."

"You can't tell me what to do." With that, she struggled to sit, then slumped over clutching her wound and crying out.

I pursed my lips. I said nothing, but helped her back on her pillow.

"Oh," she said. "Why is it so hot?"

I touched her forehead. "You have a fever. You must drink willow bark tea." At least she was conscious long enough to take the tea. I sent Robert for Ibrahim.

When he arrived, I said, "She was awake long enough to drink willow bark."

"Hmm," he said, examining the wound. "She's pulled out the stitches."

"Yes, she tried to get up."

He shook his head. "I don't see much pus, but we'll clean it out."

This time we used alcohol to cleanse the wound. Then we dabbed honey across it to fight the infection. Ibrahim sewed it shut again.

"This isn't a good sign, is it, Ibrahim?" I asked.

He answered slowly. "I'm puzzled as to why infection is flaring up at this point. Perhaps she is not as strong as she was when she first received the wound."

"She's not awake enough so I can force her to eat," I said.

"Let's try strong beef broth with liver blood in it." He said. "And keep up the willow tea. Please ask your mother to administer the next rounds of liquids. You are doing all this properly, but perhaps the voice of authority will keep her more biddable. She's not doing as well as I would like."

I knew that she wasn't, but hearing his "doctor voice" made it all too real.

I sent Mary to Mother's house. Thankfully, Mother came quickly and shooed me out the door and into the cool October day. Greg was in the backyard working with Robert to put the garden to bed.

When he saw me, though, he wiped the sweat from his face and arms. "Gwyn, let me change my shirt and let's go for a walk together. Your mother will have Ardath in hand."

"Oh that sounds wonderful!" I said. It seemed that my life was nothing but the tedium of nursing Ardath lately.

When he rejoined me in the yard, I said, "Thank goodness for a reprieve. I think I'm a better doctor than a nurse."

"Well, you've been a wonderful nurse, but you've had too much of it this year," he said. His warm arm around my shoulders cheered me.

"How are the babies doing?" he asked as we walked. He hadn't been to see them in a while.

"They are all right, I believe. It's fortunate that they knew the nanny well before Ardath was hurt."

"So not unduly upset."

"I think not, but what will happen if she doesn't recover?"

"I hope she will, but it will be James's decision what they need if she doesn't. Are you all right?"

"I feel oddly calm about it right now, just looking ahead in case the worst happens," I said.

"Until James returns, it should be the decision of your family and Elizabeth, as the children's next of kin."

"How would you feel about us taking them in if Ardath dies before James returns?"

"In his will, James names you and me as guardians if both parents die, so it would make sense for us to take them in."

"Yes, but how would you feel about that?"

"I would do it without hesitation. I would love them as our own."

"Yes, we would make room, wouldn't we? Elizabeth is too far gone in her pregnancy at this point. Her husband John should be back soon, but they have had too little time together. Margaret the nanny would need to come."

I amazed myself with this calm acceptance. It was reassuring to think the children could survive without their mother. After all, this was a commonplace happening, with death in childbirth being so prevalent. I didn't let myself mourn yet; but what an awful loss Ardath's death would be to us all.

Chapter 44

James/Sammy
Late September-
October 1754

How I wished I could tell Ardath that I was hurrying home to her, but any missive I sent would take as long as I would to get there. Charlotte (that saint of a woman!) and I had gotten Richard home without too much difficulty. He was greeted at the door much as I had been by Mrs. Bailey, who promised to make him and Charlotte feel right at home.

She let me know that the countess had free range of the estate while I was gone, with Mary as her constant companion.

"Ah, your ladyship," she said, bowing as Mother appeared in the foyer.

I braced myself for the usual abuse from her, but her eyes were on Charlotte.

"Charlotte, how I have missed you," Mother said, to my amazement. "Do come into the parlor so that we may talk."

They turned into the parlor with Mary, who nodded at me. We could still hear their conversation.

"Wherever is Stephen?" Mother asked.

"Oh, he is still in France, overseeing our interests there. He sends his love, but will not be able to return home for quite a while. He asks that I help the agents run the estates here as I did for Howard, so that you may enjoy your leisure. However,

Richard has returned with us, and Samuel is here temporarily."

"Oh, Richard. He won't be of much help. He's a rather silly boy, you know. And I must tell you the dreadful thing that Sammy has done." Here she lowered her voice. "You know he went to the colonies and married a woman of low estate! It's a fortunate thing that Stephen is earl, to prevent the shame of the other boys inheriting the title."

"Oh, I see," said Charlotte. "Well, he will be returning to Pennsylvania soon, so you mustn't worry about that."

"Well, then. You must stay in the Blue Room. I'll have it freshened for you. Also, I've been riding every day. I hope you will join me in that, and I look forward to our cribbage games in the evenings."

"So do I. I have been quite lonely in London lately."

"Stephen will love that you are staying here. We'll have a good time."

"Richard," I said as we relaxed later over sherry in the library, "I can't believe Aunt Charlotte thought of going along with Mother's delusions."

"Certainly I would never have thought of that, but it did calm her down," he said.

"True. You must be at ease and enjoy your time here. I will continue as earl, so you will not be pressured in any way. I have spoken to old Henry, our gardener. You remember him, I think."

Richard nodded, with a slight smile. Henry had been a favorite with us in our boyhood and I thought Richard would feel comfortable with him. "Well, he is getting older and can use some help in the gardens. Also, you have learned many new things working in France that could be done here. You could work with him on making improvements."

"I'd like that very much. I noticed there are some hedges growing rather tall that should be pruned soon."

I inwardly sighed with relief. "As you know, Charlotte has been craving some time in the country. I hope you and the staff will entertain her when she needs it."

"Of course, Sammy, I rather like the old girl."

"Don't let her hear you call her that !" I said. "Your very life might be in danger."

"I suppose Mother will want me to dress for dinner." He actually grinned.

"I didn't promise you could be a complete barbarian." I smiled too. Richard was so much better if not faced with the duties of the earldom. Given that condition, Ensleigh seemed to soothe him.

It was beautiful in late September in the Cotswolds, with maples beginning to turn red and orange, though the oaks were yet to come, but I became anxious to get on the ocean before winter set in. It would be at least eight weeks before I could be home to Philadelphia, and in that time, the waves could become wild and fierce. As soon as I introduced Aunt Charlotte to Appleton and Staton she quickly learned the essentials that she needed to know. I was impressed with her experience and intelligence. Of course, she couldn't stay forever, but she could send me more news of how my family members were faring than could Appleton.

Richard took my leaving easily. Mother seemed to tolerate him well. Having Charlotte there helped us all.

A Weave of Old and New

Thus I began my trip to the New World, with a cleverly hidden false bottom in my trunk that carried gold and silver. In addition, I had my household seamstress sew the largest coins into my coat lining separately so that the pieces didn't jingle. I had to pack more clothing this time, as I planned to be a man of business in Pennsylvania. I thought of Ardath, with her lovely face and figure, again glowing with health and vitality, waiting for me. Of course, I could only imagine the changes I would see in the babes. I still thought of them as tiny creatures, but they would have been growing rapidly in the months I had been gone.

Of my voyage to America, I wish I could say that it was smooth and even boring, but alas, my worry about the rough seas turned out to be accurate. The gales we endured caused the ship to plunge and lurch, especially as winter advanced. I had weathered this before and gave the captain what help I could. He was a congenial man and we got on well between the hard times. We didn't lose any hands or passengers at least. My trunk got soaked a number of times, but I didn't lose the most important items I had lodged in the bottom.

In any case, I prayed that my voyages to England in the future would be as rare as possible. Charlotte had taught me that I might fool myself at times and not even know it, but I still wanted to be hopeful rather than downhearted.

It had been a long time since I had received any news from Philadelphia about the conflict with the French. I spoke to the captain about what news he had.

"Things move slowly in political circles, that is sure," he said as he smoked his pipe in his cabin aboard ship. "Washington's attack on Jumonville really started it, back in late May. The militia that were sent thereafter to Washington from Virginia and North and South Carolina were untrained at best, some even being prisoners let out of jail, showing no real discipline or military experience. The French moved great numbers of troops into the area and had a strong Fort Duquesne."

"So, has war been declared between France and England?"

"I don't have an official answer to that," replied the captain. "It's so hard to tell, from conflicting reports, what is really happening." He reached across the small table to pour more wine. "I do know that there have been few trained officers to help our side."

I felt a stab of guilt. Our settlements in Pennsylvania and other colonies were at risk of being stopped where they were, barely farther than the coastline. I had the experience they needed and should go to the rescue of our troops, if they could even be called that.

"It strikes me that Washington has held on admirably, given these circumstances," I said.

"In the end, we British will have to send trained troops, I believe. Anyway, no campaigns can be fought in the winter."

"Hmmm," I said. "True. The outlook seems bleak if King and Parliament don't send soldiers, unless in spring the militiamen somehow can be better prepared for war."

In the nights following, I became convinced that I should get involved with the English efforts, perhaps going to the frontiers if needed.

Chapter 45

Ardath

I couldn't believe I was alive. The scouring pain in my abdomen, however, convinced me. I understood that. I could bear that. It was the weakness that overwhelmed me, that made me want to crouch inside myself, to be immobile, until I could die or otherwise be relieved of it.

"Oh, Ardath," said Gwyn as she walked into the room where I lay at her house, "I'm glad to see you awake. We must get you some broth. Do you feel able to sit up?"

I shook my head.

"I understand. You must feel very weak. I'll be right back," she said.

Now I was to be stuffed full of anything I could tolerate. I had been through this before, and again it was my own fault. Why did I dismount when those squatters threatened me? I could have dominated them from my horse. Stupid again.

Mother arrived with a steaming bowl. She sat down beside the cot I was on, laying the bowl on a small table. "I will need to turn your head and shoulders so you can eat," she said. I knew they had sent Mother because I wouldn't refuse her.

"This will hurt, but it is necessary," she said, lifting my shoulders from the pillow and adding another cushion under me.

The pain was searing. I panted like a woman in labor.

"Take a minute," Mother said, patiently, while I tried to breathe.

The process was slow, as she had to feed me by hand with spoonsful of soup.

"That's good," Mother encouraged me. "It's hard to be patient, I'm sure."

"I'm hungry," I said. "And I'll do my best not to scream at people who are trying to help me."

"A good plan," said Mother. She felt my forehead with a cool hand. "Let's get some willow bark tea in you, and then finish the soup. When your fever is gone, we can get you back to your house so you can see your children."

After some days, I actually don't know how long, my fever passed. Robert and Charles took me in a stretcher to my house. A worse journey I have never suffered, though they tried to carry me gently. I felt better when I was installed in my own parlor with its familiar teal walls and creamy lace curtains. A book lay on a small table and reminded me that someday, I could hold a book and read again.

I happily greeted Margaret, the nanny, who offered to bring in the children. This she did, and I smiled to see them. Ed was almost walking if he could hold onto furniture. Did his curly blonde hair have a hint of red? Lily stared at me with her beautiful eyes. She was getting plump and looked healthy. The nanny played with them on the quilt she put on the floor. I felt stricken that I couldn't move enough to play with them.

Margaret lifted Lilly onto my lap. I reached out to hold her, but the pain brought tears to my eyes. Lilly wiped at them, but I had to ask Margaret to take her down.

When Gwyn came in to welcome me home, Margaret took the children away. But Gwyn saw my tears.

"Gwyn, I don't know what to do. I can't even hold little Lilly in my lap; the pain is too great. I feel so sad and cold and flawed."

She held her head to one side in sympathy. "We can do more about the cold right away. I will build up the fire. We must put more clothes loosely around your middle, and eventually give you more support there. You lost a lot of blood and that tends to make you feel cold. We can build up your body with food. As to flawed, you are the bravest and most beautiful person I know. Just think about all you did on the Atlantic journey and on the wagon road—"

"But in doing those things, I took risks that affected other people, all because it was what I wanted. I only trusted in myself. I was impatient and impulsive and I should have thought more of those I might hurt."

"I believe you have grown since then. Didn't you say the squatters only saw you by accident?" she said.

"Well, yes. I had planned to go for help. Even though James isn't here, I could have asked Charles and Robert to come back and confront the squatters."

"So I thought," she said. She moved around the room to rearrange some chairs.

"Gwyn, have you had any word about James's return?"

"No, but you know how the post is. He might be here sooner than a letter could reach us. He could be home at any time. For him and for those babies, let's get you stronger. You can start by eating all your soup and getting ready to walk."

"Agreed," I said. "Bring on the soup!"

Thus we began our "regimen," as Gwyn called it. She had me stretch my trunk a little more each day, so that I could breathe and stand up better. We practiced speaking louder and breathing deeper. We walked in circles inside the house, through the parlor and dining room, down the hall, and back. I ate whatever small meals they served me five times a day. I didn't complain about the pain. If I grumbled about the work all this took, Gwyn said one word, "James." It was enough to stop my protest.

We held a meeting with Charles and Robert, who had been patrolling our outer lands for squatters. They and Ahmed and Omar had put up rudimentary fences around the plots to show they were not open lands. Charles and Robert said all was well. They had seen no squatters or evidence of them during their rounds.

Though not strictly part of the "regimen," that report put me in better spirits.

Of course, the most important work came as I spent more time with the children. Ed loved to perform his newest skills for me. At about ten months, he pulled himself up on the nanny's knee, gazing at my face, then toddled his first few independent steps before falling. We laughed. I was thrilled to see that moment. We all clapped for him. Then Lilly scooted to me and said her first word, "Mama." Tears pricked my eyes. We clapped for Lilly too.

To help my voice develop, I told them children's stories. I drew the line at trying to sing to them, as I never had a talent for that!

A Weave of Old and New

Gwyn had to visit less often as I got better. When she blew in with the cold weather, I could sit up, though still living in the parlor, and ask about her life.

She shook out her dark blue cloak and placed it near the fire, where steam rose from the wet wool. "I'm seeing some patients on my own, and I feel more confident. I have set many broken bones from icy falls this fall and winter, I can tell you. Both Greg and I are humming along, happy with our lives, and taking pleasure in learning more every day."

"That's good. You both have complicated professions. Hmm, how do you think Mother and Mrs. Perry are doing? I thought Mrs. P would want her own shop by now."

"Oh, I wondered about that too, but she wants to stay at the cabin. Now that there's only the three of them there, there's plenty of room. It works well, as Mother has someone to watch Dougie when she's out delivering a baby, and Mrs. Perry has company and people to fuss over. Dougie is thriving; he's very smart, you know, and seems to be over his naughty stage. Mother is teaching him numbers and letters now."

"And Elizabeth?" I asked.

"As you know, she's very big with child. It seems to please both her and John. I don't see them in this weather, though. John came home from the West Indies in a good mood because his shipping business is growing apace. He even found our friend Alex and has begun to work with him," Gwyn said.

"Oh my goodness. What a web we weave with all these friends. But, of course, it's James I miss so terribly," I said.

Gwyn looked thoughtful. "Well, it is December. I hope he has been on a ship these last few months and will be home soon," she said.

Chapter 46

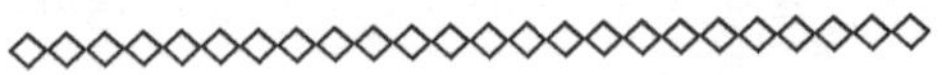

James

The wind tore at our faces, driving needles of sleet and freezing snow into our eyes as we entered the harbor at Philadelphia. It was the worst of the storms that had pestered us since leaving England. At times, we could not see anything, even a few feet in front of us, in the howling, turbulent haze.

The best hope I had was that it would hurry our inspection at the docks, which it did. While the harbormaster or inspectors could have kept us on the ship, my friend the captain shouted to those on the docks.

"The Earl of Redfern is aboard. You dare not hinder the disembarking of his person or his property," he said.

I stood at the gangplank, rising to my full height and assuming a regal air. I saw those on the dock conferring and nodding heads.

"My lord, welcome to our humble city," said the harbormaster. "Let me apologize for the foul weather that greets you."

"After all, even the best of us cannot control winter weather," I said with a slight gracious bow. "I commend our captain on his handling of the ship, but I must get out of this weather and to my home posthaste."

"Yes sir," they chorused. One gestured to some roustabouts

who had huddled under the eaves of a shack. They came running to take my trunks onto their wagon.

"Shall we call a carriage for you, sir?" asked the harbormaster.

"No, thank you. I will ride with the driver," I said. It was a complete farce of course, but I must say I enjoyed putting on this show for the officials who would cheerfully charge me outrageous taxes, if they knew what I carried.

The driver had put up a protective oiled canopy over the bench seat we occupied, but the snow flew under it and plastered our bodies like a vengeful Fury. The streets were nearly empty and the wagon made good time to our house, with only a few slips and slews. With groans, the men unloaded the heavy trunks into the hallway. Warmth and the excitement made me happy and I rewarded their work generously.

Standing alone at last in my home, I dared not shout as the babes might be sleeping. Gwyn, my dear sister, came into the hall to investigate the noise from the unloading.

"Oh, James, how wonderful to see you! Oh my!" She clasped me in her arms, while I apologized for being wet and frozen.

"Oh, you mustn't worry. Come by the fire to melt," she said. We went into the drawing room where the flames roared. "You must wonder where everyone is," she said. "I'm glad I have found you first." She busied herself with tending to my coat and hat.

The way she said that caused my heart to lurch. "What is it, Gwyn? What has happened?"

She raised her head to look into my eyes. "Your children are well, but Ardath sustained an injury in September and has struggled to regain her health since then. I know you will want to see her, but you must be prepared. She doesn't look like the hearty person she was when you left."

"Oh, God! I should never have left her. I knew it. She didn't want me to go, and I should not have." All my plans for military work on the frontier vanished like a chimera. Nothing mattered now but family.

"James, please don't blame yourself. You had to follow up on your responsibility."

"But I should have been with her, to protect her, help in her care, to console her, to…." I pounded my right fist into my left palm, until Gwyn touched me lightly.

"Don't berate yourself. You are here. That will give her reason to grow healthy even more quickly."

"I must see her now."

"Please wait to get in dry clothes and have some tea. Have you eaten today?"

"Dear Sister, you are right. I must calm myself before seeing her, though I don't feel hungry, knowing this."

Gwyn brought tea with cheese and bread and excused herself. While I ate and stilled my shivering, she sent my man Charles with a suit of clothes, and shoes as well, which he helped me don before the fire. One of the reasons I liked Charles was his quiet ways. A chatty servant would have irritated me while I tried to think how I would approach Ardath. Gwyn returned shortly.

"Ardath is awake and eager to see you," she reported.

"Thank you, dear Sister," I said. Once again she had been a good friend to me.

I followed her down the hall to the sitting room, where Ardath sat upon a chaise lounge. Gwyn withdrew. I tried to keep my face still as Ardath's appearance pierced my heart. The woman before me hardly resembled my beloved at all. Her ca-

daverous face and huge lackluster eyes, her frail arms and dull hair all seemed to belong to some aged creature who had stolen away the great love of my life. I sat by her side, cuddling her against me, both arms round her slight figure.

"Oh, Ardath, how I have missed you," I whispered.

"James, I am not as I was," she said, tears flowing down her face. I held my handkerchief to her cheek.

"You will be again. I am right here with you. We will get you back to yourself in time, my dearest one."

"I have tried.… I haven't been much of a mother either."

"It's all right, my love. I'm so sorry I wasn't here to help. I believe we can start again, do it together. Lean on my strength, as I have leaned on yours so many times."

"I don't know." Her head drooped even lower.

"I do know. You are my heart and I am yours."

I held her while she cried, willing her to feel my love and my confidence. I did not allow that confidence to waver. I must believe for her, until she could believe for herself.

After she stopped crying, she straightened. "You will understand that while I was unable, our family and the nanny have taken excellent care of our children. You will want to see them; they are much grown, of course."

"I am prepared that they won't know me," I said.

"We have showed them your miniature and talked about their father," she said, "but they are still so young." She sighed.

"Of course. Perhaps Gwyn and Margaret can bring them in."

"Yes, good," said Ardath in a stronger voice than I had heard this day.

When the children were brought, they had just waked from their nap and were all rosy-cheeked and beautiful. Ed toddled beside the nanny and Gwyn held Lilly in her arms.

"Our children are truly wonderful, Ardath!"

This brought the first smile of the day. "Yes, they are," she said, as if she had just discovered that herself.

They eyed me as a curiosity. Ed let go of Margaret's hand. I knelt on the floor and he walked to me. I hadn't shaved in a few days; he patted my cheeks and seemed fascinated by my stubble. After he smiled at me, he turned to some of his toys spread on the rug by the nanny.

Gwyn approached with Lilly. She stood her up on the floor next to the lounge. Lilly plopped on her bottom, but reached up to me.

"She has the most marvelous eyes," I said. I put out my arms; she scooted closer to me, wrapping her little hand around my pointer finger. Suddenly, she giggled, as if I were a great toy. That giggle said it all. She was glad to see me. My heart lurched up to my throat and I found myself close to tears. "Could she recognize me, do you think?"

Gwyn answered. "I believe your little girl has an expansive and intelligent spirit."

I looked up to see Ardath smiling at the scene. "You should be proud," I said to her.

"We should be proud, and so should all the family that has cared for them and for me during these last months."

"Oh, I haven't even asked about Elizabeth, " I said.

Gwyn answered, "She is doing very well. The baby is due any day now. John has been back about a month. They will be happy to see you."

"When this storm abates, I must go to her."

"She will love that. In this weather and in her state, she doesn't go out," said Ardath.

We were interrupted by a knock at the door. Charles brought back to us two very welcome guests, Smythe and Mrs. Rhys. I rose to embrace each of them.

"What a wonderful surprise!" said Smythe. "Did you just arrive in this terrible storm?"

"Yes, it is vicious out there," I replied. "Mrs. Rhys, how are you?" I gave her a bow.

"Very well, thank you, and very grateful that you are here."

"Is it possible I was missed, then?" I asked.

Ardath rolled her eyes. Smythe smacked me on my shoulder and Gwyn shook her head at my foolishness.

"Well, joker, tell us of your Old World news," said Smythe. "For one thing, are you an earl? Should we bow and scrape before you?"

"You should always scrape before me, but yes, I am an earl. That doesn't mean I must be in England, though. My brother Richard is back at Ensleigh and I think will do well enough, living there and representing the family, though not holding the office. My Aunt Charlotte is there also and I have two reliable agents in charge. I shouldn't be needed for a very long time."

Here, I watched Ardath relax against her pillow. This is what she had been waiting to hear. Her complexion became pink again and she looked more like herself.

"Yes, what I want to do is become a man of business here in Philadelphia and watch over my family, until the war is over, and we can explore new lands."

Ardath and her family had woven bright threads of joy and color into the stiff strands of my English background. Now that sturdy Old World background would provide the wealth with which we would weave a vivid future in the New. It seemed we might have the best of both together!

I looked at Ardath with love in my eyes and she gazed back at me with complete trust. "I have brought some riches from the Old World to purchase and protect more land here, in the New, but I can not do that without your help, Ardath."

Her smile widened, shedding a radiance on us all.

fini

About the Author

Now that she has retired from her practice of psychotherapy, Susan Posey enjoys searching the woods for wild plants, studying family history and, especially, writing historical fiction.

Her first book, *A Home on Wilder Shores*, was well-received by readers. She wrote *A Weave of Old and New* in response to requests for a sequel — and to reveal the fates of her beloved characters.

She lives in the Western North Carolina mountains with her husband and pets.

Historical Note

Philadelphia had a series of yellow fever outbreaks over the years. While the one described in this book was the most serious, it didn't occur until 1793. The outbreaks were probably caused by mosquitoes riding from the Caribbean on fruit imported into the city.